Forbidden

Books by Amy Miles

The Rising Trilogy

Defiance Rising

Relinquish

Vengeance

The Arotas Trilogy

Reckoning

Redemption

Evermore

The Immortal Rose Trilogy

Desolate

The Withered Series

Wither

Captivate

In Your Embrace

Amy Miles

Forbidden

an *Arotas* novel

For my family, whose love and support
carried me through the long
hours and restless nights.

Prologue

Romania, 1689

Roseline Dragomir peeks out from her hiding place behind the altar, searching for the man who led her wedding guests to slaughter. From the moment she had been presented to him, she saw evil in her suitor's eyes. His stance was firm, overbearing, and far too possessive for a casual introduction. His skin was frightfully pale, his smile leering, as if she were a meal to savor. She'd tried to warn her father against Vladimir Enescue's marriage proposal, but he was blinded by Vladimir's vast wealth, a castle, and a bloodline to rival any in Romania.

All her father got, in return, was a sword through his chest.

Roseline's gaze darts about the room, flitting high over the lifeless faces that stare at the ceiling. She dares not focus on any of them for fear of her nerve crumbling entirely.

Her fourteen-year-old sister, Adela, trembles in her arms. Tight straw-blonde curls quiver against her face; pink bows sit askew in her hair. Blood and soot smudge the freckles from her heart-shaped face. Roseline must remain strong for her.

Vladimir's older brother, Lucien, blocks their only exit. His maniacal gaze sweeps the aisles, searching for survivors.

The rectory at the front of the church was set ablaze during the massacre and acrid smoke now hangs thick in the air. It coils into Roseline's lungs, grating against her throat. Small wisps of smoke rise from the tips of her loosely curled bronze hair. She beats the embers against her white corset, wincing at the blood that clings to her narrow waist and trails down to bare feet. This blood came from her father.

There is nowhere to go and no one left to help them. She and Adela are the only ones left alive. Roseline's chest rises and falls rapidly, her pulse thumping in her ears as she fights back tears. Her parents are gone. Her beloved brother and friends too. Her new husband has murdered everyone she has ever cared for...except Adela. Roseline vows to do whatever it takes to save her sister.

The wailing cries of the dying faded away a few minutes ago, only to be replaced by an odd slurping noise. Vladimir's giddy laughter ricochets off the church walls as he celebrates with his brother.

Roseline cradles her sister, lifting desperate prayers for protection heavenward. Fear seeps into the marrow of her bones, rooting her in place. Where is Vladimir? Why has he not finished them off yet?

Wide baby-blue eyes stare up at Roseline. Adela's delicate fingers claw at her arms, pleading with Roseline to flee. To make the bad men disappear. Oh, how she wishes this was all just a terrible dream.

"Roseline," Vladimir croons. His boots squelch in the lifeblood of her friends and family. From this vantage point, she can see her father's family ring exposed in the aisle. Its eagle crest drips with drying blood.

Vladimir tsks as he slowly mounts the steps toward the altar. "This is no way to treat your husband, Roseline. Your mother would be shamed by such abhorrent manners."

Adela trembles in Roseline's arms as the sound of Vladimir's sword, trailing along the stone floor, draws near. Her pale pink lips quiver as she presses into Roseline's chest.

Heat from the flames licks Roseline's face while cool moonlight filters through the church windows above. She closes her eyes against the fear that threatens to handicap her mind. They cannot wait much longer. Soon the tapestries will engulf in flames, and then the pews, and then the...bodies.

An eerie silence hangs over the room. Roseline shivers, fighting to stave off the terror encroaching on her mind. She must be brave for Adela.

"Come out, my love. It is time," Vladimir calls, his words disgustingly intimate.

Roseline shifts, tugging the soiled hem of her dress back from view. Her skin crawls. She peeks out around the edge of the altar. Someone is watching her. She can feel eyes upon her.

Only a few feet away, Vladimir stands, twirling his bloodied sword. His chin and jaw are painted crimson, staining his pale flesh. A severe nose makes his face appear gaunt, and his crazed eyes far more fearsome than she remembered, but his eyes are not on her.

Roseline arches her back to look to the rear of the church. Vladimir's older brother posted himself near the exit when the massacre began, slaughtering any who dared to attempt escape. Her brother fell to Lucien's sword, as did so many of her friends who begged for mercy. They were shown none. Now, Lucien is missing.

She looks up. There, perched in the crossbeams of the rafters, is Lucien. A wide, gruesome grin stretches across his face. A crazed glint darkens his eyes. His lips peel back to reveal bloodstained teeth. His long hair spills over his shoulders, matted with blood. Fingernail claw marks along his arms and face make Roseline shudder. Who lived long enough to rake flesh from his cheeks?

Adela's hands flail as Roseline cups off her scream, squeezing her sister into submission.

"Come out, Roseline. It is time to begin our wedding night celebrations." Vladimir twirls; drops of blood, clinging to his three-quarter-length coat, splatter the altar. Roseline gags. She would rather die than let this monster touch her.

Adela whimpers behind her hand. Roseline shakes her head, begging her sister to remain silent. Her pulse thunders in her ears as she searches for a weapon. A golden cross lies ahead, trapped under the sacrament plates.

Her mind screams for her to snatch up the cross and protect her sister, but Lucien is overhead. A rash movement will no doubt bring Adela's end.

"Stay here," she whispers, pressing her sister tightly up against the altar. Roseline stands and faces her new husband.

"Ah, there you are," Vladimir grins. He steps toward her, bloodied hands outstretched.

Roseline's legs tremble as she forces one foot in front of the next. The closer she draws to Vladimir, the more unprotected Adela becomes, but what choice does she have?

"Please—" her voice cracks. She clears her throat, willing strength into her words. "Please do not harm my sister. She is all that remains."

Vladimir's fingers slide around her wrist, pulling her to him. Roseline crashes into his broad chest, grimacing at the blood dripping from the tips of his white-blond hair. His long fingernail trails down her cheek. "You are enchanting," he whispers.

Something lurks within his blackened eyes. Lust? Definitely, but there is something more. Something almost bordering affection.

Adela's scream wrenches Roseline back from Vladimir's gaze. She whips around, tethered to his hand. "No!"

Lucien appears from behind Adela's shoulder, fingers curling through her hair. Strands of gold part from her scalp as she strains against his hold, only a few feet away. Lucien's dark eyes enflame with blood lust. His nostrils flare as he sniffs Adela's neck.

Vladimir smirks. "Easy, brother. There will be time for that later."

Adela's wide eyes latch onto Roseline. Mewling sounds rise from her throat as she strains against Lucien's grasp. The muscles along her forearms pull taut as she fights to touch Roseline's outstretched hands.

"It is time, brother," Lucien growls, his eyes focused on the moonlight streaming through the windows.

"Time for what?" Roseline whimpers, turning to look at Vladimir.

He smiles down at her, curling his finger along her cheekbone. "Do not worry. It will all be over soon."

Adela's piercing screams tear at her as Lucien waves a blade before her sister's eyes. Adela frantically bucks the arm that snakes around her chest. Her cries give way to wailing pleas.

"No, please," Roseline begs, tears spilling from her eyes. "Take me instead. Just let her go."

Vladimir's hauntingly handsome face shows no emotion. "The pain will only be for a moment."

"Roseli—" Adela's cry gurgles from her throat as the blade slices cleanly through her flesh. A thin red line appears first, and then a shower of blood cascades down her neck, staining her pale pink dress. Her eyes bulge as she fights for breath. Delicate fingers attempt to staunch the outpouring.

As the life in Adela's eyes begins to fade away, a scream blots out all other sound in the room, wrapping Roseline in a crescendo of torment. Adela's blood spurts onto the gossamer fabric of her wedding dress, adding her lifeblood to that of her family.

She is completely alone now.

Lucien holds the dagger out to Vladimir as he steps back, releasing Adela. Roseline's heart falters as her sister pitches forward, out of her sight. Vladimir's face replaces Adela's, only inches from her own.

Roseline blinks rapidly, trying to focus. Vladimir's words sound muffled in her ears, as if spoken underwater.

"Tonight is the celebration of our union and your birth. Your sister has given her life so that you may have yours. All ties have been severed to your past now so that you may join me in molding the future."

Vladimir wipes the soiled blade on his white dress shirt. Roseline focuses on the blood, unable to tear her gaze away, even as the dagger pierces her heart. Pain ripples through her chest, making it hard to breathe as her knees buckle.

Her head smacks against the floor; her gaze locks onto the vacant eyes of her fallen sister. Roseline clenches her eyes closed, praying that death will find her quickly. A veil of numbness settles over her.

A sweet aroma tickles her nose as she teeters on the brink of consciousness. There is a rustling of fabric as something warm brushes along her lips. The scent of Adela's lavender oil disappears under the metallic scent surrounding her. "Drink, dearest."

A finger parts her lips. She gags on the thick liquid that floods down her constricted throat. Hauntingly beautiful words fill the air, wrapping tightly around her. She can feel their power as an ancient magic weaves through her being. The pain in her chest begins to recede. Cells begin to mend. The fissure, created by the knife, knits back together.

A burning begins in her stomach. Her toes curl, fingers clenching into claws, as she clings to the taste. Need gives way to unrelenting hunger. Healing warmth floods through every inch of her body.

Then…the pain begins.

One

Romania, Present Day

Roseline Enescue races down the damp corridor; her hands skim the smooth stone as she throws herself around the corner. No sounds of footsteps follow her. No cry announces her escape...yet.

The sound of dripping grows louder. She must be close.

Bright aqua eyes scan the dark tunnel. A curtain of spider webs drapes from the low ceiling. Roseline slows, clawing her way through the silky strands.

She must be careful. The sunrise approaches swiftly and her family has returned not long ago. Too many ears might catch the sound of her escape, but there is only one person she fears the most: Vladimir Enescue.

The throbbing in her jaw makes it hard to forget her most recent punishment. Refusal to join in the night's festivities has earned her a broken jaw, fractured sternum, and shattered femur. Vladimir made sure to leave his mark tonight.

Roseline was forced to wait long into the night for her bones to mend well enough for her to slip through the secret passage in her room.

Doubts plague her mind as she slides through a narrow part of the tunnel. Several feet of earth press against her chest as she wiggles through.

Can she really escape this time? Will she live through her punishment if Vladimir discovers her attempt to flee?

Death, how sweet the word sounds — an end to three lifetimes of misery. Yes, she welcomes death, if only it will reach out for her to grasp, but the chance for freedom beckons her forward. A year's worth of planning culminates on this night. True, it's a few months early. Winter has yet to set in, but she cannot stay any longer. She cannot endure another beating.

Her desperation pushes her to forego the warning signals that blare in her mind. She has no other choice. She will not suffer Vladimir's brutal tyranny any longer.

As she draws near to the end of the tunnel, her feet stutter along the floor. Roseline's limp will be a problem once she reaches open ground, but she will have to make do as she races against the sun. It is now or never.

A hint of light filters through the darkness a hundred feet ahead. Pale moonlight drifts down through the grate in the courtyard well. To her knowledge, no one knows of this passage's existence, but if she is wrong…

Her pace slows as she approaches. The sweet aroma of early morning air calls to her as she inches forward. Fall has arrived and along with it the blanket of cool that soothes her hot skin. Gone are the sweltering days that trapped her within the walls of Bran Castle. This is her favorite time of year, but she will not be around to enjoy it.

It is fall in America, she reminds herself silently. Yes, Chicago should be lovely this time of year, but she will never reach the Windy City if she does not focus.

Tilting her head to the side, Roseline strains to hear any sounds through the grated wishing well in the center of the castle courtyard. The night sky brightens as pinpricks of dawn's first light spread along the horizon.

All across the castle, mental alarm clocks alert her family to retire for the day. With any luck, most of them have already begun to slip into a drunken stupor, their bloodlust sated for the time being.

Roseline drapes her bag over her shoulder and stretches up to remove the grate covering the well. She yanks her hand back at the sound of a footstep on the flagstones overhead.

From her vantage point, she can make out a broad back and long flowing blond hair. She does not need to see his face to know who he is — her best friend, Fane Dalca.

Tiny rocks, plucked from between the stone slabs, rattle in Fane's hand. He tosses them into the depths of the well. Gravel patters against the tunnel floor, coming to rest against her shoes.

"What troubles you, boy?" a gruff voice inquires.

Roseline cups her mouth to conceal her gasp. Why is her keeper, Vasile Serban, speaking to Fane? Their lengthy history together usually ends in bloodshed and threats of beheading. Why would Fane go to him now? It makes no sense.

"How is she?" Fane asks. Roseline drops her head as guilt swells in her chest. She is the reason he risks his life tonight.

Vasile shifts, digging the toe of his boot into the ground. "You know you shouldn't ask."

"All the same, I need to know," Fane presses. He pushes off from the rim of the well, turning his back to Roseline as he leans against the circular stone. "How bad is it?"

She can picture Vasile's wild mane of marble-streaked hair, obnoxiously large nose, and the left eyebrow that perpetually twitches when he is nervous. Roseline learned long ago that it is a mistake to assume Vasile's disheveled appearance carries over into his duties. He is Vladimir's lapdog, through and through.

He is certainly not the person Fane should be speaking to about his master's wife. Especially with such emotion laid bare in his voice.

"She will be able to walk by dusk," Vasile shrugs. Roseline's fingers clench into fists beside her leg at his emotionless response. "It could have been a lot worse."

A growl rises in Fane's throat. "You speak as if you do not care."

Vasile approaches, his eyebrows furrowed. "And you care far too much." The warning edge to his tone only confirms her fear — her friend is walking a thin line.

Fane crosses his hands over his chest; his black leather jacket pulls tight across his back. Roseline stares up at him, wishing she could reassure her friend, to find some way to tell him she is safe, but her escape will have to suffice.

14

"Have you looked in on her?"

Vasile says nothing. His silence unnerves Roseline. Is he delaying? Has her escape been discovered and Vasile is buying time? She glances back down the tunnel, expecting to see Vladimir creeping silently toward her, but it remains empty.

"Leave her be, Fane. You know what will happen if Vladimir finds out you have been to see her." Vasile's hand comes to rest on Fane's shoulder. Fane and Roseline stiffen at the same time. "I will check on her when we wake. I am sure she will have healed by then."

His grip tightens as Vasile steers Fane away. Roseline commands her lungs to hold fast until the door slams behind them. Still she waits. Precious minutes pass, but she cannot risk exposure.

One wrong move and her dreams of escape will come crashing down.

She reaches for the grate, praying Fane has made it to his room on the far side of the castle. Even then, he might hear her. His hearing is the best among her brethren.

Careful not to draw blood, she bites her lip as she inches the grate up onto the path. The groan of shifting metal makes her cringe. Her muscles coil as she waits for the inevitable sounding of the alarm but none comes.

She lifts her duffle bag up through the opening and quickly follows it. Kneeling on the rocks, she wipes away any trace of her presence. She tightens the strap over her shoulder and darts across the courtyard and out into the garden grounds.

Roseline flies over the grassy hills, past blooming fall flowers still damp with morning dew. She picks her way through rocky paths until she reaches the perimeter wall.

Without any hesitation, she leaps into the air. Her feet plant firmly on the wall and race upward. Pushing from the balls of her feet, she leaps to a nearby tree, grasps the worn branch, and swings back and forth. Her fingers release and propels herself easily over the top of the wall.

The landing is far from graceful as her right leg buckles under. She goes with it, rolling back to her feet before bounding across the road. She dives behind a tree and clutches her leg, wincing at the shifting bones. It is too early to move. She needs at least another hour before her femur will heal completely, but she does not have an hour.

Someone will eventually discover her empty room. It will not take long before Vladimir rouses her brethren to search for her. Roseline glances toward the human town, cringing at the thought of entering it, but she knows she cannot just sit here.

Digging through her bag, she pulls out her most recent wardrobe addition: a black trench coat. She tucks her long bronze braid into the collar and adds a pair of wide-rimmed sunglasses to the outfit. They might help to mask her unusual eyes, but they can do little to hide her beauty. She and her family are well known in these parts. Her reputation, by association, is not the most appealing throughout the country and will only make her escape that much harder.

Over the years, Roseline has been called many things. A witch. A sorceress. Even a demon. The only name that has endured for over three centuries is vampire.

A fabricated name, as incorrect as it is vile, created to describe Vladimir's insatiable thirst for blood. Now all immortals carry the tainted name, both the good ones and the evil, but vampires exist only in nightmares and on Hollywood screens.

She cannot really blame the humans for this mistake; even she struggles to find the good in some of her family. Apart from Fane, there are few in Romania who can pass for good. Most of her immortal brethren easily live up to the vampire lie.

Roseline keeps her face tilted away as she hurries into the town center. Small shops have begun to open. The baker whistles as he prepares his tables with mouthwatering baked goods. A butcher calls out harshly as a delivery boy stumbles over the curb, spilling an assortment of meats onto the street.

A young boy rides past on his bike, tossing newspapers with wild abandon. Most land well out of range. A handsome teen with vivid green eyes and unruly dark hair glances her way from the bus stop as she disappears around the corner. All around her, Brasov is waking.

The hunch of her shoulders becomes more pronounced as she forces herself to move at a human pace along the city streets. It is infuriatingly slow.

The train station sits about two miles outside of town. She picks up speed as she moves to the city outskirts and spans the distance in less than a minute, even with a limp.

Without acknowledging the sparse crowd that lingers in front of the station, Roseline hurries for the ticket booth. "One ticket to Bucharest, please," she requests, working to make her voice sound grittier than it normally does.

The train attendant's muddy brown eyes give her a onceover. Roseline turns her chin, fearing the man's scrutiny. "You running away from something, Miss?"

She shrugs noncommittally and pulls the collar of her coat higher under her chin. He frowns, tapping the counter as she passes over her money. He stares at her for a moment longer before shrugging. He stamps her ticket and passes it through the narrow slot with her change. "Good luck to you."

With her ticket in hand, Roseline slinks out of the room. A young couple sits nearby, sipping from steaming coffee cups, immersed in their morning paper. They pay no attention to Roseline as she sinks down onto a bench at the far end of the platform.

Her knees bounce anxiously as she waits for the train to arrive. She absently peels at the chipped blue paint on the wooden slats as she darts glances at the people lounging about the platform. Her nerves fray as the hands of the clock overhead slowly tick past.

The 6:58 AM train arrives five minutes early, much to Roseline's delight. She boards and rushes into a vacant bathroom, locking the door behind. Roseline drops her duffle onto the sink and leans back against the wall.

Her fingers steady her as the train lurches away from the station, but she does not relax until the train has moved a fair distance from Brasov.

She has made it. Within twenty-four hours, she will be in a new country, with a new start to life.

She is finally free.

Two

"Psst."

Roseline swats at the voice that has been calling incessantly for nearly five minutes. Can't this girl take a hint?

"Hey, new girl. Wake up."

After a swift kick slams into her chair leg, Roseline bolts upright. Her bag clatters to the floor, pens rolling in all directions. "Where am I?" she slurs in her native tongue.

"Huh?" A bright pink mohawk fills her vision; the scent of watermelon gum overwhelms her senses.

"Forgive me," Roseline amends, slipping into an American accent. Even after her years studying the English language, her thick accent still comes through. "Where am I?"

"You're in Mr. Robert's class, and just so you know, he doesn't take kindly to students drooling on his periodic table."

Glancing down, Roseline spies the open textbook, slightly damp around the edge. She winces, rubbing her lip with the back of her arm. Her thoughts are fuzzy and the fluorescent lights overhead make her eyes water. She groans and buries her head in her hands. Jet lag is a killer.

The flights were mind-numbingly boring. Not even the bed in first class had eased the aches in her healing body as they flew over the Atlantic from London's Heathrow airport.

An epidemic of night terrors have followed her to America. Dreams soiled by pain and blood. She wipes her eyes, wishing she could bleach away the images.

"I am sorry." Roseline smiles weakly, struggling to focus on the girl across the aisle from her. "I am normally more polite when I wake."

"No biggie," the girl shrugs, pursing her lips to blow a small bubble the same shade as her hair. Roseline cannot help but wonder if the girl took a pack of gum with her to the salon as an example of what hair dye she wanted.

Amazingly enough, her obnoxious look does not stop at her hairline. Deep black circles the shade of artist charcoal ring her eyes, giving her a rabid raccoon look. Black lipstick—with nails to match—contrasts against her snow-white skin. Throw in the spiked neck collar and leather bracelet and this girl knows how to make a statement.

"Welcome to Rosewood Prep. Home of valley girl knockoffs. Don't let the fancy name fool you though—free wedgies and swirlies are handed out by the football team each morning," the girl says, leaning back on her stool.

"Are these friends of yours?" Roseline asks, amused by Mohawk Girl's running commentary.

"Hardly." The girl rolls her eyes; the ring in her upper lip rises as her lips curl to reveal two rows of perfect white teeth. Rich, but still an outcast, most likely by choice.

Kind of like me, she muses silently.

No, she shakes her head. She is nothing like her classmate. Eccentric as the girl might be, she has nothing on Roseline's dark past.

Mohawk Girl stares openly at her. "The name is Sadie Hughes. Lover of all eighties rock gods, purveyor of the right to freedom of dress, and one badass mini-golfer." She grins. "What's yours?"

Sadie's voracious chewing reminds Roseline that she failed to eat, skipping out on lunch to avoid the crowds. In hindsight, that was probably a foolish idea as she has begun to feel a tad light-headed.

Roseline rubs her temples. "I appreciate your desire for small talk, but I am only here for the class."

She turns her attention back to the tweed-loving science teacher at the front of the room. By the sound of it, he is adamantly preaching at his bleary-eyed class about why science is relevant to their lives today.

Like anyone cares.

Sadie stares hard at Roseline's profile. "I get it, you know. The tough exterior, moody rejection. You've been hurt. Join the club." She tosses her chewed pencil onto the desk, small chucks of pink rubber falling into her lap as she sits upright. "But at least I have manners."

A smirk tugs at Roseline's lip. The girl has spunk. She likes that.

"Alright." She turns to face Sadie. "My name is Rose Danbry. I detest summer, adore ice swimming, can run faster than a bullet, and can easily kill a man with my bare hands." She raises her delicate fingers, as evidence of the brute strength that miraculously lies hidden within her hands.

"See, that wasn't so hard, was it?" Sadie's mirroring grin is wide and toothy. "I'd work on your intro a bit though. It's pretty lame. And that accent? Killer, by the way! Where are you from?"

"Romania."

Sadie's eyes light up. "Europe? Awesome. Your English is really good."

"Thank you very much."

"A tad formal though." Sadie frowns. "We'll have to work on that."

Roseline turns back to the front of the room, berating herself for letting any info slip. She needs to remain focused and avoid drawing any attention to herself. She makes a mental note to focus on adapting to the local lingo.

Tilting her head to the side, Roseline listens to the whispered conversations floating around the room, barely audible over the gentle hum of the heat pumping through the vents in the ceiling. She notes each sarcastic phrase, lilting laugh, and clipped slang word. She studies the sentence structure and files it away for future use.

Several guys dart glances over their shoulders at her throughout the lecture. Some blush and turn away while others meet her gaze, openly leering at her. Roseline rolls her eyes and slumps low behind her raised textbook.

Just what she needs—a bunch of hormone-crazed teens following her around.

One of the things she hates most about being an immortal is how she naturally attracts human males. It doesn't matter their age;

they are all drawn to her. Some are more subtle, but others are downright obnoxious. She has been the source of more fights in her lifetime than she cares to count.

Each detail of her mortal body was perfected during her immortal birth for one purpose: to hunt and kill. At least that is what Vladimir has spent years trying to convince her of.

Perhaps he is right. For what other reason does she need lush ruby lips, a perfectly sculpted body, and endless legs? Her beauty is a work of art. Roseline despises it and all that it stands for.

"Earth to Rose," Sadie calls, waving her hand before Roseline's face.

She blinks, yanked back from her musings. The room has erupted into complete chaos around her. Students dart for the door, their backpacks swinging wildly behind them as they dive into the hallway traffic. Chairs screech against the hardwood floors, grating on her sensitive hearing.

"Are you sure you're okay?" Sadie asks, her lips pursed with concern. "You seem a bit out of it."

"Yes, I'm quite all right." Roseline forces a smile as she snatches her bag off the floor, retrieving a pencil that rolled two desks over. She crams her science book inside, stretching the seams, and glances up to find Sadie staring blankly at her. Roseline swears internally and focuses on making her next words sound more natural. More human. More like a chatty teen. "Just daydreaming, I suppose. Nothing to worry about."

"Good thing that bell wasn't for a fire or you'd be toast." Sadie hops off her stool and leans back to study Roseline. "The parking lot can be pretty hectic this time of day. Want some help finding your car?"

Her hesitation doesn't go unnoticed. "Let me guess, your mom is picking you up?" Sadie rolls her eyes. "Lame."

The well-rehearsed lie slips smoothly from Roseline's lips. "My mother is away for work. She took the car."

"You only have one?" Sadie arches an eyebrow.

Shrugging, Roseline throws her bag strap over her shoulder and glides down the aisle. "For now. We only moved here a couple days ago. Her job transfer was rather sudden. The movers have yet to arrive with our belongings."

Sadie gives her a onceover. "I guess that explains your crazy outfit."

Glancing down, Roseline frowns. Her black V-neck tank narrows down to a trim white skirt and black leather knee-high boots. What is wrong with that? Rolling her eyes, Sadie points to the window. "Did you sleep through the sleet this morning, too?"

Roseline inwardly groans, realizing now how much her summer outfit must make her stand out among the hoodies and parkas. She forces a sheepish smile. "This is all I brought with me. I was under the impression it would be fall here."

Sadie snorts, shaking her head as she leads the way into the hall. "Seasons mean squat around here. We have some crazy weather come off that lake. One minute it's sticky outside and then the winds shift and hello winter."

The hall is jam packed with teens when Roseline arrives at the doorway. Sadie shoves straight through the human wall, unphased by its momentum. Her voice carries back to Roseline. "I gotta grab my brother first. He won't mind giving you a lift."

"No, wait, that is not —" Roseline groans as Sadie disappears into the flood. She sucks her lip between her teeth as she glances in the opposite direction toward the exit.

"Are you coming?" Sadie calls over the din of the crowd. Roseline can barely see Sadie's head as she jumps up and down in the middle of the hall.

Roseline grits her teeth. What choice does she have? Sadie's obnoxious call has already drawn attention. Deciding it is best to avoid further peering eyes, she ducks low and dives in.

Wading through the hall is less like swimming and more like carving a path through a wave. Teens on all sides part as she approaches—some pause to stare, others are too preoccupied with making party plans for the weekend.

"Rose? You back there?" Sadie asks.

"I am here," she calls back, exiting the fast lane. She finds Sadie standing beside a wall of crimson lockers. A look of consternation pinches Sadie's face. "Is something the matter?"

"Darn thing is stuck again." Sadie slams her fist into the locker door. She swears and hops about, cradling her wounded hand.

"May I help?"

"Have at it. The stupid thing likes to stick in the middle," Sadie mutters around the fingers she has shoved into her mouth.

Roseline surveys the door, noticing the hinges and general location of Sadie's previous abuse. She places her palm against the metal. Careful not to dent the door, Roseline pushes her hand until she feels the click. When she pulls back, the door springs open and a flood of magazines pour from the overstuffed locker.

Sadie squeals and dives for the cascade of teen gossip.

"I am sorry." Roseline stoops to help collect the stray magazines. She notices a pattern as a young boy's face appears on several of the magazines. "Who is this?" she asks.

"No one," Sadie grunts indignantly, shoving handfuls of the magazines back into their disorganized home. "I certainly don't like Justin Bieber. I'm just holding these for a friend."

Roseline smirks. She doesn't even have to sense Sadie's nervousness to know a lie when she hears one. Heat paints Sadie's cheeks as she slips her hand back through the door to cram her schoolbooks inside. Maybe Sadie is not as badass as she tries to appear.

"I wanted to tell you that your offer for a ride is not —" Roseline's attempt to turn down Sadie's offer cuts off as a loud whistle rings out over the hum of students. Roseline turns. All eyes follow.

"Well, hello, new girl." A handsome blond boy emerges from a huddle of guys farther down the hall, each one sporting puffed-up chests and lettermen's jackets slung over their shoulders — the starting line-up for Rosewood's football team.

A path through the crowd opens as the boy approaches. "Did it hurt when you fell from heaven?"

His groupies chuckle at his corny pick-up line. Roseline rolls her eyes, crossing her arms over her chest. "Does that wretched line actually work on the girls in this country?"

The peroxide-loving boy's eyes narrow and his mouth tightens with annoyance, revealing a hint of a goatee. "I've never had any complaints before."

Roseline snorts. "Well, consider this your first. You are revolting."

She turns her back on him, surprised to meet Sadie's gaping face. Her eyes flicker over Roseline's shoulder, widening with shock a split second before Roseline feels pressure on her backside.

The boy howls in pain as she whips around and twists his hand up behind his back. "Lay a hand on me again and you will lose yours. Are we clear?" she growls in his ear.

His eyes water as he sinks to his knees, nodding. "Perfectly."

Roseline releases his hand and shoves him away. He sprawls to the floor. His feet struggle to grip the freshly waxed floor as he scrambles back from her. When she looks up, every eye is glued to her.

"Pervert." She shrugs to the crowds as she silently berates herself for making a scene.

Some heads dip in agreement while others stare suspiciously at her. All begin to move on as they realize the show is over. The boy's friends rush to his aid. He swears, shoving them off as he stumbles to his feet. Fiery eyes glare at her as he turns and leaves without a word, his pride obviously wounded.

"Holy crap, Rose. That was amazing," Sadie crows, patting her on the back. "I can't wait to tell Will. Totally freaking priceless."

"Who was that boy?" Roseline asks as she watches him storm down the hall and slam through the double doors.

"My ex." Sadie grins. "I've been waiting four years for someone to put Oliver in his place. I knew from the first moment you started snoring that I was going to like you."

"I do not snore." Roseline sniffs indignantly as Sadie weaves her way back into the thinning crowd.

"It sounds like someone is holding a grudge." She knows all about those.

"Duh. The idiot dumped me for my best friend, Claire, during the first week of freshman year. Can you believe that? Oliver is hot but he's a total loser. I'm better off without him." Sadie ducks around the corner.

As Roseline's foot shifts forward to follow, her back jerks ramrod straight. Her nostrils flare and her steps falter as a scent slams into her gut—sweet and utterly delicious. She inhales deeply, savoring the unfamiliar aroma. It is not like her to have a mortal call to her so strongly.

She whirls around, her gaze darting from face to face, in search of the human. No one stands out to her, but still the scent lingers. Her mouth waters as her thirst rises. The scent is potent, making her knees quiver with desire. Although she has never given in to the seduction of blood, her carnal nature longs for it. It is an urge that she has to daily suppress.

Closing her eyes, Roseline inhales deeply, searching for the source. The scent is bold—definitely masculine. One heartbeat pumps louder than all the rest, calling to her, but it begins to fade away.

Roseline's eyes fly open as she frantically searches the crowd. There. At the end of the hall. A boy, buried in a large crowd of laughing teens, ducks out of the back doors. He is gone.

Three

An arm loops through Roseline's, pulling her around the corner. "What are you staring at?" Sadie asks, rising onto her tiptoes to see.

"Nothing," Roseline says, shaking her head. "It was nothing."

Sadie's eyes narrow. "You sure? You look really freaking pale, right now."

Roseline waves off her concern. "What were you saying?"

"Oh, I was just telling you about Oliver." Sadie tugs on the strap of her bag. Roseline can tell she doesn't like to talk about it. "That was before the fall."

"The fall of what?" she asks, blinking as she forces herself to focus on Sadie's words. It's hard to pull herself away from the scent. It lingers in the air. Not as fresh, nor nearly as potent, but still enough to make her throat burn with need.

"The tragic fall of Sadie Hughes." Sadie swings her green canvas satchel over her shoulder. It's covered with patches, each one supporting a different cause or rock band. By the looks of it, Sadie has tried very hard to make the bag look worn. Roseline's keen eye notices the scissor cuts and the places where she has rubbed the material with a Brillo pad. Evidence of ample washes gives it a faded look.

"What happened?" Roseline asks, eagerly latching onto the topic—anything to help her forget the burning in her throat.

Sadie grimaces. "It's a long story. Basically I was in there, right at the top of the popular crowd, but my best friend Claire Scofield decided she wanted my boyfriend."

"Oliver?"

Forbidden

"Yep, but the stupid thing is she only wanted him because I had him. Claire figured out he was a loser pretty quick and dumped his butt on the curb. My reputation was damaged beyond repair." Sadie sighs, ducking back into the hallway's inner fast lane.

Roseline sticks with her, careful to keep her head down as she moves through the crowd. She allows herself to be jostled and bounced from person to person instead of clearing a wide path. Sometimes it takes a lot of effort to mask her abilities.

She is about to question Sadie further when the girl comes to a sudden stop, forcing Roseline to put on the brakes. Only her superior reflexes save her from bowling Sadie over.

"Will," Sadie groans, thumping a crouched boy on the shoulder. "Not again."

Roseline glances around Sadie, curious to see what has caused her to sound so put out. She can't help but giggle as the sandy-blond boy rises. His white sweater is completely stained with spaghetti sauce. "Who was it this time?"

Will's grin is wide and genuine, as if he could care less that he has worn the evidence of a tomato massacre since lunch. "It was just Conner and Oliver. You know how those guys are this close to a big game."

Sadie nods, looking less than pleased. "But do they always have to pick on you?"

Will shrugs, stuffing his physics book into his bag. "It's just for a laugh. You know I don't mind."

"Sounds like bullying to me," Roseline mutters. Two sets of eyes turn toward her. She blushes as one set widens in surprise.

"You've been holding out on me, I see," Will huffs, elbowing Sadie in the ribs as he sidles up to Roseline, offering his hand. "William Hughes. My friends just call me Will."

Roseline smiles, shaking his hand politely. "What a tragedy. William is such a lovely name. You should never shorten it."

Sadie rolls her eyes dramatically as William flushes with pride. "Oh, great. Now you've done it. The dork won't go by Will now for a month."

"I assure you I meant no disrespect." She glances between the siblings, wondering if she has just offended the only two people she has really spoken to since arriving in Chicago.

27

Sadie and her brother burst into a fit of giggles. "She's something, huh? Found her sleeping in sixth period."

"Lucky you," William says, his voice low and husky as his eyes trail over Roseline's outfit. She blushes furiously and glances away, wishing she could find a way to stop attracting guys. She is pretty sure enticing a girl's brother is totally off limits within the first hour of meeting her.

Not that William isn't cute. His brushed-over hair drifts down into his eyes. A nice tan speaks of hours spent at the pool and the lines at the corners of his lips tell her all she needs to know— William likes to have a good time.

"Oh, not you too," Sadie groans, pulling her brother away from Roseline. "I'm starting to think I should be jealous of you, Rose. You sure do have a way with guys."

Her responding laugh appears innocent enough, but Roseline works hard to mask her distress. Sadie is right. She has already attracted far too much attention on her first day of school. Maybe she should let Sadie give her a makeover. No, on second thought, Sadie does everything she possibly can to stand out. Roseline needs to find a way to blend in.

No matter how much she might try to change her appearance, it won't be enough. Hormones naturally seep from her skin. It is a scent that draws in even the most hard-core humans, like the prey fawning over its predator. They never even know the attack is coming until it is too late.

Roseline shivers and glances away. She refuses to think like that. Deep down she knows she is the monster Vladimir created her to be, but she fights it with every ounce of her being. Roseline refuses to allow herself to become a cold-blooded killer.

"So, Romeo, are you gonna offer your coat to the lady or just stand there and drool all over her?" Sadie asks, tapping her foot impatiently.

William smiles sheepishly and grabs his black wool coat from his locker. "Sorry about that," he mutters, blushing as he offers it to Roseline.

"For being a doofus or for slobbering all over her?" Sadie retorts, planting her hands firmly on her hips, looking just like a little kid who has been told it is bedtime during her favorite show.

Roseline saves him from answering. "Will you not be cold?" She hates taking away William's coat when she will be perfectly happy in the freezing afternoon air. Her skin—naturally warmer than humans—delights in cold weather. The harsh winters back in Romania are blissful for immortals.

"I insist." He grins. "Wouldn't be much of a gentleman if I let the beautiful lady freeze to death."

Sadie rolls her eyes. "I think I'm gonna be sick."

Roseline quickly follows the siblings down the hall. Her mind fumbles through several arguments to get her out of this predicament without appearing rude but now that she's huddled within the warm layers of William's coat, she sees no escape.

Once outside, she effortlessly maneuvers the icy front steps but remains close to Sadie just in case her feet decide to take the fast way down.

Logic tells her that she should not care one way or another about Sadie and her brother. They are mortals and as such should not matter. As an immortal, Roseline ranks far above them on the power scale but, then again, she has never really been one to care about hierarchy. Sadie has touched a nerve within her and already Roseline finds her poorly constructed defenses weakening.

Sadie is fun and bubbly, and her enthusiasm has easily drawn Roseline out of a depressed funk. Would it be so bad to have one friend? What about William? If she can keep him at bay, wouldn't it be nice to have a guy friend again?

Life without Fane has been a hard adjustment. She took it for granted that they could always sneak away for a private conversation among the castle grounds. She is desperate to hear his voice but refuses to give into her selfish longing, knowing that his life depends upon her actions.

As they cross a large patch of black ice leading to the parking lot, the siblings' laughter warms a part of her soul that she has not felt since Adela was taken from her. Sadie, with her crazy clothes and boisterous attitude, reminds Roseline so much of her rebellious younger sister that she simply cannot pull herself away.

"Nice vehicle," she says, nodding approvingly as they pause in front of a brand-new SUV. William grins, his lips noticeably darkening against the cold. A twinge of guilt stabs at Roseline as she shifts inside his coat.

"It was a birthday present," he says proudly, motioning towards his blacked-out Escalade, covered with a light sheen of freezing rain. His teeth begin to clatter together. "Sadie got a Mustang."

Roseline does not have any clue what kind of car that is but, judging by the gleam in Sadie's eyes, it must have been exactly what she wanted. "Your parents are very generous. I am sure they felt you have earned such an extravagant gift."

The automatic door lock sounds and Sadie shoves Roseline into the backseat, laughing. "There you go again. If I didn't know any better, I'd think you were my parents' age."

Roseline winces, making another mental note to work harder to fit in. Her appearance is that of a seventeen-year-old, so she had better start acting and speaking like one. She takes a deep breath and regurgitates some of the slang she picked up on earlier. "Sorry. It has just been Mom and me for a while. She's rubbed off on me, I suppose."

Better but still needs some work, Roseline mentally groans. Fitting into the human world is much harder than she imagined it would be.

"Tragic." Sadie shakes her head. "Hate it when parents do that."

"Maybe you just need to get out for a bit. You should join us for tea and crumpets later," William cackles, slipping into the driver seat. He rubs his hands together to warm them before slipping the key into the ignition. The engine roars to life. Freezing air bursts from the vents, eliciting a few choice words from him as he rushes to close them off.

"She's not British, you idiot. She's from Romania," Sadie says.

William glances back over his shoulder as he backs the car out of the narrow space. The rear windshield is almost completely glazed over. "Either way, I think the way European chicks talk is hot with a capital HOT."

Sadie groans, shaking her head. Roseline smiles, enjoying their playful banter. If her brother, Petru, were still alive, he would have loved William. Staring out the window, Roseline secretly wipes a stray tear from her eye. Her heart aches for the brother and sister she lost so long ago. For the country she left behind. For Fane.

"So where do you live?" William asks, glancing at her in the rearview mirror. He frowns when he notices her sullen face.

"On Raven's Court," she replies absently.

William nudges his car out into the long line of traffic. "Is that in Wildwood Estates?"

Roseline pushes the faded memories of her family away, locking them back into her heart where she keeps them safe and untouched by Vladimir's wickedness.

"I believe so," she responds, managing a somewhat genuine smile.

The home she has rented is not extravagant by any means. It is a simple two-story bungalow in a nice, older neighborhood. She was lucky to find the daughter of a recently deceased man putting out the for rent sign in the front yard as she walked by two days ago. Although the woman was a bit hesitant about renting to a teenage girl, her fears were easily calmed when Roseline produced enough money to pay half of the year's rent up front.

The shoddy house and her school tuition has eaten up a great deal of the meager funds Roseline managed to smuggle out with her. She will need to be careful with her money from now on, but a new wardrobe is obviously a must, and perhaps a new bed. The lumpy mattress she has been sleeping on has got to go. A girl, immortal or not, needs her beauty sleep.

"So, do you have plans tonight?" Sadie asks.

"Perhaps, why?" Roseline responds warily. She glances up to find William's eyes locked onto her in the rearview mirror. His fingers clench around the steering wheel.

"There's a football game tonight and it's gonna be huge. You have to come," Sadie says. "I hate always going by myself."

She reminds Roseline so much of her little sister. Same pout, same whine, and same irresistible plea. Sadie chips away another brick from her resolve.

"Hey," William cries, pretending to be wounded by his sister's words. "I go with you."

"Yeah, but all you do is check out girls," Sadie grumbles, looking tragically put out. "It's so annoying to not have a girl with me."

Roseline shakes her head. "I am rather tired from the flight and American football is not something that I understand. Why the need for pads? Real men do not need them."

William scoffs and rolls his eyes. "If you knew these guys, you would totally get it. They put the lose in losers!"

"Come on," Sadie pleads, ignoring her brother's comment. "It's only a couple of hours and you said your mom isn't in town. She won't even know you're gone."

William's pointed stare makes Roseline laugh. "I would not want to intrude—"

"Heck no," William cuts in, a rakish grin brightening his face. "You'd be doing me a favor. After the game I usually end up with a stiff neck."

"From what?" Roseline asks.

"Ogling girls, of course," Sadie snickers.

William's smile is infectious as he raises his eyebrows suggestively. Roseline laughs. "So what do you say?" Sadie asks.

An internal war wages. Logic tells her that she should say no, disappear into her home and only come out for school again on Monday, but her heart yearns for more.

Vladimir stripped away her chance at a normal life. She never got to really live, to laugh and be carefree. Isn't this why she came to America in the first place? To try to reclaim what she missed?

How bad can one football game really be? She could just try it once and if she hates it, which she fully expects to do, she will have a good excuse to bow out of any further adventures with Sadie and William.

Sadness sweeps over her at the thought of spending the night in her empty home. She misses Fane, her sister Adela, and the friendship they both offered her over the years. Is it so wrong to want that again?

"Perhaps, just this once," Roseline concedes.

Sadie squeals. William hoots as he brakes for a red light. "So, I guess this means you might be around from time to time.

Maybe you two should have a sleepover or something." He grins mischievously. "You can paint each other's nails, have a pillow fight, and talk about how amazing I am." William ducks Sadie's slap seconds before it hits.

Sinking back into the seat, Roseline grins, watching the siblings duke it out. She is enjoying herself so much that she is surprised moments later when she recognizes her house fly by. "Go back. We missed it. It is the one two doors back."

William throws his vehicle into reverse, his tires sliding on the icy road as he backs down to her house. Sadie and William exchange a confused glance. "That's it?" William questions.

Roseline nods, grabbing her backpack off the seat. "I assure you, it is not a permanent house. It was the only place we could rent on short notice."

Sadie nods, still looking troubled as she notices the peeling paint and badly sloping front steps. Faded shutters hang at an odd angle, banging loudly against the wall. Instead of commenting, she whirls around, grasping Roseline's hand. "You're definitely coming tonight, right?"

"I suppose so," Roseline laughs. She cannot help but be infected by Sadie's excitement.

William looks pretty darn smug in the mirror. "Pick you up at seven?"

Roseline nods, ducking out of his coat. "Thank you for the use of your jacket," she calls as she hops out of the backseat and runs to her front door, easily maneuvering the black ice clinging to the cracked steps. She turns back when Sadie sticks her head out through the window.

"Make sure you wear something warm. It's gonna be freezing tonight."

Four

Gabriel Marston bounces on numb toes, his gaze darting around the growing crowd. It's a full house in the stadium tonight. Not a big surprise since it's the homecoming game against Rosewood's biggest rivals—the Stanton Greyhounds. It looks like everyone in town has come out to see the game.

But Rosewood's team captain and star quarterback can't concentrate to save his life. Not since he noticed her: the girl with amazing aqua eyes and skin as pale as the snow that threatens to escape the clouds tonight. Gabriel caught sight of her the moment he exited the locker room but the crowd swallowed her before he could reach her.

He can't explain what it is about the girl that calls to him so fiercely. Obviously, she is gorgeous…but it goes beyond that. It's almost as if some lifeless portion of his heart has begun to beat. The pull toward her is so magnetic that it takes all his strength to put one foot in front of the other to head out onto the field and away from the stands.

"Dude? Are you okay?" Gabriel's best friend Connor Bennett asks, clasping his arm. Connor's charcoal hair is plastered to his forehead, slicked down from the falling rain whose texture is more sleet than liquid. "You look tense."

"It's just nerves," Oliver West snickers as he yanks his chest pads into position under his jersey. "Gabe's just worried about the scouts."

Gabriel snorts, shaking his head. "You guys know I couldn't care less about getting into Notre Dame. It's just—" he trails off.

"There was this girl." He shoves Conner out of the way to continue his search.

Conner and Oliver roll their eyes at each other. Despite the fact that their friend is dating the hottest girl at Rosewood Prep, he has always noticed the fairer sex.

"Dude, Claire will kill you if she hears you're checking out another girl."

It's no secret that Oliver holds a grudge against Claire Scofield for dumping him a few years back, but that doesn't stop him from wanting her or for feeling snubbed by his friend because of it.

Gabriel ignores Oliver, stretching up on his toes. "I know she's out there."

Oliver turns on the bench, scanning the crowd as well. "What's she look like?"

His sudden interest annoys Gabriel, but he lets it go as he scans the stream of fans pouring in from the south side of the stadium.

"Do you even know if she goes to our school?" Conner asks, bending to tie the laces on his shoes. His fingers are red from the cold, quaking as he tries to maneuver the tiny laces.

Gabriel's heart sinks. Maybe he's looking at the wrong side. What if she doesn't even go to Rosewood?

Just as he's about to give up, he spots her. Gabriel's chest warms, pushing every hint of cold from his mind. He stops bouncing as his gaze locks onto the mystery girl.

"Find her?" Conner asks, standing when he notices the odd stillness that has fallen over his friend. Conner's handsome features tense as his hazel eyes scan the crowd for Gabriel's missing beauty.

"Sixteen rows up, all the way down at the south end. It looks like she's sitting by Sadie."

Oliver nearly swallows his chewing gum. "Sadie Hughes? That freak show I dated for a week?"

Gabriel nods, ignoring the worried glance his friends share behind his back. He doesn't stop to worry about Sadie's geekdom or the fact that by even thinking of associating with her his reputation will be sorely tarnished. "She's in the blue coat."

His friends cup their hands around their eyes, blocking out the glare of the overhead lights glinting off the drizzle. Conner whistles, nodding his head appreciatively. "Man, you've got good taste. That girl is smokin' hot."

"So what?" Oliver scowls as he crosses his arms tightly over his chest pads. "She's gorgeous, no doubt about that, but she's off limits." Gabriel turns toward his friend, biting his tongue against his protests. "Sorry, dude, but you gotta face it. You're with Claire."

Conner winces. "Yeah, but Claire's got nothing on that girl. Look at her!" He drools. "Dude, if you don't go for her I will!"

Oliver's eyes narrow with anger. "Trust me, she's a real witch."

Gabriel nearly loses his balance. "You've talked to her? At school?"

With a shrug, Oliver turns his back on the girl. "Yeah. I mighta said hi or something."

Conner stares at his friend, lips curling into an amused grin. "She turned you down, didn't she?"

Oliver growls, chucking his helmet onto the ground as he shoves into Conner's face. "I turned her down," he roars, spittle flying from his lips. "I could have that girl any day I want."

Conner shrugs, but the humorous glint doesn't disappear from his eyes.

"Oliver's right. I'm with Claire." Gabriel breathes out a weighted sigh, pulling his friends toward the field. "But that doesn't mean she's fair game for you two."

"Oh man, no way," Conner complains. "Why not?"

"Because I know you. You'll just use her and walk away," Gabriel retorts. The thought of their hands on that girl makes his fingers curl into fists. He can't explain the strange need to protect her from his friends. Only that he can't imagine letting them hurt her. "Just leave her alone, okay?"

"That's so not cool," Conner mutters. He winces under Gabriel's stern glare. Conner throws up his hands in defeat. "Fine, but I think it's wrong, man."

Gabriel turns to glare at Oliver. His scowl is followed swiftly by a shrug. "Whatever."

It's the exact response Gabriel anticipated. His "friends" are only by association. He can't trust them further than he can throw them. Gabriel vows to keep an eye on them…and on the girl.

"We've got a game to win, guys," Gabriel calls as the countdown buzzer sounds. "Focus."

He jogs alongside his friends, determined not to think about the mystery girl until after the game is over. That is easier said than done.

Five

Despite Roseline's reservations about Sadie and William, she finds herself naturally longing for their company. The football game, although mildly exciting, pales in comparison to the enjoyment she got just from watching Sadie root obnoxiously for the team. Even William's antics delighted her.

The weekend following the game was painfully boring. Even clothes shopping alone for a new wardrobe failed to lift her spirits, but she was determined not to let the time go to waste. She ventured out into the mall and sat for hours, studying the movements of other teenagers. She filled a small notebook with slang terms that she picked up on and would hopefully remember to use. Having a thick accent is bad enough, but speaking like a grandparent is unforgiveable.

When her alarm blares on Monday morning, Roseline is more than a little excited to shed the confines of her lonely home for the obnoxious halls of school.

Freedom. Dangerous as that freedom might be for her, she is desperate for it.

She rushes through her morning routine, shoving an apple butter bagel into her mouth as she hops into the living room with only one shoe on. She has just finished zipping up her knee-high boots when a horn blares outside Roseline's front window. She smiles. William has not only kept his word to drive her to school this morning, but he is also early, by nearly twenty minutes.

Roseline laughs to herself. "Seems someone is rather anxious."

Tossing the remains of her bagel into the trash, Roseline snatches her bag and hits the door. William waves his hand behind the glass window, obviously refusing to allow in a tiny sliver of arctic air. Roseline shakes her head, amused by his enthusiasm.

"Morning," William drawls as she sinks into the soft leather. He scrunches down in his seat and blasts the heater to steal away the chill in the air.

Without missing a beat, Roseline leaps into their playful banter, taking Sadie's side about how great Rosewood's team did at the game on Friday night. Although Roseline really can't care less about the outcome, it feels nice to be normal for a change, almost human.

They part ways as the first bell rings and Roseline settles into her second day of school. She quickly discovers that the teachers think they know it all, and the students don't give a hoot. Most spend their time chatting about the football game. She sinks back into her chair and observes. Apparently, American football is a pretty big thing around here.

When the bell for lunch echoes down the hall, Roseline is the first to emerge. She hits the double doors of the cafeteria and brakes just in time to slide into the food line and snatch an apple, a soda, and something that barely resembles a taco salad. She hands over her money and hurries to find a seat at the back of the room.

Students filter in over the next few minutes. It's obvious how the hierarchy of the cafeteria is set up. The jocks and cheerleaders command the use of the center tables, and the rest are designated for the outer circle—the uncool kids.

Roseline rolls her eyes. Obviously some things never change.

Sadie's squeal pulls Roseline from her thoughts. Her new friend slams into the chair next to her, grasping her chest as she forces huge gulps of air into her lungs. "Are you alright?" Roseline asks, leaning in toward her friend.

"I...just...wait," she gasps. Roseline sits back as Sadie gets herself under control.

Sadie's lips peel back into a wide grin. "I've got news."

"I assumed," Roseline says with a laugh. What on earth can be so important? The poor girl is practically hyperventilating.

Sadie runs her hands over her spiked hair and nods in approval. "You're not alone."

"Excuse me?"

William rolls his eyes as he sinks down onto his chair. His styrofoam plate is absolutely heaping with the surprise meat taco goo. "What she's trying to say is that you are no longer the new kid on the block."

Roseline's eyebrow rises. Sadie's cheeks flush with excitement as she leans forward. "He arrives this morning. Mom and Dad went to pick him up at the airport before we left for school. Can you believe it? I'm going to have a hot foreign exchange student living in my home!"

"It's not that big of a deal," William mutters around a massive bite of greasy meat. "She's probably going to scare the poor kid anyway."

Sadie slaps him on the arm. William winces but manages to turn it into a private wink for Roseline.

"Don't ruin it for me," Sadie squeals, bouncing on the edge of her seat.

Roseline chuckles. "You are rather excited."

"Darn right I am." Sadie pounds on the table. A few people cast curious glances her way but she remains oblivious. "I've got dibs on the hottie."

"And which hottie might you be referring to?" a voice squeaks from just behind Sadie. She whirls around and her expectant smile instantly droops. The boy's thick Romanian accent rolls over Roseline's back, chilling her.

"You have got to be kidding me," Sadie groans. "This is what they sent me to work with?"

As Roseline glances up at the tall boy standing behind Sadie, every muscle in her body locks down. *Oh no*, she moans silently.

One of the attributes that Roseline has honed over the years is facial recognition, with a side of voice recognition. Although she has never heard this boy speak before, she instantly recognizes his face.

It's the boy she noticed in Brasov waiting for the bus on the morning of her escape. She glances down at the table, not needing to look into his startling green eyes to draw up the mental image.

A human from her hometown? It can't be a coincidence. It just can't be. He must be here for a reason…but why?

His appearance is drastically different here. Gone is the designer sweater and fur-lined coat. His eyes now lie behind cheap plastic-rimmed glasses, which constantly slide down the bridge of his nose. His hair is greased, slicked down into a horrendous cowlick at the back. An oversized, second-hand, green knit sweater dwarfs his lean frame, giving him a frumpy look. The holes in his faded jeans were obviously not added by the designer.

The boy stumbles over his feet as he hurries into a chair between Sadie and William. His gaze flickers toward Roseline, eyes pinching at the corners when he meets her steely gaze, but he turns his full attention onto Sadie. "Nicolae Dalma, at your service."

"Oh man," Sadie grumbles, pulling away from the offered hand. She leans toward William. "Can we send him back?"

William glances at the four-eyed nerd he will be sharing his bedroom with and sighs. "I think Mom might frown on that idea."

"Figures." Sadie scoots her seat as far away from Nicolae as she can.

Roseline watches as he darts a glance in her direction. She knows exactly what he sees— unveiled beauty. The hitch in his breath betrays him. He obviously knows what she is, at least to the extent of the rumors that are passed from father to son. "And you are?" Nicolae asks with forced politeness.

"Leaving," Roseline says; her voice trembles slightly as she slings her bag over her shoulder.

"Aren't you going to eat that?" William calls as she leaves her tray of untouched food behind. She does not wait to see if Sadie is following her as she rushes from the cafeteria.

The moment she exits the room, Sadie falls back against the wall and throws a hand tragically across her forehead. "I'm doomed. This was supposed to be my year. My dreams of a hot live-in boyfriend are ruined."

Roseline clamps her hands tightly on her bag strap, stilling the tremor that threatens to spread to her extremities. Does he know who she is? Surely, he has heard stories of her kind, but does he know her exact identity?

Even if he does, who would he tell? Chances are the kid is wetting himself right now. His parents probably thought it would be safer in America with drive-bys and gang wars as opposed to living in "Dracula's" hometown. Boy were they wrong!

Her stomach coils on a new thought. What if he has been sent here to spy on her? No, that is ridiculous. He's too young to be a hunter.

"Where are you going?" Sadie calls as Roseline stumbles down the hall, away from him, away from humans. She needs to be alone.

"Bathroom," she manages to say just before she ducks inside the bleach-soaked room. The smells that inundate her nose do little to still her stomach. She throws open the handicapped stall door, locks it behind her, and embraces the porcelain throne. When the contents of her stomach have been forcefully expelled, Roseline sits with her head back against the cool tile wall.

At some point, the bell rings ending lunch. Voices come and go as the next period begins. Roseline makes no move to leave. What does she care about skipping class? It is not as if these teachers can teach her anything she does not already know. She has lived through the wars, gone to the parties, and studied her way through the entire library at Bran castle. Roseline is well educated, impeccably so.

A couple hours pass in a blur of fears and doubts as Roseline silently rocks, cradling her knees to her chest. Could one boy ruin an entire year's worth of planning? If Vladimir finds her here…

Roseline wipes the tears from her eyes. No, she won't let some stupid boy steal away the life she's trying to make for herself. She will wait and watch. She's not above threats of dismemberment to keep his mouth shut.

When she can no longer stand the eye-burning chemical smell, she emerges from her stall.

She vaguely remembers the bell ringing two more times. Judging by the empty halls, it must be the middle of last period. She breathes a sigh of relief. The risk of running into Nicolae has diminished.

Roseline dreads trying to explain her actions to Sadie. No doubt, she looked like a complete nutcase as she dashed into the bathroom. Knowing Sadie, she will ask too many questions that Roseline will not want to answer.

"Watch out!" The shout rings out through the deserted hall.

A football whizzes through the air, heading directly for her face. Roseline's hand snaps up just in time to save her nose from being rearranged. Heavy footfalls announce the arrival of the football's owner.

"I am so sorry about that—" the boy's words choke off as he finds Roseline staring back at him. "Hey, it's you."

Her eyes narrow. "Pardon me?"

"No, I mean…I saw you at the game a couple days ago."

"And?" Roseline questions, curious as to why his pulse has sped up. The boy has not even been around her long enough to be affected by the hormones leaking from her pores.

Rubbing the back of his head, the boy smiles sheepishly. "And I was hoping to run into you sometime."

Roseline tosses the football into the air. She catches it easily and hands it back over. "Well, it looks like you have succeeded." She turns and heads away.

A tall dark-haired guy at the end of the hall calls out, waving his arms for a return pass, but the boy waves him off. His partner disappears around the corner with a shrug.

"Wait a second," he calls after her, jogging to catch up. "Aren't you going to let me apologize?"

"I believe you have already done that," Roseline points out, not slowing her pace.

"My name is Gabriel, by the way. What's yours?" He reaches out, gently placing his hand on her arm to stop her.

Roseline gasps, jerking away as she feels an intense heat radiating out from his hand, like a blowtorch on her bare skin. No mark, no searing flesh, but the same intense feeling. Gabriel's eyes widen as he reacts to the burn.

She stumbles back, shocked to find her senses impaired. Her nose crinkles as she fights to pick up even the tiniest hint of body odor coming from the boy's locker room. The lights overhead dull before her eyes. Her skin feels clammy, heart thumping wildly in her ears. Her throat constricts as she fights to regain control.

"What was that?" he gasps, staring hard at Roseline.

She doesn't know but she has no intention of sticking around long enough to let him try it again. The final bell of the day rings, saving her from fumbling through an answer. Doors slam open and a tidal wave of students spills into the hall.

Sadie bursts out of the room at the end of the hall, shoving people out of her way as she rushes up to Roseline. She takes in Roseline's furrowed brow and Gabriel's glassy-eyed stare.

"Come on," Sadie demands, yanking her down the hall. Roseline looks back as Gabriel is swept away by the hoard.

"Thanks," she mutters. Her labored breathing begins to ease.

"Where the heck have you been? And with Gabriel Marston, no less," Sadie hisses, huddling close. "What were you thinking?"

Roseline blinks, trying to clear away the confusion fogging her brain. "We were only speaking..." she pauses, planting her hands on her hips. "What is it that you are implying?"

"I'm implying that you're messing with the wrong guy, Rose," Sadie snaps. "That's Claire Scofield's boy toy back there and you know what happened when she messed with Oliver."

Roseline nods, clearing her throat. "I do, but that does not change the fact that it was an innocent introduction. He was simply apologizing for nearly hitting me with a football."

Sadie rolls her eyes scathingly as she slams through the side exit and stomps toward William's car. "Oh, don't try to patronize me, Rose. I saw the look on his face. If that guy is not smitten with you, I'll give my car to charity."

Six

"Oh not again," Oliver groans, watching Gabriel frantically search the growing crowd. "I thought we were past this."

Gabriel waves off his friend. "I met her. I mean, I nearly took her head off a couple days ago with a football, but I finally did it. I was starting to think I'd dreamed her up."

"Definitely not, man," Conner says as he plops his helmet down over his head. "That girl is out-of-this-world hot. No way could you dream her up."

Oliver punches Conner's helmet, jarring his brain. "Shut up," he hisses as a group of cheerleaders walk by. They might hide their giggles behind pompoms but there is no mistaking the object of their gaze—Gabriel Marston.

There is not a girl in school who would dare go behind Claire Scofield's back to talk openly with Gabriel, but the desire is definitely there. Not only is he the most popular guy at school and a super star on the field, but there are rumors circulating that he is pretty amazing off the field too.

"Dude, get your head in the game," Oliver reprimands as their coach shouts at them to huddle up. "Tonight is the state qualifiers. Don't screw this one up."

Conner nods as they move toward the huddle. "I heard from Sara McClintock that if you win the game tonight, Claire's gonna make it worth your while."

Gabriel spits to the side in disgust. Claire is head cheerleader and his longtime girlfriend…but not by choice. Sure, she's pretty to look at, but that's where her attributes come to a grinding halt. Her annoyingly petty personality and slutty manner have never sat well with Gabriel. She flaunts her looks at any guy that walks by. It sickens Gabriel.

Not long after they started dating, false rumors began flying around the school about them. Gabriel was furious when he discovered Claire was making their relationship out to be a sordid love affair, but there was little he could do about it. The more he denied it, the more Claire ramped up the dirty details.

Every male in the entire school envies him. If only they knew the truth.

Gabriel is trapped. His father, Steve, would throw him to the curb if he ever dared embarrass him in front of Claire's dad, a snake of a politician who is known for having Steve's law firm tucked securely in his back pocket. Gabriel has spent the past four years despising Steve for placing him in this situation but, at his mother's request and for the sake of peace in their fragmented family, he submitted—but only for his mother's sake. Steve could take a flying leap for all he cares!

This is not the life Gabriel wants, but no one seems to notice. Everyone views him as some rich playboy with a bright future. After this game, a full ride scholarship to an Ivy League school is almost a sure thing and his dreams will be long gone.

Steve has long since stopped listening to what Gabriel wants in life. All he cares about is his image. Pride will not allow him to let Gabriel pursue the career he wants. Gabriel has been set up for the "perfect life" and along with that comes the shackles of Claire Scofield.

"Whatever, man. Let's just get this win," Gabriel says as he calls his teammates around him. This game is too crucial to let someone like Claire ruin his mood.

Seven

"Can you believe it? We're going to state!" Sadie squeals, bouncing up and down on the metal bleachers. The crowd lingers; no one wants to leave after such a spectacular game. The final score was 21-14 and Gabriel Marston is the talk of the night.

This topic is one that Roseline would rather avoid. Especially since she can't seem to get his face out of her mind. His electric touch has begun to haunt her dreams.

Roseline rubs her arms, trying to hint at a chill that she does not actually feel. As if her nerves weren't already frayed enough, she now has to deal with the green-eyed monster sitting behind her. She can literally feel Nicolae's gaze boring into the back of her head. If she is not careful, she might just be tempted to maim the boy.

Thankfully, Sadie forced him to sit two rows behind them after she went ballistic on him for spilling hot chocolate on the back of her coat.

"For the life of me, I cannot imagine why you invited him," Roseline mutters, hunching lower in her coat. She flips up the collar and stares fixedly away from Nicolae.

Sadie groans. "My mom made me. She seems determined to make me play nice."

William scoffs. "Yeah, like that's going to happen."

A grin spreads across Roseline's face. Perhaps she can just bide her time and Sadie will rip Nicolae's head off for her.

"The guy is really creepy," Sadie shudders, her spirits visually plummeting. "All he does is ask about you."

That is exactly what Roseline has been afraid of. "What does he want to know?"

Sadie shrugs. "It's all really random stuff. Like do you ever go to church, do you ever go outside on sunny days, or if you like garlic on your bread? I'm telling you, Rose, the guy is totally off his rocker."

Roseline ducks her head, hiding her frown. So, he thinks he knows all about her. Too bad he has been sucked into all of the silly vampire myths. When will humans ever learn that vampires don't exists?

"I'm just sorry that you're stuck with the guy," Roseline mutters.

Sadie and William exchange a glance. Their silence pulls her attention back. "What?"

William grins. "You used a contraction."

"I did?"

Sadie smirks. "Not too bad. Maybe we can Americanize you after all."

The corners of Roseline's lips lift with pleasure. Maybe she really is starting to fit in, even if her slip-up was an unconscious one.

"Don't forget that it's not just Sadie that has to suffer in all of this," William whispers as he climbs down onto their bleacher and ducks in low to dish the dirt. "I'm the one that has to share a room with the freak. He's like, anal to the max."

Roseline frowns. "Pardon?"

William grins. "Sorry. Um…he's freakishly neat. The guy even rolls his underwear. All of his socks are color-coordinated and don't even dream of touching his picture album. The guy totally went loony toons last night when I accidentally knocked it off the bedside table."

Roseline makes a mental note of that. If she can get her hands on his family photos she just might be able to figure out who he is and why he's so nosy.

"It is a tad chilly out here." Roseline shivers for added effect. She will stoop to just about anything at this point to get out of here.

"No problem. I'll go grab us some hot chocolate." William leaps to his feet and heads for the stairwell, taking the steps two at a time.

"Wait up," Sadie calls, whipping around to follow her brother.

"Aren't we leaving? The game is over," Roseline calls to Sadie's fleeting back.

She grins back over the head of a little girl dressed like a Rosewood Prep cheerleader at the base of the stairs. "Leave? This is when all of the fun begins."

Roseline groans and sinks back onto the cold bleacher seat. "Great. I knew I should have remained home," she grumbles. She shoots a glance back over her shoulder and finds Nicolae staring straight at her, unblinking.

She takes a deep breath and turns back to face the field. *Ignore him*, she mentally berates. *He's not worth it.*

The field is nearly empty now. A few stragglers remain along the sidelines, mostly parents of the players by the looks of it. Small clusters of students hoot and holler in the stands all around, but Roseline tunes them out. Her senses focus completely on the boy two rows behind her. She counts his breathing, hears the rising flutter of his heart as he leans toward her.

Crap.

Roseline whips around. "What is your problem?" she growls, slipping naturally into her native tongue.

Nicolae's eyes widen as he instinctively shifts back. "Pardon me?"

"You heard me," Roseline says, stomping up the bleachers to where he is sitting. "You are staring at me and it is really starting to tick me off."

Oh, wouldn't Sadie be proud if she had heard those words pass Roseline's lips!

Nicolae holds her glare for a moment longer than he should have done. Roseline's eyes narrow. "I'm sorry. I didn't realize," he mumbles, finally averting his gaze.

Donning her best Sadie impression, Roseline steams ahead. "Cut the crap, Nicolae. We both know you saw me in Brasov. Now I want to know who you are and why you are here."

Although her words are spoken barely above a whisper, she can see the glint of fear in his eyes. The threat in her voice is unmistakable.

"You saw me?" Nicolae scowls. His fists clench against his leg.

"I see everything." Let him stew on that one for a while.

"I didn't know it was you," he protests.

Roseline leans over, meeting him at eye level. She can smell his anxiety, but there is something in his eyes that she doesn't like—defiance.

The glow in her eyes reflects off his dilated pupils. It doesn't matter that he can see it. He already knows what she is, or at least he thinks he does. "If you tell anyone about me, I will enjoy ripping out your spine."

Nicolae's jaw clenches, anger exploding from his eyes like fireworks, but he simply dips his head. "Understood."

"Good." She smiles, patting Nicolae on the head like a child. She turns to leave but shifts back. "And leave Sadie alone. You are annoying her almost as much as you are me."

Nicolae manages a curt nod.

Roseline glares for one moment more before shifting to return to her seat. Her forward momentum carries her right into the arms of Gabriel Marston.

"Oh!" she cries, faltering backward off the bleacher. She falls, rather ungracefully, into the space between the seats. *Smooth,* she inwardly groans.

Gabriel is instantly at her side, offering a hand up. "I'm sorry to scare you like that. I just wanted to say hi."

Roseline thrusts herself upward, rising to her full height. She sends a scathing glance back at Nicolae and heads away, practically running from Gabriel. He trails behind her. "Aren't you going to say something?"

"Why?" Roseline says through gritted teeth as she rubs her sore hip.

"Huh?"

Roseline bites her lip, annoyed that she forgot to adjust back to English. "There is nothing to say."

Her limp is slight but it's enough to encourage Gabriel to offer his hand. Roseline stops and warily glances up at him. Towering well over six feet tall, she has to crane her neck back to see him.

"I won't bite," he grins, holding his arm steady for her. Roseline hesitates. She glances around, noting several curious eyes have shifted their way. Why does she keep attracting so much attention?

Gabriel stands before her, commanding her attention. She can see the stubborn set of his jaw. He isn't going to let this drop.

With a sigh, Roseline allows her gloved hand to wind around his arm. Even through the thick material, she can feel heat radiating from his skin. The intensity is shocking, but what is even more shocking is that instead of running away from the heat, she is drawn to it like a moth to a flame.

She has never felt such heat in a human before. What is it about him that calls to her?

"Thank you," she mutters, allowing him to help her reach the bottom of the steps. She breathes a sigh of relief as her boots hit level ground, one step closer to the parking lot.

"So..." Gabriel clears his throat, glancing at the watchful eyes following their departure. No doubt, word will spread quickly about their conversation. "You're a very mysterious girl. Do you know that I've asked all around school and no one seems to know your name?"

Roseline shrugs. "I mostly keep to myself."

She darts a glance up at him, amazed at how blond his hair looks under the stadium lights. His breath hangs in the air, pumped from lungs buried under a broad chest and a band of rigid abs that press enticingly against his thin sweater. He must be freezing.

"I noticed that, but it seems like you're pretty close with Sadie Hughes."

"Oh, so people do know her name," Roseline laughs. "I was beginning to think I was the only decent person at this school."

Gabriel chuckles. "Sadie's great, but I didn't peg you for the type to hang out with a girl like that."

"A girl like what, exactly?" Roseline asks, crossing her arms over her chest. She juts out her hip and waits for what needs to be a really good explanation.

"I didn't mean anything by it. It's just...Sadie's not really a football fan," he covers lamely.

"Well, neither am I," she snaps. Like an alpha wolf, Roseline can feel her hackles rising to Sadie's defense

51

Gabriel tugs gently on her arm and they resume walking. "Then why *are* you here?"

Roseline shrugs, wishing for the hundredth time that she'd had the sense to remain home tonight. Although she has enjoyed regaining the teenage years that Vladimir stripped away from her, she has to admit that all of the teenage angst can be very wearing. It's hard not to long for a normal adult conversation. "I didn't have any other plans."

Gabriel's stunning grin takes her off guard. She is used to seeing beauty. It has surrounded her every day since Vladimir transformed her, but immortal beauty and human beauty are two very different things. This teenage boy is appealing in ways Roseline never dreamed possible.

The softness of his hair, the smooth curve of his lightly stubbled jaw, the tantalizing scent of cologne, and his easy smile all add to the charm that are irrevocably sucking her in. She blinks, shocked to find herself actually leaning into him.

A light mist of freezing rain glints off Gabriel's sun-streaked hair. His eyes are the palest blue she has ever seen, so pale they could pass for transparent. In the light they appear iridescent, a quality she finds deeply appealing.

It's obvious Gabriel takes pride in his looks, from his body-hugging cashmere sweater to his designer jeans and rain-dampened leather shoes. He knows he looks good and yet, oddly enough, he does not come off as overly cocky. This surprises Roseline. She thought a boy of his social status would be different.

"So does that mean you're free now?" he asks, pausing as they reach the rear end of the bleachers. He takes a step closer to see her. Gabriel's eyes linger on hers; the hope shining from them steals her breath away.

Roseline braces for it. The inevitable is about to happen. The harder her heart pounds in her chest, the faster the hormones will seep from her skin. Any second now, he will be putty in her hands.

She watches his pulse thump against his neck. The tender flesh commands her attention as her nostrils flare, inhaling his masculine scent. As his eyes lock on to hers, the world disappears. Her senses go into a frenzy and she forces lead into her legs to keep from moving toward him.

The instant her feminine scent hits Gabriel, his eyes dilate. Pheromones leech from his skin in alluring volumes. Beads of rain mingle with the sheen on his forehead. Heat stains his neck as he licks his lips. Roseline waits for him to give in to his desire...but something is wrong.

He has all of the usual symptoms but is annoyingly in control of his muscles. Instead of dragging her under the bleachers for a spicy make-out session, he remains rooted in place. He should be pleading to touch her, begging to be near her, but he isn't. His restraint is deeply unsettling.

Roseline frowns. She decides to test his resistance. "What did you have in mind?" she asks, her voice low and sultry as she steps closer. She marks the increase in his pulse and still he resists.

He wants her, there is no doubt about it, but somehow he is able to keep his wits about him. Gabriel shrugs and, instead of moving closer to her, he actually backs off. Leaning against the bleachers, he glances away.

Roseline bites her lip to silence her cry of indignation. No man, human or otherwise, has ever backed away from her once she decides she wants him. Gabriel, unknowingly, has just physically rejected her.

She has seduced many humans over the years, each time to spite Vladimir, but never once has one of them had so much control around her. Gabriel is not only holding his own, he is actually making Roseline beg for *him*.

"Oh, there you are, Rose," Sadie gasps, holding the stitch in her side as she rounds the corner with William right on her heels. Her eyes open wide—rain-streaked mascara lines her cheeks—as she notes Gabriel's presence. William glares openly at the quarterback, obviously not the least bit happy to find Mr. Popular moving in on Roseline. His fingers dig into the Styrofoam cups; cocoa flows over his fingers.

"Nicolae said you wandered off with some guy, but I didn't think it would be him," Sadie says, jerking her head toward Gabriel.

"And what were you two doing back here in the dark, Gabe?" William asks.

"What's it to you?" Gabriel challenges, turning to face off with William.

"Enough," Roseline snaps, quickly inserting herself between them. "Gabriel and I were talking. That is all."

"So, you do know my name," Gabriel grins, backing away. "And you're Rose, right?"

Roseline nods, painfully aware of the tense situation she has caused. She glances at her friends before turning toward Gabriel. "I guess that answers your question."

"Yeah." Gabriel frowns, his smile drooping with disappointment. "I guess it does. I'll see you around."

She turns her back on him, refusing to give in to the urge to watch him walk away. Sadie pounces before he rounds the corner. "What on earth are you doing back here with Gabriel Marston? Didn't I warn you about him?"

"Of course you did, but it was completely innocent."

Well, almost innocent, she silently amends.

"Nothing happened," she insists, annoyed that she has to defend her actions.

"Sure, that's all Gabriel ever wants to do with beautiful girls," William scoffs.

Roseline eyes him up. His possessive nature is beginning to grate on her nerves. Her brief meeting with Gabriel has really thrown her for a loop.

To add more fuel to the fire, Nicolae chooses this moment to pop his head around the corner. "Everything alright?"

Sadie groans loudly, whirling around. "I said wait by the car, Nicolae. Can you not understand basic English?"

He raises his hands in surrender and turns, but not before glaring icily at Roseline. He has made his presence known and that irks her. Nicolae is checking on her or, more accurately, he is checking on Gabriel.

William chucks the nearly empty cups aside as they head toward the parking lot. "So, are we gonna party or not? Sophie Reynolds is throwing a huge bash at her house tonight. Wanna crash?"

"I'm game," Sadie grins, wiping the mascara smudges from her face. Instead of looking like a raccoon, she almost resembles a zombie on Halloween. Roseline is pretty sure that is not the look Sadie is going for.

Roseline shakes her head. "I think I would prefer to return home. I'm feeling a tad flushed at the moment and should probably retire for the evening."

Sadie rolls her eyes. "There you go again. I thought you had that proper lady talk tucked into bed. What's with you?"

Holding her forehead, Roseline winces. Her face feels warm, boiling actually. It isn't possible for her to get sick, and yet there is an obvious fire burning deep within her. "I'm sorry. I don't feel very well."

William cuts off Sadie's protests as Roseline wavers on her feet. He scoops her into his arms and carries her across the parking lot. Roseline's head lolls to the side as a jacked-up Jeep guns past them. Gabriel's eyes lock onto Roseline from the passenger seat.

Her stomach flips. She pulls out of William's arms and drops to the curb. Dry heaves attack and acid burns her throat as she gives in to this mystery illness.

"Holy crap," Sadie gasps as she wraps her arm around Roseline's shoulders. "She's burning up. Will, get the car."

Her voice fades as Roseline passes out.

Stuttering brakes rouse Roseline. She groans and peels her cheek off William's leather backseat. "Want me to carry you inside?" William offers.

"No. I can manage." She slips from the car, unlocks her door without a goodbye wave, and crawls up to her bed.

Eight

"What's with you, man?" Oliver asks, shoving his friend in the shoulder. Gabriel is zoned out, completely oblivious to the blaring music, the stench of vomit wafting from the overflowing toilet down the hall, and his wanna-be pole dancer girlfriend using his leg for an impromptu dance. "Claire is all over you."

Gabriel pushes up off the couch, spilling a very drunk Claire onto the floor. He stumbles over her, not caring to stick around to hear her shrill ranting. He needs air. He pushes through the back door and falls onto a plastic lounge chair.

Staring up at the stars, all he can see is Rose. Her silky skin, long delicate bronze tresses, gorgeous eyes that see right through him, and the full lips that he knows will haunt his dreams. He doesn't want to be at this party. He does not want Claire dry humping his leg like a dog in heat. He wants Rose—beautiful, mysterious Rose.

What is it about her that feels so right? He has dated several girls over the years, but none have ever gripped him so tightly. Nor have they felt electric to the touch.

Gabriel buries his head in his hands. He clamps his eyes shut as the world begins to spin. Drinking was a really bad idea, but he needed to take the edge off. Now all he's managed to do is compound his problems.

He sinks to the ground, disappearing into the shadows as he crawls on hands and knees to the cool damp grass. It feels like slipping into a refreshing pool on a sweltering day. His skin is on fire, fueled by a bubbling volcano in the pit of his stomach.

Something is wrong. Very wrong. This isn't because of drinking—something much worse is happening.

Pain radiates through Gabriel's chest, squeezing his heart and wringing the air from his lungs. His fingers claws in the dirt, inching toward the floodlight illuminating the deck. He can see people dancing just beyond, their movements distorted in the strobe lights. Loud music rattles the windows, blocking out his cries for help.

He rolls onto his back as the pain spirals out from his heart, racing through his veins. His fingers fumble in his pocket for his cell phone. It falls onto the grass beside him. Gabriel grits his teeth against the pain as he tries to still the trembling in his fingers long enough to dial 911.

It's a struggle to breathe as he writhes on the ground. His shirt and pants soak through but it does little to ease the flames under his skin.

He feels something shifting—as if his entire genetic code is adapting. The fires begin to smolder, retreating back to his core. It rounds his heart and shoots out through his eyes. The pain vanishes as a pure blue light explodes from between closed eyelids.

Energy floods through his body. His mind screams in ecstasy as his cells erupt with sensitivity, overwhelming his senses.

Gabriel passes out.

Nine

Roseline tosses and turns in her sleep, plagued by the same dream that has repeated every night since her encounter with Gabriel after the state qualifiers. Images of him bathed in a brilliant blue light burns into her retinas. The sensation of being cocooned in his arms brings tears to her eyes. Some part of her brain acknowledges that it is a dream, but it feels like something more—something tangible.

Blinking away sleep, Roseline groans as she sits up on the edge of her makeshift bed. She rubs her neck, feeling the familiar ache she has come to expect each morning from her lumpy mattress. She vows to go bed shopping before the week is out.

Her bedroom, if she could really call it that, is sparsely furnished. A long, solid wood slab runs the length of the far wall. A rickety stool stands under the makeshift table. On top of it lies a computer she purchased the day she arrived in Chicago. Standing in the sleazy pawnshop, Roseline had promised herself she would only use it to contact Fane in case of an emergency, but her self-control is beginning to wane.

There is only one reason why she would give in now—Gabriel. It has been a week since they spoke at the football game and she has done her best to avoid him since then. Sneaking around behind his back is beginning to wear thin, especially when a huge part of her wants nothing more than to snatch him into the janitor's room and kiss him until he faints, but she cannot even think about letting that happen. A relationship with a human, especially this human, is far too risky.

But that risk, the thrill of "what if," has brought her to this moment. Staring across the room, Roseline eyes the machine that can instantly connect her with the only person who truly understands her. Of course, Fane will think she is crazy. A growing obsession with a mortal? Ludicrous. Fane would listen and try to help her, but he would also try to track her down.

"Not today," she mutters as she slips into her robe and steps out into the hall. Her fingers trail lightly over the aged wooden banister. The stairs creak underfoot, echoing loudly through the empty house.

Stepping nimbly over the cigarette burned carpet in the living room, Roseline heads for the fridge. The heavy metal door squeals as it swings open. "Drat," she groans, remembering that she was supposed to have gone grocery shopping.

When was that? Yesterday? The day before? Roseline rubs her palm against her forehead. The days of the past week have passed in a blur. Gabriel consumes her thoughts far more than he should and she can't figure out why.

With a heavy sigh, Roseline heads back through the living room, not even caring to glance at the sparse boxes stacked in the corner. They are not her stuff and, from the musty odor coming from the loose lid, there is certainly nothing of interest in there.

The dining room holds the most furniture in the entire house. A painted hutch sits in the corner, layered with an inch of dust. An old wooden farmhouse table fills the rest of the room, its long benches tucked underneath. Past that, a bathroom stands off from the main hall, its pink tiles glaring obnoxiously at anyone who dares to enter the time warp.

"I really should get out today," Roseline mumbles as she gives up her aimless wandering and heads back upstairs. Rounding the banister, she heads into one of the spare rooms. She uses this one as her makeshift closet. Designer store bags stack high in one corner, empty of their purchases. Piles of clothes, laid out in perfect condition, litter the floor. New wardrobe: check.

Sighing, Roseline grabs an outfit from the top of a pile and heads to the bathroom. Her love for all things fashion refuses to allow her to don a baseball cap so, twenty minutes later, she settles with combing her hair straight around her face to help conceal her identity. Checking one last time to make sure her makeup has helped tone down her appearance, Roseline heads out.

She is not sure where she is heading until she looks up to find that her feet have taken her right to Sadie's doorstep. It's only been a couple days since she was last here, although she struggles to remember why at the moment.

Movement in the upper window of the house next door catches her eye but the curtain flutters back into place before she can make out the person concealed within. Roseline frowns.

"Well hello, Rose. Did you do well on that Chem test you and Sadie studied so hard for? Sadie swears she aced it but I have my doubts." Mrs. Hughes smiles as she opens the glass-paneled door. Her sapphire blue robe is tucked tightly around her slender figure.

"I believe I did well enough," Roseline says, thankful for the reminder as she steps over the threshold and dips low to slip off her boots.

The scent of vanilla invades her senses. Sadie's mom appears to have the same affinity for scents as Sadie's does for wardrobe changes. "Sadie, Rose is here."

Thundering footsteps race down the carpeted hall. Roseline smiles as she hears abuse slung about from upstairs. "Back off, she's my friend."

"How do you know she came here to see you?" William protests.

Sadie snickers as she rounds the corner. "You are so desperate."

"Hi." Roseline grins, amused by their state of dress. William stands in the doorway, wearing only plaid pajama bottoms. His hair is heavily tousled, sticking up in the back like a peacock. Roseline tries not to admire William's bare chest, but it is smooth and toned, far more appealing than she would have guessed under the ratty t-shirts he loves to wear.

What amazes Roseline the most is Sadie's transformation. Without her dark eye shadow, rocker shirts, and cutoff jeans, she actually looks lovely. "Wow, Sadie, look at you."

Sadie rolls her eyes. "I know. I look terrible without makeup."

"No." She shakes her head. "You look amazing."

"See, told you so. No one likes your Goth look." Mrs. Hughes grins as she pokes her head into the room.

"Mom," Sadie hisses, shooing her mother away. Mrs. Hughes takes the hint and disappears, but not before she plants a kiss on Sadie's forehead. "She's so embarrassing."

Roseline smiles, wishing she could've had that kind of relationship with her mother. "I apologize for the early hour. I couldn't sleep and decided to take a walk."

William throws himself onto a leather couch. Reaching for the remote, he switches on the massive flat screen over the fireplace. He flips through several channels before settling on an animated children's show. Roseline raises an eyebrow but Sadie just waves it off. "He's still into cartoons. Loser."

"I heard that," he calls from the other side of the couch. He has sunk so low Roseline can't see anything more than his leg slung over the end.

Sadie heads back toward the stairs. "Come on up. I gotta get dressed anyways."

Roseline follows Sadie up to her room. Glancing toward William's partially open door she stiffens when she realizes the room is occupied. Nicolae has his back turned toward the door. She spies a mass of scars along his back before he rushes to pull his shirt down over his head.

When he turns toward her, his gaze is harsh. Roseline gets the "mind your own business" message loud and clear before Nicolae shuts the door in her face. She frowns and follows Sadie into her room, closing the door behind her.

"What's with Nicolae?" she asks, watching her friend belly flop onto her bed. Roseline settles for an oversized neon pink beanbag by the window.

"What do you mean?" Sadie asks, instantly bored with the topic.

"The scars. Haven't you noticed them before?"

Sadie sits up. "What scars?"

"On his back." She begins to question what she saw when Sadie's brow knits together. "You've never seen them?"

"Nope, but I'm not exactly trying to see him with his shirt off either." Roseline can't help but think that if Sadie had seen him back in Brasov she might have a different opinion of meek little Nicolae. "That guy gives me the creeps."

Roseline nods in agreement, but she knows her reasons are much different from Sadie's. "So is he still stalking you?"

"Night and day. The guy won't leave me alone for a second. He's always watching me."

"I think he likes you."

Sadie grits her teeth at the thought. "Yeah, well I'm off the market. I am officially done with boys. Besides, he's kinda freaky, ya know? Like how he is always offering to help me out of the car or get my lunch tray? It's almost like he's trying to be the perfect guy."

"Maybe I should talk to him," Roseline offers, rising from her seat.

Sadie laughs, rolling out of bed. She grabs a rumpled towel off her computer chair, giving it a quick sniff test before shrugging and tossing it over her shoulder. "What could you possibly do to scare him off?"

Roseline grins. "You never know."

She slips out into the hallway as soon as Sadie disappears into her bathroom. She turns and bumps straight into Nicolae.

"Do you mind?" he mutters as he bounces back against the wall. He tries to move away but Roseline's hand lashes out, clamping tightly around his forearm. Nicolae flinches at her warm touch but says nothing. Roseline can feel his anger radiating off him.

"I thought I made myself clear the other night," she growls in her native tongue as she pulls him close.

"Ah, there you are, Nicolae. I was beginning to wonder if you were up as well."

Roseline instantly releases his arm as Sadie's father exits his room at the end of the hall. "Morning, Rose. It seems I have you to thank for my family's early rising." Mr. Hughes yawns, plodding past them in his stripped PJs and slippers. He descends a couple of steps before turning back.

"I'd forgotten that you two were from the same country. Small world, eh?"

Roseline smiles as he disappears down the stairs. She turns her attention back to Nicolae. He meets her icy glare head on. No backing down. Roseline's lip curls into a snarl. Her mind explodes with imaginary red warning flags. Nicolae is far more than he appears, certainly not a typical school boy.

"Leave Sadie alone."

"Or what?" Nicolae challenges. "You'll kill me?"

"Don't tempt me." Roseline's face clouds with anger. "You know I can. In fact, I think I would rather enjoy it."

"I don't doubt that, but I doubt you would do it here, with witnesses." Nicolae's smirk tightens as he takes a step toward her. "I'm not afraid of you."

"No?" Her lips peel back over her teeth as she counters his challenge, positioning herself an inch from Nicolae's nose. His eyes widen but he holds his ground. Roseline pauses, taking in his strong stance and the muscles rippling under his shirt. "Who are you?"

"I'm the guy that's protecting Sadie," he says, grinding the words out through clenched teeth.

Roseline blinks, surprised. "You think I want to hurt my friend?" Nicolae's jaw clenches as he nods. She blows out a breath, easing back onto the pads of her feet. So that's what his whole stalker mode is about.

"You may think you know me, but you are wrong," Roseline says, leaning back against the wall to put space between them. "I give you my word, I would never lay a finger on Sadie."

"Your word means nothing me," Nicolae growls. "I will be watching you."

He turns and steps back into his room, slamming the door in Roseline's face. She stares at the closed door. Fear tickles her spine. Just how much does Nicolae know about her? Deciding there is nothing she can do about it, Roseline slips back down the stairs. Noticing William is still slouched in front of the TV, Roseline decides to join him.

"Budge up." He straightens, allowing her some room. "What are you watching?"

"Phineas and Ferb. This show is awesome."

Roseline watches for a few minutes, amused by the platypus that is a pet by day and secret agent by night. "Creative."

"No kidding," William nods, eyes glued to the screen. "It's brilliant."

"Do you watch children's shows often?" She fights to conceal her amusement.

William switches off the TV and retracts his legs from the armrest. "Hey, I know what you're thinking. What's a genius like me doing watching a show like that? Well, let me tell you, missy, brainiacs need a break too, you know."

Roseline giggles as William thrusts his thumb into his chest. "I see. Wow, I didn't realize I was in the presence of greatness."

William nods solemnly. "And don't you forget it."

"Is he trying to hit on you again?" Sadie calls as she bounces down the stairs. Her usual spiked collar has been replaced by a dog choke chain. It clangs loudly as she lands on the ground floor. She wears jeans two sizes too big, drooped at the waist, and a Pink Floyd t-shirt.

"Oh, not again," William groans. "Aren't you done with this phase yet?"

"Nope. I'm still exercising my civil rights."

Roseline grins. "Protesting the school dress code on the weekend, too?"

"You bet." Sadie nods, slinging herself into the armchair. "Someone has to make a statement."

"Well, I'd say you're covering that for the entire school," Mrs. Hughes says as she carries in a plate of freshly baked biscuits into the living room. "Hungry, Rose?"

"Yes, ma'am. I forgot to eat this morning."

"No kidding. It's like five AM." Sadie groans, shielding her eyes from the bright sunshine streaming in through the bay window nearby.

"Oh, stop being such a sour puss," William cries, tossing a pillow at his sister. "It's at least seven AM."

"It's a tragedy, that's what it is," Sadie says mournfully. "I never get out of bed before ten AM on a Saturday."

Roseline's brow furrows, thinking over her words. "Then why are you awake so early?" Obviously, Sadie and William were awake when she arrived. A mischievous grin spreads across Sadie's face. She glances over at William with a conspiratorial gleam in her eye. Roseline stares at the siblings with increasing suspicion. "Alright, what's going on?"

Ten

"How could you say yes without even asking me?" Roseline cries, leaping to her feet. When Gabriel stopped by Sadie's house the night before to invite them to a party at his house she actually agreed. Roseline leaps through feelings of betrayal and straight into panic. This is the complete opposite of avoiding him!

"I thought you'd be happy." Sadie's grin phases into a frown. "You sure seemed to enjoy talking to him last weekend."

"Yes, talking is fine..." Roseline agrees hesitantly.

Sadie scans her growing blush. "But he wants more, doesn't he?"

William jerks upright, suddenly very interested in their conversation. Roseline tries to appear as if her shrug is innocent. "He asked if I had plans. That's all."

"So what stopped you?" Sadie asks, leaning forward.

"Besides you, you mean?" William snorts. His face takes the brunt of Sadie's couch pillow missile.

Dozens of reasons flood Roseline's mind. Like the fact that she's an immortal with a husband who has a vicious jealous streak and will happily rip Gabriel's limbs from his body? Or because Gabriel is a mortal and totally unsuited for her life? Or that simply by being around him, she gets all warm and mushy and her predatory senses are shot to pieces? Or maybe it's that she can't even figure out why she is so drawn to him. This fact alone is enough to make her want to run and hide.

Roseline stares pointedly at Sadie, choosing the only excuse that won't make her sound like a lunatic. "He has a girlfriend and that is where I draw the line."

William grins triumphantly but Roseline ignores him. His enthusiasm over her decision makes her groan inwardly. Although she has given him no reason to hope for a relationship, apparently those dreams are still burning strong.

"It's just a party, Rose," Sadie says, throwing up her hands. "I'm not asking you to marry the guy."

Unable to remain seated any longer, Roseline rises to pace the room. She hates how unsettled Gabriel makes her feel. Just thinking about him is bad enough, but after a week's worth of dreaming about him, she is afraid she will jump him the instant she sees him.

"What if you went with a date?" Sadie suggests, breaking into Roseline's thoughts. "That way you wouldn't be tempted to break your moral code."

"A date?" Roseline laughs. "Where could I find a date on such short notice?"

William trips over his own feet trying to stand. His arm shoots straight into the air. "Me. I'm free."

Definitely need to discourage this, she sighs inwardly. "Thank you, William, but I will be fine."

"Are you sure?" he asks, his face drooping with disappointment.

"Definitely."

William is cute, no doubt about that, but he needs to take a hint. He has brother vibes wriggling all over him!

Roseline turns on Sadie, still trying to find a loophole to get herself out of the party. "I thought you hated the in-crowd. What is with the change of heart?"

"Oh, don't give me that look," Sadie pleads. "I know what you're thinking and, yes, you're right. Partying with snobs isn't exactly my scene anymore...but it's the first time since freshman year that I've been invited. I gotta go, Rose."

"I don't know." Roseline chews on her lip. Sadie buries her head in a pillow, wailing dramatically.

William rolls his eyes. "I don't see what the big deal is, Sadie. She doesn't want to go, so she shouldn't. We can chill out here, or something. We can rent a couple movies, pop some corn, and snuggle." He raises his eyebrows suggestively.

Roseline laughs at Sadie's horrified expression. "Are you insane? There will be girls there. Girls!"

William cuts a glance over at Roseline. He shrugs. "I'm good here."

"Un-freaking-believable," Sadie cries out, thrusting herself back into the couch cushions. "All I'm asking for is one night of teenage bliss. You two hate me."

"Oh, don't be like that," William says.

"No, she's right." Roseline lets out an exaggerated sigh. She cannot fault Sadie for wanting one night to fit in, but that doesn't mean she thinks it's a good idea. "Don't forget that you have spent four years rebelling against these people. I hate to think you would give all of that up just for one stupid party."

Sadie's upper lip tucks behind her lower lip, creating a pathetically endearing pout. "You think I don't know that I will still be the leper of the party? I do. I get it, but I still want to go. Can't you give me just one night to live out my delusions?"

Roseline drapes her arm over Sadie's shoulder. "According to your own advice, the in-crowd is just a bunch of miserable drug addicts, alcoholics, and sluts. You really wannabe like them?"

"Well now that you mention it..." Sadie trails off, grinning mischievously.

Roseline laughs. "You are shameless."

"And proud of it." Sadie crows, not looking the least bit contrite. "So what do you say?"

"Are you in on this too?" Roseline glances over at William, whose pout over her rejection lingers.

He shrugs before stuffing another biscuit into his mouth. "Yeah, it could be good. I'm game."

"I don't have anything to wear," Roseline protests, knowing it's such a pathetic excuse that Sadie will shoot holes through it in an instant.

She is wrong. William jumps first. "No problem. Sadie has a load of clothes that she never wears. I'm sure she has something that will fit you."

Roseline's gaze darts toward Sadie, not wanting to be rude. Sadie giggles. "I don't always dress like this you know. I do own *some* normal clothes."

"I didn't say a word," Roseline holds up her hands in mock surrender.

"You didn't have to," William chuckles. "Why don't we pick you up after dinner? That should give you about an hour before the party starts to get ready."

"Like that's gonna be enough time," Sadie scoffs, grinning conspiratorially at Roseline as she ushers her friend toward the front door.

Eleven

"Sexy," Sadie says, grinning as Roseline hesitantly steps out from behind the bathroom door. She walks lightly, careful not to twist an ankle on the mountains of clothes that have been carelessly discarded around the room.

Roseline smoothes her hands along the tight black strapless dress. It hugs her figure with perfection. For the first time since she became an immortal, she feels overly self-conscious about her looks. "You're sure about this? It seems a bit over the top."

Sadie's smaller stature means every outfit Roseline tries on is a tad too short. This little black number is no exception. The dress falls along the upper portion of her thighs, revealing far more than she would have preferred.

"Oh yeah!" Sadie grins, giving her an enthusiastic thumbs up. "Gabriel will love you in that one."

"That is exactly what I am afraid of," Roseline groans, reaching behind her to unzip the dress. Sadie shrieks and shoves her hand away.

"Don't you dare," she commands.

"Why not?" Roseline tries to use her arms to cover her slender waist. The tight boning is beginning to dig into her side. Not that she can't handle it. She has worn dresses much tighter and heavier than this, but that was a long time ago. In Roseline's opinion, the invention of the jeans and t-shirt look was the best thing since electricity.

Sadie shoves Roseline in front of the mirror. "Because you look freakin' amazing."

A knock at the door startles Roseline. She grinds her teeth at letting someone slip up the stairs unnoticed. Her concern over the dress has made her lose her edge. She has to find a way to stop thinking about Gabriel.

"Are you girls ready yet?" William asks through the door, checking for the third time in ten minutes.

Sadie throws a hiking boot at the door. "Go away. We're not done."

Roseline smirks as William lumbers back down the stairs, not making the slightest effort to hide his exasperation. She can sympathize. They have been playing dress up for nearly two hours now and Sadie shows little sign of tiring.

"So...strappy or closed toe?" Sadie holds up two pairs of black high heels. Roseline chews on her lip. She would normally go for the strappy, but they are a bit too sexy. "Definitely closed toe."

"I thought you would say that." Sadie rolls her eyes as she yanks her window open and chucks the closed toe shoes straight out of her second story room. Her cat, Patches, howls as they land nearby. Sadie giggles and holds out the strappy ones. "I think we need to work on your fashion sense."

"Look who's talking." Roseline jabs a finger at Sadie's mix-matched outfit. She is wearing a shredded Metallica t-shirt over a purple tank top, green feather earrings, bright yellow mini skirt, and red flip-flops. Her normally spiked hair is tamed and braided with black leather straps. Sadie looks like the rainbow threw up on her. "No offense, but that outfit is horrid."

"You think you can do better?" Sadie challenges, spreading her arm towards her walk-in closet. "Be my guest."

Roseline disappears into the messy room. "You really need a maid."

"Tell me about it. I have been begging for months but Mom thinks it's a waste of money. Can you believe that? All you have to do is take one look at my room and see the value."

Moments later Roseline reappears, a triumphant grin lighting her face. "This is perfect."

Sadie's eyebrows rise as she nods appreciatively. "Rose, you've totally redeemed yourself." She grabs the outfit from her hand and dances off into the bathroom. Roseline perches on the edge of the bed and begins winding the straps of the high heels around her ankle.

She is still trying to find a way out of attending the party when the bathroom door creaks open. Roseline glances up and whistles as Sadie twirls in the doorway. "Oh, you look smashing."

Her friend smiles shyly as she spins back around. The bright pink and black zebra-striped dress is an amazing match to Sadie's pink braided hair. Black teardrop earrings dangle from her earlobes, gently caressing her pale cheeks. "You think so?" she asks, her voice unusually soft as she blushes.

"Definitely," Roseline assures her, throwing a pair of black knee-high boots at her. "You are definitely gonna turn some heads tonight."

"Not if I'm standing next to you," Sadie snorts, shoving her feet into the shoes and zipping them. She stands back up, smoothing out her dress. "All set. Let's go before William breaks down the door."

Sadie takes the stairs at a breakneck speed. *Someone is way too excited about this party*, Roseline silently muses. She has barely touched the final step when Sadie howls indignantly. "You have got to be kidding! No way is he coming with us."

Standing less than a foot from the front door, Nicolae winces, shifting back and forth nervously. His buttoned-up shirt looks rumpled, his glasses slightly askew. He appears less than thrilled at the idea of going to a party, but the moment Roseline hits the bottom step his spine straightens and his defiance leaps to attention. He stares her down with open hostility but the electric chemistry in the room that Sadie has created covers their silent showdown.

"Sadie, don't be rude to our guest. You know Gabriel invited everyone to his party," Mrs. Hughes calls from the living room. The smell of popcorn filters throughout the ground floor. Apparently, Sadie's parents are planning a date night of their own and judging by the tone of her voice she is not about to let her teenage daughter spoil it.

"I cannot believe this," Sadie growls under her breath. "Fine, just try not to act like a loser." She grabs Nicolae by the arm and yanks him outside. He splutters and stumbles after her, nearly tumbling as she races down the front porch steps.

William holds the door for Roseline, grinning stupidly as he eyes her dress. "Wow, Rose, you look amazing."

"Thanks," she blushes and ducks out onto the porch. Unwilling to hang around while William openly ogles her, Roseline rushes across the side yard and directly onto Gabriel's front driveway. She still cannot believe that Sadie actually lives next door to the one guy in all of Chicago that she is trying hardest to avoid. Isn't she already being tortured enough?

Roseline comes to a grinding halt behind Nicolae as the door opens. A feeling akin to that of a battering ram slams into her stomach as Gabriel emerges from the dim interior. Why does he have to look so gorgeous?

"Sadie, Nicolae, how nice to see you. Come on in," Gabriel smiles. Sadie drags Nicolae over the threshold, apparently unaware of how intensely Gabriel gazes at Roseline. She blinks, wishing she could break the hypnotic stare. "Are you coming in too?"

Roseline flushes and nods as she shuffles past him into the beating heart of her first high school party. It is louder than she could have imagined, which is really saying something since the speakers aren't even in sight as she skirts along the wall. Gabriel starts to close the door behind her, but a hand shoves through the gap. He pulls open the door to reveal a perturbed William.

"Will, nice to see you could join us." Roseline smirks at the rough edge to Gabriel's voice.

"Sure thing. Wouldn't want to miss a famous Gabriel Marston party. I've heard so many great things."

He lets that loaded statement hang in the air. Gabriel clears his throat, shifting uncomfortably in the awkward silence.

William saunters up to Roseline, inserting himself between her and Gabriel. "Would you like me to grab you a drink?"

"Uh, sure. That would be great." Roseline blinks, severing her connection with Gabriel as William brushes past. Although his commanding eyes no longer fixate on her, she still feels drawn to him.

"I'm glad you could make it," Gabriel says, letting his eyes flicker down the front of her dress only for a moment. He swallows and turns to close the door.

"It was really nice of you to invite us," she says, darting a glance over at him as he leads the way into the foyer. Her stiletto heels clack against the tile entry. The instant they meet up with the newly waxed wood floor she releases a small cry of alarm. Her legs fly apart as she reaches out for the wall to stop her descent, but Gabriel grabs onto her first.

The feel of his hands on her arm only increases the fuzziness of her senses. Her Jell-O-filled legs refuse to obey as Gabriel's free arm wraps around her waist to hold her upright. "Are you okay? You haven't twisted your ankle, have you?"

Ankle? Of course not. It's her pride that is bruised.

Her fingers curl around the edge of the wall as she eases out of his hands. "I will be fine. Thank you." She smiles as heat stains her cheeks. Even though his fingers no longer brush against her skin, she can still feel the remnants of the electrical current that vibrates along her skin.

"This should be safer for you." He grins as she steps onto the plush carpet.

"I swear that I am normally more graceful," Roseline laughs, shifting her head to the side to allow her hair to fall in a protective wave over her face. "Maybe not the best choice in shoes, huh?"

"Oh no," Gabriel shakes his head, risking a glance down at her calves. "They look great." He clears his throat. "So, um, do you like to dance?"

Roseline pulls the silky veil back from her eyes to look at him. "You cannot be serious. I think I might injure someone with these shoes."

Gabriel chuckles. The sound warms the pit of Roseline's stomach. "Well, if you change your mind, the dance floor is downstairs. The snacks and drinks are in the kitchen and the back deck has some loungers if you need to cool off. You're free to roam the rest of the house, but I'd stay clear of the third door on the left upstairs."

Roseline's brow crinkles with confusion. Gabriel laughs. "It's my room."

"Ah," she nods. "Are you afraid I might see your bed unmade?"

"Nope," Gabriel shakes his head. "The last time I looked, it had been turned into the hook-up room. Just trying to save you from walking in on something you really don't want to see."

"Right." Roseline shifts beside him, unsure of what else she should say or where she should place her hands. Awkward does not even begin to explain how she feels. That, in and of itself, is enough to throw her off. Normally she is completely in control of herself, especially around humans.

"Well, I guess I should probably go." The wistful tone in his voice is undeniable as he glances toward the crowd of teens spilling from every corner of his home.

"I don't want to steal away the host," Roseline nods in agreement. A part of her wants to protest, to keep him close by, but logic tells her to flee before she does something she might regret, like yanking him into the coat closet by the front door.

"Well..." he pauses, waiting for Roseline to give him a reason to stay. When she doesn't, he steps back. "I'll see you around."

Roseline tosses him an awkward wave as he disappears into the crowded family room. Wincing at how poorly she handled herself, she slips around the corner and straight down the basement stairs to find a dark corner to hide in until Sadie is ready to leave, but when she arrives, she discovers a manic scene. Strobe lights dance over the heads of a throng of underage drinkers. They grind against each other, moving in ways that she has only ever seen at nightclubs back in Romania. She was always forced to sit and watch. Anytime someone asked her to dance, Vladimir would scare them off with a threat of dismemberment. It worked like a charm.

The heat and nearly visible cloud of teen hormones drive Roseline back up the stairs. She maneuvers her way through the packed kitchen, skirting the group crowding around the island chanting like cavemen as two boys compete to see how many cheese curls they can shove in their mouth. Deciding she doesn't want to fight through the crowd for a soda, she peeks out the window at the deck. It appears to be empty. She sneaks through the backdoor and closes it behind her, sucking in a cleansing breath of fresh air. Solitude.

"I should have known you would be drawn to the dark."

The hair on the back of Roseline's neck rises as she whips around, coming face to face with Nicolae. His shirt is unbuttoned, his glasses vacant from his face; his hair ruffled into messy spikes. If she didn't loath him so much, she might actually be able to appreciate the handsome boy before her.

"Looks like I'm not the only one who likes dark places," Roseline retorts, moving away from him.

"That's because you and I have much to hide."

Roseline turns, narrowing her eyes. "And what is it that you are hiding, Nicolae?"

His gaze grows cold. "You don't know?"

"Should I?" she counters. *Who is this boy? Why does he seem to know so much about me?*

He steps into the light flooding from the kitchen window. The harsh set of his face takes Roseline back. "I know what you have done, Roseline Enescue. You will pay for your sins, and those of your family."

The color drains from her face. "You don't know me," she whispers. Her throat chokes off the last of her words. Her stomach roils as she steps back to lean against the railing.

"I don't have to. Your kind are all the same," he spits out. Blackened fury captures his eyes as he closes the gap between them. The scent of alcohol is heavy on his breath, but he hasn't been drinking long enough to be drunk. This crazed anger is rooted elsewhere.

His hand wraps around her arm, squeezing to the point of near pain. Her eyes narrow at his strength. "Who *are* you?"

"What the heck is going on?" William calls. The red plastic cup in his free hand falls to the deck as he yanks Nicolae back.

Nicolae's face shifts instantly as he grabs his glasses from his shirt pocket. He settles them into place and smoothes down his hair before William turns him around. "What's wrong with you?"

"Nothing," Nicolae adopts a meek voice. "We were just talking."

William glances back at Roseline. Her hands shake as she presses them tightly to her stomach. William's back teeth grind as he sees how frazzled she is. "Get out of here. If I see you around her again tonight I swear you will regret it."

For a split second, Roseline thinks Nicolae will challenge William. She watches the shift in his stance as he rocks onto the balls of his feet, the quivering of his jaw as he grinds his teeth, and the way his fingers flinch by his side. William squares off with him, inserting himself between Roseline and Nicolae.

"Whatever," Nicolae mutters as he turns and stalks off.

William waits until Nicolae slams the door behind him before turning toward Roseline. "Are you okay?"

"Yes," she replies, wincing at the tremor in her voice. "It was nothing really."

"You're as white as a ghost. That's not nothing."

Roseline shrugs, blowing out a deep breath. The need to be alone nearly overwhelms her. "I'm a little thirsty. Think you could grab me another drink?"

"Sure," William smiles, releasing his grip on her arm. He steps over the spilled soda near the door. "I'll be right back."

Roseline sinks into the lounger and covers her face with her hands. Deep steadying breaths help to calm her. Nicolae knows too much. *Do I run again?*

Even as the thought crosses her mind, Roseline's anger fuels. No. She isn't going to run again. She can't give up the life she has begun to build just for one teenage punk.

But if he says anything...she will have to deal with him.

"Feeling any better?" William's voice cuts into her thoughts.

She smiles up at him, accepting the punch cup. It reeks of cheap alcohol but she downs it anyway. What does she care? She has a high tolerance for the stuff. The cool liquid soothes the burning in her throat. "Yes, thank you. That guy just really irks me."

She looks beyond him to the living room where Nicolae stands, glaring openly at her. Instead of backing down, Roseline meets his icy gaze.

"You know, if it weren't for his creepy obsession with Sadie, I would say the guy has a thing for you."

Roseline nods. "Poor Sadie."

"Tell me about it. The guy even mumbles about her in his sleep. If he touches one hair on her head I swear I will lose it."

Roseline stiffens as she watches Nicolae's facial features harden. At the rear of the room, Sadie ducks toward the basement stairs with a guy in tow. Nicolae's jaw sets as he storms after her. "You might want to follow him then." She points to Nicolae's fleeing back.

William groans. "Are you sure you are alright?"

"Yes," Roseline manages a grin. "Now go kick his butt."
And if you can't do it I will gladly help out, she silently adds.

William throws open the door and darts for the stairs. Roseline moves to close the door but stops cold in the doorway. There, less then fifteen feet away, is the sight she had most wanted to avoid tonight—Claire and Gabriel together, as a couple.

One glimpse of Claire grinding against Gabriel's lap sends all thoughts of Nicolae running. Her jealousy skyrockets to the moon.

"He's just a human. He's just a human," she growls as she slams the door and turns away.

Twelve

Roseline's gaze sweeps Gabriel's backyard. The scent of fragrant herbs filters through her senses from the manicured beds below. A frost hangs thick in the air, giving the spluttering fountain near the center of the yard a halo effect. Beige paving stones create a pathway to a small wooden swing that hangs under a tall oak tree near the back fence.

A cottage-style playhouse in the far right corner of the yard has been transformed into what appears to be a garden shed. Little blue shutters framing the windows are adorned with small window boxes filled with colorful fall mums.

Her heart clenches at the thought of how much this backyard resembles the grounds of Bran Castle. Beautiful. Tranquil. Deceiving.

"I couldn't help but notice you look lonely out here by yourself. Would you like some company?" a masculine voice calls to her from behind. Roseline turns slowly, reluctant to give up her solitude. The guy standing before her looks vaguely familiar, but she can't place him. "I'm sorry. Do I know you?"

"The name's Conner." He moves to lean against the railing next to her. His casual demeanor is appealing. "I'm Gabriel's friend."

"Oh," she says, dropping her gaze she he would not see the flicker of pleasure pulling at the corners of her lips.

Conner leans in. The scent of his cologne draws her in as she breathes deep, savoring the aroma. "Gabriel would be ticked if he knew I was out here."

Surprised, Roseline glances up to meet Conner's gold-flecked hazel eyes. "Why?

He shifts closer. "Haven't you wondered why none of the other guys have hit on you tonight?"

"Um...no?" Roseline isn't quite sure how to take that question. Is he playing a joke on her? If so, what would be the point? Did Gabriel set him up to this?

Conner's chuckle is deep and throaty. "You must know that we're being watched right now."

Roseline's spine straightens as she follows his gaze to the windows. "All of the guys want you and all the girls would kill to be you," he whispers near her ear.

He is right. Numerous people are watching their interaction. Some stare enviously at Conner but nearly every hostile glare is blasting at her from the girls in the room as they fight to draw the attention of their guys back to them.

She crosses her arms over her chest and focuses on Conner. "So what about you? Are you here just to chat me up?"

"Well, that depends." He grins, leaning in so close she can smell the mint on his breath. His gaze droops to take in the appealing curve of her low-cut dress.

"On what?"

He reaches out and runs a single finger down the length of her bare arm. His smile is enticing, filled with experienced promise. "If you want me to."

The thought of leaning in and pressing her lips against his is tempting, but only because she would give anything to push the image of Gabriel with Claire from her mind. Passing the time cuddled up with this human might not be a bad way to pass a few hours. It is certainly a better idea than standing around here feeling completely out of place.

Conner shifts to face her. His hands slowly wind around her waist. She lets him press up against her, intimately molding his body to hers. His breathing becomes heavy as he looks down into her eyes. "You are so beautiful."

His murmur should draw her in, but it feels wrong. Not the words. They are fine. It's who is saying them.

"Gabriel," Roseline murmurs softly. She places her hands on Connor's chest and presses back gently as he leans in to kiss her. "This isn't—"

Movement over his shoulder makes Roseline gasp. Conner stumbles back a step as she shoves him away. Gabriel stands in the doorway, eyes glued to her flaming cheeks. Anguish fills his face as his fingers clamp tightly around the door. Roseline feels his pain slam into her. "You should go," she says to Conner, without breaking her gaze from Gabriel.

Conner turns and scowls. Gabriel's wounded stare shifts to encompass his friend before he turns on his heel. The glass-paned door slams shut behind him.

"Are you kidding me? He's been all over Claire tonight and you still want to hold out hope the guy wants you?"

"What I want doesn't matter. But this," she motions between them, "is wrong."

"Why?" he challenges, pulling her hand into his. "I'm not seeing anyone. It's not like I'm cheating."

"No." Roseline shakes her head. "But you just betrayed your friendship with Gabriel."

Connor shrugs indifferently. "Well, it wasn't fair for him to claim you and Claire. No guy deserves that kind of luck."

Roseline sighs as she notices the line of teens pressing against the windows. Great. Now her reputation is tarnished here too.

"If you change your mind—"

"I won't," she cuts him off, yanking her arm out of his grasp.

Conner spins and reenters the house to a rousing cheer and congratulatory pat on the back. Roseline turns away, sickened. She sinks down onto a lounger. How can this night get any worse?

People come and go as the hours pass. The moon slowly moves across the sky, bathing her in its luminescent glow. Finally, when the ache of sitting sinks deep into her bones, she rises wearily to her feet. It is time to go. Now if only she can find her friends.

"William," she calls as she slips through the backdoor. He casts an apologetic glance over his shoulder as he follows a cute blue-eyed, mini-skirted girl up the stairs. The sheen on his flushed skin tells Roseline all she needs to know. "Typical."

She moves down the hall, wrinkling her nose at the smell of vomit wafting from the bathroom. It is much worse than when she first arrived. At the entrance to the family room, Roseline pauses, straining up on tiptoes to scan the crowd for Sadie. It should have been easy to spot her neon-pink hair, but among the mass of spinning colored strobe lights it is an impossible task.

She closes her eyes, stretching out her senses as she searches for Sadie's voice. The room is bursting at the seams with sweating, hormone crazed, drunk teenagers. Ear shattering music rises from the basement below.

"Hey, new girl."

Roseline groans. She is really beginning to hate that title. She turns and watches as a guy barrels his way toward her. His broad shoulders shove people out of the way as he carves a wide path straight through the room. One thick finger hovers in the air before him, pointing directly at her. His steps are heavy, no doubt trying to compensate for the booze coursing through his blood stream. This guy she recognizes.

Crossing her arms over her chest, Roseline stands her ground as he lumbers up. "You're that girl that threatened me a couple weeks ago, aren't you?"

Roseline rolls her eyes. This is obviously going to end badly. "Yeah? So?"

"So I think you should apologize," he burps, beer sloshing from the plastic cup as he wipes his mouth. His forehead is clammy, eyes slightly glazed. Only his resentment appears to be keeping him lucid.

"I will do no such thing. You were acting like a brute so I put you in your place."

As Oliver slams his fist against the wall near the side of Roseline's head, a spray of beer rains down onto her dress. "No one puts me in my place," he growls.

His head cocks to the side, enjoying the view down the front of Roseline's dress. "You know, there is something about you that I like though."

Roseline chortles. "I wonder what that could be."

Oliver grins. "You've done a real number on Gabriel," he tsks. "Poor guy can't stop thinking about you. I wonder why that is," he murmurs as he slides closer, pressing the length of his body against hers. His sweaty clothes stick to her bare skin. "Maybe he's already had a taste."

Roseline spits in his face, disgusted. She shoves him away. "I warned you before...don't touch me."

Oliver grins maliciously. Roseline is unable to stop the shiver that races down her back. That look is one she has seen thousands of times on Vladimir's face. Empty, unmerciful rage, and each time it is followed by pain.

Instead of Oliver leaning over her, she sees her husband's livid face. That is all it takes to immobilize her.

Vice-like hands cup her face. Rank breath washes over her nose, turning her stomach sour as Oliver closes in. "I think it's only fair that I get a piece of the action too," he leers down at her, his tongue flickering over his lips. Carnal lust gleams in his eyes.

He withdraws one hand, sliding it around her waist to pull her tightly against him. It's not the feel of him shoved against her that snaps her out of her paralysis, or the way his breathing grows haggard as his thumb brushes over her lips. It's not until Oliver's head slams into the wall next to her that she blinks away the fear.

"Are you okay?"

A single tear slips from Roseline's eye as she turns toward her savior. "Gabriel?"

He reaches out the steady her as she struggles to remain upright. "Did he hurt you?" All Roseline can do is shake her head.

"Oh, thank God," he breathes a sigh of relief. "I was afraid I'd be too late.

Roseline blinks, trying to focus on him. "Where did you come from?"

Gabriel glances away, the muscles along his jaw clamped down tightly. "I was worried about you. When I saw you weren't on the deck..." The words pinch off as he grimaces.

"I didn't go with your friend."

Gabriel nods solemnly. "I know. He's over on the couch with Rachel Lutz."

Roseline glances to the far wall, snorting as she watches Conner shove his tongue down the cheerleader's throat. "Well, he bounced back nicely," she replies sourly.

"Yeah. He always does," Gabriel says through gritted teeth. His gaze falls back on her. "Are you sure you're alright?"

His concern touches her more than she wants it to. "Yeah, just a little shaken up."

"Want to get out of here?"

Roseline nods, following Gabriel's lead faithfully. His fingers entwine with hers as he leads her through the crowd. It is not until they start up the stairs that she begins to question his motives. "Where are we going?"

Gabriel turns at the sound of her concern. His smile is warm, trusting. "Don't worry. I just want to show you something."

Roseline follows him to the end of the hall. The third door on the left is closed, shrill giggling escapes from under the door. Gabriel groans. "I'm gonna have to sanitize everything."

Roseline smirks, pausing as he reaches overhead. He grasps a thin cord and a pull down ladder appears. "After you," Gabriel offers, waiting for her to go up first.

Her blush comes fast and furious as she glances down at the dress that up until this point has seemed only mildly inappropriate, but with its painfully short hem, there is no way she is going to go first. "I can't," she says, burning with embarrassment.

Gabriel's eyes lower to her dress, widening as he comes to the same realization she has. He clears his throat, fighting to tear his eyes away. "Uh yeah, right. I'll just go up then."

Roseline glances around to make sure the shadows are pervert free before she races up the ladder after him. Once inside, Gabriel swiftly closes the hatch.

Thirteen

The sight before her is unlike anything Roseline would have guessed. Gone are the spider webs, scurrying mice, and three-inch-thick dust covering teetering boxes of abandoned junk. Instead, the room is warmly lit by the moonlight streaming in through the skylights above. A lamp perched on top of an overflowing bookcase casts a warm glow on the couch nearby.

A thick beige shag rug fills the center of the room, leaving exposed hardwood floor around the outside. The ceiling and walls have even been completely finished, painted a warm vanilla color. A table overlooks the window above the garage. Adorning the top is a full bouquet of orange roses.

Her gaze is drawn away from the beautiful flowers to the easel standing next to the window, the perfect spot for letting in southern exposure. "You're an artist?" she whispers, twirling around, noticing for the first time that the walls are lined with charcoal sketches.

Gabriel remains silent as Roseline examines each piece, carefully noting every skillful stroke. City streets filled with people, a mother cradling her child, a little boy wrestling with his dog, and a toddler girl with bouncy curls gleefully riding a merry-go-round. "These are amazing, Gabriel," she whispers.

Turning, she notices him watching her. The delicate skin of his cheeks reddens as he smiles. "I spent all my spare time last summer finishing off this space so I could turn it into my own private art studio…but you're the first person to see it."

"Really? You're parents haven't even seen it?" Roseline gasps, shocked by his admission.

Gabriel shrugs, sinking down onto the black leather couch at the other end of the small room. "If it's not about football or anything to do with Notre Dame, they don't really want to know. They have plans and I'm not allowed to ruin them."

Roseline slips out of her heels, treading through the lusciously soft fibers of the carpet as she sinks down next to him. The despair in his voice feels all too familiar. "I'm so sorry."

Gabriel's shrug does not fool her. She can see how he has put his heart and soul into every detail of the room and to be unable to share it with anyone...

"I love the roses," Roseline points at the beautiful arrangement. Another surprising detail.

"They're my favorite," they say at the exact same time. Roseline smiles shyly, lowering her lashes as she feels a blush spreading along her neck.

Her eyes light on an open sketchbook between them. Gabriel scrambles to close the book, but Roseline gets there first. Snatching the book away, she carefully runs her hand across the edge of the page. "Is this me?" she whispers, amazed at the beauty staring back at her.

"It's just a doodle," he mutters, reaching for the book. "It's not very good."

Wide, beautiful doe eyes look demurely down at the folded hands in the girl's lap. A delicate floral skirt lies across her shapely calves. The low V-neck shirt fits snugly to her curvy frame. Roseline blushes. "Wasn't this what I was wearing the first time we met?"

Gabriel nods uncomfortably. "I uh...I was trying to remember you, just in case you slipped away again."

"It's very flattering," she whispers, amused by the varying shades of red clinging to Gabriel's ears.

"It's how I see you," he mutters.

Roseline allows him to pull the book away. He clutches it to his chest as if she might snatch it back. "I'm not sure I really look like that, but thank you. It is beautiful."

His eyes dart up to meet hers but struggle to hold long. Roseline is drawn in by his vulnerability. It is so different from the image he puts forth at school. "Thank you for sharing this with me."

She can hear the leather shift as he sinks deeper into the couch, his jeans rustling as he crosses his legs. Somehow, in that innocent movement, he closes part of the gap separating them. Fingering a loose thread on his pant leg, Gabriel speaks. "I knew you'd understand."

Roseline tilts her head to the side. "How? You don't even know me."

"True," Gabriel agrees, bobbing his head. "But I feel..." he trails off, wincing. "Never mind."

"What?" Roseline presses, annoyed by how desperately she wants to hear his next words.

Gabriel sighs, finally meeting her gaze. "I feel like there's something between us. Like a past that I have no memory of."

Roseline sucks in a breath. Should she admit the same? The dreams that feel like memories, the longing she has begun to feel for him, and the way just thinking of him sets her body on fire? Yes, there is something there, but why? It doesn't make sense.

Running his hands through his hair, Gabriel blows out a breath. "Sorry. I know how lame that probably sounded."

Stretching out her hand, Roseline gently lays it on top of his. "No. Not lame at all."

Gabriel stares down at their hands. "I think you've bewitched me, Rose."

She feels the tremble in his fingers as his gaze lifts to search the faint rosy tint of her cheeks and darts to everything below that. She can see the question in his eyes, as if he verbally asking how she was coerced into wearing such a bold dress.

Electricity spikes each time they touch. Skin to skin. Spark to spark. She can't explain what it is about him that makes the air around them feel charged.

"I've known many a witch, Gabriel," Roseline says, releasing his hand to shift away. She perches on the edge of the couch, yanking on the short hem of her dress, wishing it would magically grow another couple of inches. "But none of them have ever had much luck getting the right guy to fall for them."

His fingers tap idly on the couch cushion. "That's a shame. I quite like the idea." Roseline blushes, turning away from him.

"Have I embarrassed you?" he asks softly.

She shakes her head as she fights with her emotions. Being near Gabriel is intoxicating. She breathes in deep, enjoying his blood's aroma. It calls to her, winding silky tendrils of desire through her belly. A deep ache begins in her toes, worming its way up through every nerve in her body.

Why does his blood call to her? Why does she feel like her fate rests in his hands? He is a mortal, for goodness' sakes. It doesn't matter what she feels or how her body betrays her. Gabriel Marston is off limits.

"Please don't," she whispers, fighting to keep the tremor from her voice. "We both know you have a girlfriend, and I'm…I'm not good for you."

She dips her head, allowing her bronze strands to shield her face from him. His fingers grip his thigh, as if he wants to reach out to touch her, but instead he thrusts to his feet. Roseline breathes a silent prayer of thanks. She needs space and an eternity of time to think. Even then, she doubts she would have time to get a grasp of her feelings for this mortal boy.

Gabriel paces. The boards underfoot creak in protest of his heavy tread. His sigh captures her attention. She watches as his shoulders sag under the invisible weight of obligation. "You're right. I am with Claire."

"You don't sound too happy about that," she murmurs. She knows she shouldn't care, that she should flee from this room as fast as humanly possible, but she can't bring herself to move.

It's not as if they can ever be together. This longing is pure torture but reason fails her as Gabriel drops to his knees before her.

"I'm miserable, Rose." Despair pinches his handsome face. "I don't want to be with her. I never have. I only want one thing," he pauses, rising up to meet her eye to eye. "I want a chance to get to know you."

Her lower lip trembles at the implications that request could have. Hope? Love? Perhaps, but she cannot overlook the reality of what such a choice would mean. Relations of the heart with a human are strictly forbidden and intensely enforced. The immortal world must remain secret.

She has been taught since birth into immortality that humans are meant for only two things: bloodletting and sex. Even then, it is frowned upon for a married immortal to seek out such physical relationships.

Which is exactly why Roseline has sought them out every chance she could get over the years. To prove to Vladimir that he does not own her mind, even though he lays claim to her body.

Could she enter into this form of relationship with Gabriel and manage to walk away unscathed? No. Getting close to him is sure to burn her.

Gabriel bows his head. "I know all of this feels so sudden but in my gut I know that it's right. We are right." He pauses, blanching slightly. "I have tried to forget you. To move on and pretend that you don't exist but I can't. You are in my every waking thought."

Her groan is silent but it feels like it resounds through the heavens. Why is he doing this to her? The urge to yank him into her arms is nearly unbearable as she turns away. With tears in her eyes, Roseline speaks the words that her heart forcibly denies. "I'm sorry, Gabriel. I don't want to be with you."

A stunning smile slowly spreads across Gabriel's face. "Liar."

"Well, that is rude," she bristles, shifting her body away from him.

Gabriel laughs. "You're a terrible liar. Besides, I know when a girl is crying. Trust me, I've had plenty of experience with that."

"Why, because you've broken so many hearts in your time?" she snaps, swiping away her tears, annoyed with herself.

"Touché. I'm sure you have a few sob stories you could share yourself."

She sucks in a breath, shocked at how easily she has gone from distressed to irate. "Are you always this obnoxious?"

He grins. "Sometimes. The truth hurts."

With a feather-light touch, Gabriel reaches out and brushes his fingers over her hand. Roseline bites down on her lip to still her cry. Her eyes are glued to his fingers as they slide around to the underside of her wrist and begin drawing delicate circles along her sensitive skin.

Never has anyone's touch affected her so fiercely. She can feel the animalistic growl rising in her throat as her pores ooze her heady scent. His touch is addicting.

"I get it," he whispers, his voice taking on a hoarse tone. "You don't want to hurt me or yourself but I am right and you know it. There is definitely something going on between us."

Although his fingers are calloused from countless hours on the football field, his touch is like the finest silk against her skin. The warmth radiating from him feels like a warm blanket on a cold winter's night. She would give anything to snuggle up to him and let the world pass her by. It's a warmth that is comforting and enticing at the same time.

It is getting harder to resist him. The longer she lingers with him, the more intense the attraction becomes. Roseline's mouth begins to water, savoring Gabriel's scent.

Her eyes fly open wide as she rears back. She snatches her hand away as the scent of rain and cut grass washes over her. *It's him. The boy I smelled on my first day,* she thinks.

It is more than that though. The same scent is tied to some of the most realistic dreams and tantalizing fantasies she has ever experienced. How is this possible? It can't be him. It just can't be!

"What's wrong?" Gabriel asks, leaning close. His brow furrows with concern.

Unable to stop herself, Roseline closes the gap between them. "Shh," she breathes as she nuzzles against his neck, embracing the warmth of his throat. His pulse jumps madly against her cheek.

Gabriel rolls his neck to the side as she presses her lips against his artery. The sensitive skin beneath her lip quivers. Her heart beats harmonious with his. His breathing adjusts to match hers. A contented sigh escapes his lips.

Reality crashes in as Roseline throws herself to the other end of the couch. She commands her lungs to stop moving as she fights to remain in control.

"Why'd you stop?" Gabriel groans, his words slurring.

Roseline glances hesitantly at him. Her body begins to tremble as she looks deeply into his eyes, terrified by the faint blue glow radiating out from them. It is not possible. Humans can't do that.

What the heck is going on? She silently panics.

Maybe it is the moonlight streaming in from overhead, or a trick of light from the lamp glowing on the bookcase, or maybe her mind has finally snapped, trying to convince herself that Gabriel is something more than a mortal, but try as she might to convince herself of these possibilities, the truth continues to gnaw at her.

Gabriel's heart drums loudly in his chest. Hormones leak from his dampened skin, mingling with hers in the air. The scent of their desire permeating the air is nearly more than she can handle. Roseline's lips part, allowing one final agonizing breath to enter her body. She groans, burying her face in her hands, as she tastes Gabriel's essence.

"That was amazing," he whispers, his mind slowly escaping the fog. "It's never been like that before."

The reminder of his time spent with other girls snaps Roseline out of her trance. "I barely touched you," she murmurs, trying to sort out what they have just experienced. It has certainly never been like that with other humans she seduced.

"Really?" Gabriel frowns, blinking away the last of the haze. "That's not what it felt like."

A thought, so irrational she nearly discards it, flashes across her mind. It blooms into full-blown hysteria as she begins to rock on the edge of the couch. Warm tears slip between her fingers. "This isn't possible. It can't be true."

What other explanation could there be?

She jumps as Gabriel's hand settles on her bare arm. Scorching fire licks against her skin as his blood calls to her. No, not just calls to her, it invades her. Her whole body burns with need, yearning for his touch, to feel him pressed up against her.

This, whatever this is, is not some sadistic hunger or a physical need for blood to aid in healing. This is lust in its rawest form. It hardly compares with a far more terrifying discovery-buried love. "Are you okay, Rose?" he whispers. His breath tickles against her ear. Goose bumps leap to attention.

"No," she croaks. "I have to go. I have to leave. I have to—" she chokes off, completely unsure of what she can do to stop this unnatural bond.

It's too late, her mind whispers. *You already belong to him.*

Fourteen

Gabriel's disappointment hits her like a wrecking ball, but she refuses to be swayed. She has to leave, to get some fresh air to clear her mind before she does something she will really regret. Like seal the bond that's not even supposed to be possible with a human!

Why didn't anyone tell her this could happen? Maybe it's never happened before. What if she is special somehow? Or Gabriel? Whatever he is, he is obviously not human.

She takes a deep breath. He smells human…only slightly off. Like he is somehow something more than just human.

His scent lingers in her nostrils, making her head spin. "Please let me go," she begs.

A strange cold lingers where his fingers were only a moment before. Roseline rubs her arm, refusing to acknowledge the yearning of her soul.

Gabriel crouches beside the hatch, finger hooked though the door. "I'm sorry. I never should have…I didn't mean to…" he sighs, shaking his head. "I'm sorry."

"It's not you," she whispers softly.

She bites her lip as his face droops. She doesn't want him to feel guilty. In fact, she wishes he didn't feel anything at all, but the rebellious side that risked life and limb to escape from Vladimir wants Gabriel to fight for her. To tell her that all of this is happening for a reason, that there just might be a way to make it work.

She knew if he did, she would lose herself to him. It takes every ounce of strength she possesses to not pull him back as he opens the hatch. She cannot trust herself. Not with him. Not in this moment.

She knows he is not in any real danger from her. No matter how good he smells she would never bite him. Blood is the source of life, for humans and immortals, but taking the lifeblood of another being comes with a terrible curse.

Although she and her family do not actually feed off the blood of others, like so many of the vampire myths claim, it does happen from time to time to help speed healing. Like any prescription drug that can become addictive, so can too much human blood. Personalities begin to change, behaviors become more violent, and the result has been the creation of the vampire myth.

A myth that Roseline fights against daily.

The need she now feels for Gabriel goes beyond fleshly desires. Even her lust for him has begun to fade against the presence of the bond somehow formed between them. As if their souls have somehow entwined and that fact scares her, more than she could ever admit. She cannot fall for a mortal. It is forbidden. And yet...

Her heart tells her it is already too late. The bond is sealed. But how? They have not shared any physical intimacy, which should be the moment when two become one. So how is this even possible?

"What do you think you're doing?" a shrill voice screeches from the hallway below.

"Claire," Gabriel gasps, teetering toward the hatch opening. Roseline's hand shoots out, gripping his shirt as she pulls him back from danger. He gives her a weak smile of gratitude before rushing down the ladder. "What are you doing here?"

Roseline dashes across the room and snatches her heels. In a flash, they are wound around her ankles and she is back at the attic hatch. Neither Gabriel nor Claire notice her movements.

"Looking for you, duh," Claire snaps, swaying slightly on her feet. Her blood-red lipstick is smeared; her breath reeks of alcohol and something else. Roseline leans through the opening and sniffs the air, her nose scrunching with disgust when she recognizes the scent.

"How dare you cheat on me, Gabriel Marston," Claire shrieks, slapping him across the face. Roseline bares her teeth and hisses but her reaction goes unnoticed as Gabriel rubs his reddening jaw. "Your father is going to hear about this."

Claire turns and stomps toward the stairs, wavering precariously on her silver stiletto heels. Her hands wave wildly just before she tumbles end over end, landing in a heap on the landing. Groaning, Claire rights herself and scoots down the remaining steps.

Roseline hurries down the ladder, peeking to make sure no one will see her descent. Gabriel appears deeply embarrassed by his girlfriend's state. "Sorry about that. She probably won't even remember this tomorrow morning."

"I sure hope she doesn't remember what else she's been up to," Roseline mutters under her breath as she smoothes out her dress.

Gabriel's eyebrow rises. "Oh yeah?"

Roseline chuckles. "Well, by the smell of that aftershave, I'd say your girlfriend just messed around with Oliver."

Gabriel grimaces. "Yeah, that sounds like them. I'm gonna have to do something about her."

Sensing an awkward moment rapidly approaching, Roseline steps toward the stairs. No way can she handle a talk about his crumbling relationship with Claire. "I should probably get going," she mutters. "Thanks for the tour."

She turns to head down the hall but Gabriel catches her arm. "I meant what I said earlier. I really want to get to know you."

Roseline struggles to pull her gaze away from him. She can already feel the gravitational pull building between them. She clears her throat, annoyed by how flustered he makes her feel. "I'm not sure that's such a good idea.

"Me either," he admits. "But I don't care."

She hates how easily those five words change her life. Roseline knows it is wrong, for so many reasons, but she refuses to care, at least for tonight. She nods with a tiny smile and slips down the stairs.

"Where have you been?" Sadie moans as soon as she arrives on the ground floor, relying heavily on the wall to remain upright. "I've been looking all over for you. I think I've had too much to drink." She belches loudly and swipes her arm across her mouth. Her hair is matted with crushed chips and gooey chocolate. She must have gone in headfirst to the pudding bowl.

"I think you've had a bit too much fun for one night," Roseline says as she pulls Sadie toward her. "Your mother is going to kill you when she finds you like this."

The only answer she receives is a gentle snore as Sadie passes out in her arms. Roseline darts a glance around to see if anyone is watching before she lifts Sadie's legs and carries her out of the house. Judging by the moon's location overhead it is well past two in the morning. The house is dark as she approaches but Roseline can hear Sadie's parents whisper complaints from their room on the backside of the house.

Clutching Sadie tightly in her arms, Roseline kicks off her high heels and easily scales the tree. She slips in through the cracked window, gently tucking her snoring friend under the covers. Roseline hesitates, smiling down at Sadie. It is amazing how sleep can tame the wild beast.

"Goodnight," she whispers from the window before leaping to the ground.

Deciding it would be best not to go back through the door she exited only a couple minutes before, Roseline slips down between the two houses. An eight-foot privacy fence stands between her and Gabriel's back yard. Roseline steps back then jumps straight over the top, landing silently on the other side.

"How can you embarrass me like that with Oliver?" an angry voice calls out through the night. Roseline ducks behind a tree, wincing at her bad luck. She has just landed in the last place she wanted to be—right in the middle of Gabriel and Claire's confrontation. Fate is obviously having a laugh at her expense tonight. Roseline peeks out, unable to stop her curiosity.

"Oh, that was nothing," Claire replies from where she is slumped on a lounger. "Why do you even care? You were fooling around with that slutty new girl."

"Take it back," Gabriel growls, yanking Claire to her feet. His face contorts with anger.

Claire's high-pitch laugh grates on Roseline's nerves. "Are you serious? You are actually defending her honor? Oh, that is too good."

"I said, take it back."

Claire's laugh cuts off. "What's gotten into you, Gabe? You fall for some new girl and now you are ready to give up everything for her? Have you even seen who she hangs with? Sadie-Freakshow-Hughes."

"You know what," Gabriel says, releasing Claire's arm. "I'm glad Sadie got out. At least she didn't have to stick around and let you dig your claws into her."

Claire spits at him, unwilling to take that comment lying down. "We both know you haven't changed. It's all just an act to get in that girl's pants."

Gabriel rolls his eyes. "Sure. That's my motive. Just like I've worked so hard to get into yours." His voice is rising right along with his blood pressure.

Roseline is sure all of the neighbors can hear Claire's howl. "You jerk. How dare you talk to me like that?"

"Why? It's the truth." Gabriel's response is surprisingly emotionless. Roseline cannot help but pump her fist in triumph. Gabriel has not fooled around with Claire. That's nice to know.

"You're just trying to ruin my reputation. Everyone knows you can barely keep your hands off me," she screams, making sure all of the questioning ears plastered to the windows can hear. "You can't get enough of me."

"We both know how much you'd like to believe that." His bitter laugh masks Claire's cry of indignation. "And it's not like you work hard to make everyone believe that you're an upright girl. You spend more time on your back than you do shopping."

The sound of Claire's slap does not surprise Roseline. In fact, she is surprised it didn't happen sooner. "We're through. Do you hear me, Gabriel Marston? I never want to see you again."

"Fine by me," Gabriel replies, slamming the glass door in Claire's face. The eavesdroppers scatter, diving behind couches or slipping down the basement stairs as Gabriel stalks past.

Roseline remains crouched, wondering how long Claire will linger on the back porch. She really needs to get inside and find William.

"Hello? Yeah, it's me, Daddy. Gabriel just broke up with me," Claire cries into her cell phone. Roseline rolls her eyes at Claire's exaggerated sobbing. "I don't know what happened. He just blew up and started accusing me of messing around with some other guy."

There is a brief pause before Claire cries indignantly. "How can you even ask me that? Of course it's his fault."

"Whatever, Daddy. Just come get me." Claire snaps her phone shut and stumbles toward the fence at the side of the house.

Roseline sneaks out of the bushes as Claire unlatches the gate with great difficulty. Claire loses her balance and plops to the ground as the gate swings closed behind her. Roseline silently races across the moonlit yard and eases the glass door open. Most of the drunken students have begun filtering out of the house now that the show has ended. That should make it much easier for her to find William and get the heck out.

"William?" she calls, cupping her hands around her mouth. She wanders through the house, stepping lightly over snoring teens.

"He's over there," Gabriel whispers as he slips up behind her. He points to a crumpled heap on a couch in the basement.

Roseline rolls a snoring William over. His face is covered with bright red lipstick and an impressive bruise has begun forming on his neck.

"Well, at least someone had a good time," Gabriel chuckles, sounding impressed. She nods and bends down, bracing to lift William. Gabriel's electric touch stops her. "Let me. He's probably heavier then he looks."

Frustrated with Gabriel's intervention, Roseline is forced to watch him struggle to lift William's dead weight. "It's no problem. I'm sure I can manage him."

Gabriel laughs, struggling to stand upright. "You'd just crumble under him. Especially in those shoes." His gaze trails back down the curve of Roseline's calf but quickly shifts away.

Relenting, Roseline settles with following his slow pace up the stairs and across the side yard. He knocks on the door before Roseline can stop him. Her ears perk up as light footsteps approach.

William's mother looks livid when the door opens to reveal her son passed out in Gabriel's arms. Roseline can tell she is fighting back the urge to scream at Gabriel as she moves aside to let him pass. "Put him on the couch please. I won't have him ruining my new carpets upstairs."

When she turns to look at Roseline, she manages a weak smile. "Nice to see you on your feet, Rose."

She tries to find some response that might lessen the grounding William is sure to receive by morning but comes up empty. She settles for a simple nod. Mrs. Hughes' lips press into thin lines. "Have you seen Sadie?"

Roseline nods. "She left over an hour ago. Said she was tired and wanted to get some sleep. I think she might have had a headache from all of the noise."

Gabriel gives Roseline a sharp look as he passes by Mrs. Hughes. "Yeah, it must have been all that dancing. She sure did tear up the dance floor."

Mrs. Hughes smiles tightly at him, her disapproval barely restrained from the tip of her tongue. "Do you need a ride home, Rose?"

Before she can speak up Gabriel interjects for her. "Not to worry, Mrs. H, I can drive her." Her eyes narrow as she takes in Gabriel's steady stance and clear gaze. She nods. "Alright. Goodnight then."

"Oh, and Gabriel?" she calls as he steers Roseline away from the porch. "I expect that party to clear out now, you here?"

He dips his head. "Sure thing, Mrs. H."

Fifteen

"My car's this way," Gabriel calls back to Roseline as he heads toward the far right side of his parent's three-car garage. Flipping open a hidden panel, made to look like the rest of the bricks on the house, the door slowly clatters open.

"I'm really not sure this is a good idea..." she trails off as her lips pull up into a smile. "A Range Rover? I have one just like this back home."

Fane talked her into buying it on a whim a couple years back and it'd quickly become her favorite, although her cherry-red Ferrari is a close second.

Gabriel shrugs. "It's just a car." Roseline glances at him over the hood. Her slender fingers glide over the smooth paint as she fights back a stab of longing for her own car. "It looks expensive, it's foreign, and it makes Steve look richer than he really is. That's the only reason I have it."

"Sounds like you two don't get along so well."

Gabriel smirks, shaking his head. "Not at all. Jump in. You must be freezing out here." He hits the automatic unlock button and climbs up into the driver's seat. Roseline follows, somehow managing not to expose herself as she makes the leap into the car. "So...where to?"

Her mind is still screaming at her to jump right back out and run away, but she thinks that plan might make Gabriel a tad suspicious. Instead, she resolves to get out of his car as fast as she can, while holding her breath of course. "Um...you can just drop me off at Jimmy's on Brendon Street. I can walk from there."

Piercing blue eyes gleam out from the dark as he appraises her. "What are you afraid of? Think I'm gonna stalk you if I know where you live?"

Stalking? No, but if he ever looks in her windows, he will certainly start to ask questions that she is not ready to answer.

"Of course not," Roseline laughs, wincing at how forced it sounds. Her palms feel clammy, her forehead beads with sweat. "It's just that I'm kinda embarrassed about my house. It's a temporary thing until my mom can find something better, but she's always gone for work so she's barely even seen the place."

Gabriel's gaze softens. "The first thing you should know about me is that I'm not hung up on status. Sure I might look like I am, but it is just a mask I wear to get through the day. Under the designer clothes, expensive house, and flashy car, I'm just a guy that wants to be normal. I don't care about the money. Actually, to be honest...I hate it."

"You hate money," Roseline scoffs, rolling her eyes. "Well I have learned one thing tonight. You're a terrible liar."

"Okay. Well not money in general," Gabriel chuckles. "Just Steve's money."

Roseline nods slowly. "I see. You don't like feeling like something you're not."

"Exactly," Gabriel agrees, turning over the engine. He backs smoothly out of the drive and pauses in the street. "So? Where to?" he asks again.

"Jimmy's."

Gabriel laughs. "All right. If that's what you really want." He maneuvers the empty streets with confident ease. "So you're from Romania right?"

"Yes," she replies, frowning at the tension she hears in his voice. There is something there, something he's not telling her. She can't help wondering why this topic makes him uncomfortable.

"Ever see Dracula?"

Roseline splutters. "Are you serious?"

"Sure." Gabriel shrugs. "Isn't that what all Americans ask you? Vampires are all the rage here, you know."

How can she not know? Everywhere she looks, handsome movie stars bare their teeth on movie posters and book covers.

Teenage girls fight over which guy should win the human girl. T-shirts, calendars and even key chains promote the romanticized idea of the vampire world but it is all so painfully far from the truth.

"Yeah I think I've heard about it but it's all just fantasy. Vampires aren't real," she whispers, feeling a lump form in her throat.

"Really? That's a bummer."

Roseline laughs at his pained expression. "Oh, don't tell me you actually believe those stories."

"No way. But the idea behind it is pretty cool." Her wince does not go unnoticed. "You don't agree?"

"In my experience, there are many different forms of evil. Some are much older than others, more sinister and devious than humans can ever imagine." Roseline's voice drops to a whisper as she speaks of her past life. Gabriel leans in, visibly drawn in by the husky passion radiating from her. He pulls the car into the first spot in Jimmy's parking lot. The neon bar sign overhead provides enough light from for Gabriel to see Roseline clearly.

"So you *have* seen something?"

Roseline blinks, as if waking from a trance. She smiles, grasping the door handle. "Nothing worth mentioning. I'll see you around." Roseline leaps out of the car and slams the door behind her. Icy winds curl around her with delightful vengeance.

"Wait a second," Gabriel cries, scrambling to exit the vehicle. "You have seen something, haven't you? You gotta tell me." Roseline laughs, shaking her head.

"Oh, man," Gabriel groans. "Come on. That's like telling a guy that you've actually been to Area 51 and then refusing to spill. That's so not cool."

Roseline pauses, wondering how much she can say. Obviously, the truth is out of the question, but a part of her wants to let Gabriel in, just as he did when he shared his artwork. "The things I've seen in Romania are a smoke screen. A hidden world veiled behind human reality."

"Why?" Gabriel leans in closer. His eyes widen with anticipation.

"Some things are not meant to be understood. People don't need to know the horrifying truths that are hidden from them. It's for their own good."

Despite the fact that the solemn tone in Roseline's voice obviously creeps him out, Gabriel is hooked. "You've seen this hidden world, haven't you?" he whispers.

Closing her eyes to the pain, she nods. "But that is a story that I reserve only for my dearest friends…and you, Gabriel Marston, are still a stranger."

His pout is endearing, but Roseline shakes her head. "Fine. Then I'll have to see about changing that."

"Somehow that doesn't surprise me," she chuckles as she turns and leaves him standing next to his purring car. The winds whip around her, tangling her hair about her face, but she doesn't notice. Her thoughts have drifted away, to a time so long ago. To when life was simple and death meant the end, not the beginning.

Sixteen

"Great news," Gabriel crows loudly as he slides into a seat next to Roseline little over a week later.

After the party, she tried her best to avoid Gabriel. The more time she spent with him the more confused she got. The worst part was discovering that he is not just a pretty face. She really enjoys spending time with him, which makes it so much harder to keep up her abnormally rude pretense.

Not only has Gabriel begun meeting her in the hall to escort her to class, but he has also managed to slip in a few lunches as well. Her fight to remain indifferent is a losing battle. Just seeing Gabriel makes her stomach flutter and the hairs on her neck stand at attention. Makes her feel like the giddy schoolgirl she is trying to portray. Every nerve in her body is tuned with his presence and fighting her natural urges is really wearing her out. Her willpower is fading quickly.

"Aren't you going to ask what the great news is?" he presses, his stunning smile too inviting to refuse.

Roseline rolls her eyes and uses her finger to mark her place in her book. She is reading Pride and Prejudice for the millionth time. As she sits there, huddled away in the corner of the high school library, she finds herself wishing fate had allowed her to find her own true love before she turned into a monster.

Despite her lot in life, Roseline has never lost the hope of finding love. Fane certainly tried his best to fill that role, but it never felt truly right to Roseline. Now, with Gabriel in the picture, everything has changed. Maybe it is the lingering essence that wafts past her in the hall or the dreams of him that are so vividly tempting that made her pick up the classic book again.

Or maybe it was because she had to. That is what she likes to think at least. Her English teacher, Mrs. Carlson, instantly noticed Roseline's meticulously well-educated background and managed to persuade her into volunteering as a tutor. Why, oh why, did she agree?

The answer to why she is willing to teach some simpleton the eloquent words of Jane Austen is painfully simple—she is trying to avoid Gabriel. Looks like that plan backfired.

The sad thing is, the pimple-faced pencil pusher she is expecting, who no doubt hasn't developed a single romantic bone in his body, is late for their session. No, not just late, he is utterly absent. At least Gabriel will distract her from gnawing her fingernails to a nub as she waits.

Roseline sits back, tucking her bookmark within the slightly wrinkled pages. "I'm a bit busy at the moment, Gabriel. Can this wait?"

"Humor me."

With a heavy sigh and exaggerated rolling of her eyes, Roseline concedes. "Fine. What can possibly be good enough to have you bouncing in your seat?"

Gabriel's smile broadens at her obvious sarcasm. "I signed up for a tutor."

"Okay..." she frowns, wondering when he is going to get to the punch line. Gabriel is the last person to need a tutor. He is a shoo-in for valedictorian. "You have lost me."

"An English tutor—" he presses, his eyebrows bounce suggestively.

His words hit Roseline like a ton of bricks. "Oh no," she groans, burying her head in her arms. "Please tell me you didn't."

"Of course I did," he laughs, digging into his backpack from his own copy of Pride and Prejudice. The binding creaks as he opens it. "So, where should we begin?"

"With you leaving," Roseline snaps, shoving her book forcefully into her bag. How can he do this to her? To manipulate her teacher with those gorgeous ice-blue eyes of his. The fact that he even attempted it is remarkable, but the fact that he managed to pull it off is downright infuriating.

103

"If you think I'm going to waste my time teaching you about love, you are sadly mistaken," she says as she rises to her feet. Curious students glance their way as Gabriel latches on to Roseline's wrist.

"Please, sit down. You're making a scene."

It doesn't take a genius to know this gossip will be spread across campus by the time the final bell rings. It is for this reason alone she sinks back into her seat.

"Thanks," he whispers, leaning in close.

"I'm not doing it for you," she snaps, tossing her bag back onto the table. "So what is your angle, Gabriel? Think I'll ask you back to my place for a study date and you can make your move?"

The ice in her voice feels unnatural but her annoyance mingled with an ounce of outrage makes it feel completely justifiable. Can't he take a hint? What more does she have to do to get him to back off?

Perhaps it's because he knows you are lying, her mind scolds. She winces. No matter how hard she tries to tell herself being with Gabriel is wrong, her heart keeps fighting it.

"That's not fair," Gabriel counters, leaning in so close Roseline can smell his anger. "I'm not that kind of guy...but then you'd know that if you actually gave me a chance."

"A chance at what?" Roseline retorts. "You're with Claire, remember?" She would rather die than let it slip that she overhead their explosive end.

He shakes his head, sinking back into his chair. "We broke up."

"Oh, and you two seemed like such a cute couple," Roseline says, folding her arms firmly across her chest.

"What's your deal?" Gabriel questions, eyeing her up. "Did I do something to royally tick you off?"

"You mean besides this?" Her fingers begin to cramp against her arms. She hadn't realized how tightly she was digging in until her nails pierce her flesh.

"Hey," Gabriel cries, pulling her hand away. "You're bleeding."

"Thank you, Mr. Obvious," she says, swiping away the blood with little thought. "Look, it's not that I don't like you. We both know I do, but this really isn't going to work and you need to accept that."

"Why?" he presses, leaning in so close she can feel his heady scent weakening her resolve. She leans back, fighting to escape the cloud of delicious hormones. "You're not even giving me a chance."

"Yeah, so take a hint." Roseline tries to maintain her abrupt tone but her words come out more as a desperate plea.

Gabriel sits back and laces his fingers together on the top of the table. "Why?"

"Why what?" she asks, annoyed with the circular questions.

A smirk settles firmly in place. "Why can't you leave?"

Her mouth gapes open, flabbergasted. A myriad of emotions and thoughts flit through her mind, most of them teetering on the irrational side thanks to his scent filtering through her nose. "I was here first."

Smooth, she inwardly groans.

Gabriel snickers, slouching low in his chair. "Wow, that's a really mature answer, Rose."

Knowing he is right is infuriating. She buries her face in her palms. "Just please leave me alone. I will beg if I have to."

The silence that meets her feels oppressive, like an open grave just waiting to be filled. She can hear his slightly elevated breathing and the hammering of his heart in his chest, but nothing else. It is as if the fluttering of book pages and low chattering of the students around them has vanished completely.

"Why?" His whisper stakes her to the heart. It is so filled with confusion and pain that she nearly allows a whimper to escape.

Why does he make me so weak? I'm a trained killer, not some sappy school girl. I shouldn't be reduced to putty in his hands, she thinks.

Yet she is. There is no denying her need for him, to be with him, to touch him. The harder she fights the fall, the faster she tumbles out of reason and into love's madness.

His breath washes over her face as he shifts his chair closer. The hairs rise on the back of her neck as her skin quivers. She closes her eyes to the desire that slams into her gut. His scent is too strong, much too strong for her to remain in control.

"Oh no," she moans under her breath. A brief inhale is all it takes for her walls to come tumbling down and desire to flood in. In this moment, she realizes she is going to lose control in a public school, surrounded by gawking teenagers.

In less than an hour, the entire school will know she is a freak and she will be forced to flee. Again. Her toes curl painfully with desire as she looks up into Gabriel's eyes. They flicker with surprise but quickly melt into something warm and filled with promise.

"We have to go." Roseline grabs Gabriel's hand and yanks him to his feet. He barely has time to grab their bags before he is stumbling after her.

Roseline dashes for the door, desperate to get away, to hide from so many eyes. She needs space. She needs air. She needs Gabriel.

"This really isn't helping our reputation, you know," Gabriel chuckles as he struggles to keep up with her frantic pace. She ignores him as her feet slap the polished floor. The hall is crowded with students just beginning to arrive for the day. Roseline sucks in a breath of air, expelling Gabriel's scent as she tries to focus.

A set of double doors lay ahead. With little thought to Gabriel's arm socket, she jerks him around and bursts through the doors. Students scatter out of their way; a skateboarder doing tricks on the railing tumbles into the bushes as Roseline shoves past.

"Rose!"

She ignores Sadie's call as she streaks toward the parking lot. Scanning the jumble of high-end foreign vehicles, she finally spots Gabriel's Range Rover. He collapses against the passenger door, gasping for breath. "If you wanted to skip school all you had to do was ask."

"You got a problem with it?" She is nervous, insanely so, but she has to do something. Emotions are boiling up inside to fast to handle.

"Not at all." Gabriel grins as he unlocks the doors. Roseline hops in and slams the door shut before he can lend her a hand. He rounds the hood and slips into his seat. The engine purrs to life but his hands hesitate over the gearshift. "Um, where exactly would you like to go?"

She closes her eyes, fighting back the urge to rip open his shirt, sniff his neck, and give in to the fantasies plaguing her mind. Her fingers curl around the armrest. "Anywhere. Just drive."

Gabriel throws the car into reverse. The tires squeal wildly as he spins out of the parking lot. At the base of the hill, he guns the engine to fly past the guard at the gate and merges recklessly with the busy street. He sucks in a settling breath before glancing over at her. "Well, that was fun."

She smirks at the flush rising on his cheeks. "First time?"

He nods, grinning like a little boy who has just got away with sneaking a cookie from the cookie jar. "I don't know why I haven't done this sooner."

Roseline laughs. "Oh yeah, you're a real rebel now."

"You got it. I think I should do this more often," he says, settling into a relaxed driving pose. He dips and darts through the early morning traffic with ease.

She watches him from the corner of her eye as she fights to get her pulse under control. The effort is completely useless. The desire to undress him right here and now is too overwhelming to be forgotten with playful banter. "Is that coat warm?"

He frowns. "Yeah. It's wool, why?"

Fingering the window button Roseline thrusts her head outside. Even over the gush of wind, she can hear his cursing. She sucks in huge gulps of fresh air to clear her senses. Just before she raises the window she stills her lungs and prepares to endure the close quarters with him.

"What the heck are you doing?" he gasps as the glass seals out the arctic winds. "It's freezing out there."

"Just needed to clear my head."

"And you can't do that without turning me into a popsicle?" he grumbles, reaching to flip the air as hot as it can go.

Roseline drops her gaze and settles into her seat, making sure to leave plenty of room between them. She might not have to smell him, but his presence alone is enough to throw her off.

Gabriel clears his throat and taps his fingers against the steering wheel. "That, um, was quite a scene you made back there. For a second I thought you had something else in mind for this drive."

107

"I did," she mutters to the window, unwilling to meet his gaze.

"Oh," he says. His knuckles pop. "So should I try to find a back road or something?"

Roseline bursts out laughing. "I thought you weren't that kind of guy."

Gabriel's lips pull up at the corners. "Neither did I."

She wants to laugh it off as a joke but the serious undertone is far too prevalent to miss. Clearing her throat does little to clear her scattered thoughts. Gabriel darts a couple glances toward her but Roseline stares out the front window. No way is she going to risk saying anything now.

The weight of his gaze makes her uncomfortable. The silence even more so. Why did she drag him out here with her? She could have run, alone, to get some air.

"So…" Gabriel fiddles with the air controls. "Are you really mad about being my tutor?"

"Not really." She allows a small chuckle. "Actually, I'm rather impressed. Do you have all of the teachers wrapped around your little finger?

"Most of them," Gabriel admits proudly. "I've always had a way with women." Roseline glances over at him as he grimaces. "No. I didn't mean it like that," he stammers. "I just meant…"

Roseline settles her hand lightly on his arm. She fights to ignore the heat rising from beneath. "I know what you meant, although, if you want to keep that reputation of yours, I probably wouldn't freak out like that again."

Gabriel rolls his eyes. "Yeah, like I care about my reputation. The hottest girl known to man has just yanked me out of the library, and I am sure the rumors are already raging like a forest fire. By the end of school, everyone will know that you violated me."

"And I'm guessing you won't do a thing to slow that one down."

"Are you kidding?" Gabriel scoffs. "I'll be a hero."

Roseline snorts. "Whatever."

"It's true. Every guy in the school has been after you." Gabriel laughs at her puzzlement. "Really? You didn't notice?"

She shrugs, glancing out of the window. "They're not my type."

"Oh, so you have a type now. I can't wait to hear this." Gabriel pulls into an overflowing parking lot. She glances around, confused.

"Where are we?"

Gabriel opens his door and hurries around to her side. "Come on." His fingers entwine with hers as he helps her down. She blushes, pleased at how warm his hand feels against her skin. "So...?"

Roseline smirks, pleased that the heaviness in the air has been abated by gentle teasing. "Not gonna let that one go, huh?"

"Not on your life." He leads her toward a large stone building. A massive banner with a picture of a beluga whale sprawls across the front. "Want to see some whales?"

"Why not?" She shrugs and mounts the steps next to him.

Gabriel sweeps her to the side as he moves to open the door. "After you, my lady."

Amused by Gabriel's showmanship, Roseline steps into line for tickets to Chicago's Shedd Aquarium. Although she has never given any thought about going before, Roseline has to admit she is excited. Gabriel ducks in front of her just as she reaches the ticket booth and pays for their entry fee. Handing her a ticket, he eases them toward the entrance.

As soon as they have maneuvered through the slow moving crowd, Gabriel takes her hand again. "This is nice," he whispers near her ear.

Roseline knows she should not agree with him, but she does. She knows she should not be there with him, but she is. She should not crave his blood, his very essence of life, but she does...more than anything else in the world. This is a bad idea but she can't make herself part from his side.

"So...you're a pretty good football player," Roseline says. The words sound just as lame aloud as they did in her mind but she is desperate to break the silence that has fallen. If he is anything like her, his thoughts are no doubt focused solely on the heat building between them.

His hand comes to rest on the small of her back as he steers her toward the Shark Exhibit. "Yeah, so they tell me."

She watches him closely in the dim light of the fish tanks. There is a nearly invisible tick in his right eyelid. His lips are set into a firm line and his fingers tense ever so slightly against hers. "You hate it though, don't you?"

"I have ever since the first day Steve made me try out. I never wanted to play sports. As a kid, I was terrible. I think Steve had almost completely given up hope until he saw me goofing around with Oliver in the backyard right after school started my freshman year. After that he just became obsessed." Gabriel's lip curls with disgust.

"He wants me to go to Notre Dame. It is where he spent the best years of his life. At least that's the crap he's shoved down my throat for four years."

The hall in front of them darkens and the air cools slightly as they move farther underground. A pale blue light shines on the carpet, lighting the room ahead. Gabriel leads them past fish tanks with dancing tropical fish and beautiful coral to an empty bench near the back of the shark room. They sit, staring at the beasts of the deep as they glide lazily past.

"What do *you* want, Gabriel?" Roseline asks softly. She knows he is talented—he proved that with the makeshift art gallery in his attic—but she wants to know more. What drives him? What thrills him? What makes him get out of bed every morning?

"I want freedom. I want the chance to decide what's right for me." His voice is soft as he turns to look at her.

Her throat clenches at the glint of pain in his eyes. "It's not easy to accept when that choice is taken from you," she whispers, dredging up memories she would rather remain hidden. Her pleas for her sister's life fell on deaf ears. Her own pleas for death had been met with callous laughter. Repressed anger bubbles in her chest. The warrior within begs to strike back, to avenge the life she lost. *Someday*, she vows silently.

Her thoughts fragment as Gabriel pulls her hand into his lap. He traces small circles along her inner wrist, slowly trailing a fiery vine toward her elbow. "Somehow I knew you would understand. From the first moment I saw you, I knew."

"Knew what?" she asks.

"That you're a fighter. I can see it sometimes. But I can also see that you're afraid..." His gaze falls to their hands. "I know you're running from something. I just don't know what."

Roseline pulls her hand from his grasp. "You don't know me."

He turns to face her, gently lifting her chin with his finger. "I know enough. I know pain when I see it."

Tears sting her eyes as she fights to keep them back. How can he know, just by looking at her? Sadie and William hardly noticed her morose moments over the past few weeks. Heck, they hardly questioned her about her home. No doubt, Nicolae's annoying presence dampened their excitement over her foreign culture, but Gabriel sees too much.

"Don't you get along with your mother?"

She blinks, trying desperately to gather the shreds of lies that she has dangled since arriving in Chicago. That's the problem with lies, they eventually unravel around you.

She offers a tight smile as his finger drifts along her cheekbone. His gaze holds her in place. "Sure, she's great, but I don't know how long I will be here."

He tenses, his fingers halt in their path. "But you just got here."

"My life isn't very stable right now. My mom's job moves a lot and I never know when I will have to leave."

Gabriel watches her closely. "What are you afraid of?"

Besides leaving you, she cries silently. "Nothing."

He sits back. "You're lying."

"No." Roseline shakes her head. She does not want Gabriel to think she needs to be saved. If Vladimir finds her, and he eventually will, she can't bear the thought of Gabriel foolishly trying to protect her. "I don't want to leave..."

"Then don't," he says, twining his fingers with hers. "Stay here. With me."

Roseline is caught off guard as he stands and sweeps her into his embrace, twirling her around as if they were two people in a grand ballroom. She closes her eyes as memories of being in Fane's arms at a fancy ball in London close in around her. She pushes them back. That was then. This is now. Gabriel is here, not Fane.

She effortlessly falls into the familiar steps, matching his with perfection. "Well, aren't you full of surprises?" She blushes at the gawking bystanders who have stepped out of the way.

Gabriel gives her a knowing wink. "What can I say? I'm a man of mystery."

Her laugh cuts off as he dips her low and her hair brushes the floor. When he pulls her upright, his gaze unwavering from hers, two little girls burst into wild applause. Roseline smiles down at them before Gabriel pulls her attention back.

"Have I ever told you how beautiful you are?" he whispers.

Her palms begin to sweat against his skin. The heat is intensifying, as if she might actually combust from within. "Maybe."

His hand gently sweeps back her hair. "You are. I'm sure you've had a million guys say that to you."

"None that mattered," she whispers. Her chest rises and falls. She can almost imagine their scents spiraling out from them, entwined like a melding of auras.

His hands tighten against her back as he leans in. His eyes droop closed as his lips part, his nose brushes against hers. "We can't," she says, wiggling out of his embrace.

When his eyes open, they are clouded over with desire. "What's wrong?"

She jerks her head toward the two little girls who stand nearby watching every move they make with saucer-like eyes. The tiny Disney princesses clutched in their arms no doubt resemble the private moment she nearly shared with fate's cruel idea of her own prince charming.

Gabriel rubs the back of his neck as he steps away. He tosses a wry smile at the girls and grabs her hand. She rushes behind him, eager to be away from the children and their parents' disapproving glares.

Laughter bubbles in her throat as they emerge from the shark exhibit at a near run. Her chest heaves, sweat clinging to her skin as Gabriel yanks her into a darkened corner, pressing himself against her. "Where was I?" He grins as he leans in.

"You were about to tell me that you are like this with all of the other girls." She's stalling and he knows it.

He leans back just enough to see her clearly. "No, I'm really not. There has never been anyone like you in my life before, Rose. It's like somehow you complete me."

Roseline rolls her eyes. "Oh, come on, that is a terrible line."

The pressure of his hand on her hip increases. "I can't change the truth."

Like a moth to a flame, she is drawn in, with little fight left in her. Her body willingly molds around his, her lips quivering as they seek his out. "I barely even know you and yet my world seems to revolve around you. You're in my dreams, my every waking thought. I can't get you out of my mind and it's driving me crazy."

Roseline expels a breathy laugh. "Is that supposed to be a compliment?"

A growl rises in his throat as he crushes his lips onto hers. She locks down on her muscles, refusing to let them move an inch while his tongue parts her lips. The boiling begins in her heart, liquid fire pumping to all areas of her body. The flames lick hotter and hotter as her lips move against his, her body pressing intimately close.

The kiss lingers, their need rising and fading like the tides. Roseline's mind shifts into autopilot as she sinks into his embrace. After what feels like an eternity, she realizes something is off. Gabriel should have come up for breath ages ago, and yet his lips still move against hers.

"Excuse me—" Roseline gasps and pulls back. A middle-aged security guard, with quite an impressive paunch, stands next to them, his face stern with disapproval.

"I'm so sorry," she whispers, retreating from Gabriel's arms. He wavers but manages to hold his ground. His skin is flushed; his eyes glow brightly in the dim light, his scent searing her nose as she fights to keep her distance.

"This is a family museum, you know. I think you two should follow me," the man orders gruffly, pointing toward a door hidden in the shadows on other side of the room.

Embarrassment burns along her cheeks as she follows the guard, keeping her eyes glued to the floor. She is not upset about being caught. She is grateful for the interruption. Gabriel's taste, his touch, still lingers too fresh in her mind. If the guard had not come along...

Seventeen

Roseline sits with her hands in her lap, refusing to meet Gabriel's intense stare. The sporadic heavy sighing from the driver's seat is enough to portray his frustration. "Jimmy's again?" he asks, his voice unnaturally void of emotion.

They have spoken very little to each other after being kicked out of the aquarium with a stern warning not to return. What is there to say? The connection between them is undeniable and, if anything, it is strengthening. This is too confusing. Only Roseline understands the why but the how is remaining annoyingly illusive.

She shrugs, not trusting her voice. No doubt, it will waver at the worst moment and betray her sadness. That will only make this harder.

Buildings slide past as Gabriel weaves through Chicago. They hit the interstate at a breakneck pace that doesn't end until he slams on the brakes in the bar's parking lot. The engine continues to purr but Gabriel doesn't reach to turn it off. He just sits, waiting.

Roseline knows she has to leave. The thought of uprooting her life again is too painful to even consider. Leaving Sadie and William behind is agonizing but the thought of severing all contact with Gabriel is unbearable. Her stomach twists at the thought of it, but what choice does she have? If she stays, his life will be forfeit. She can't let that happen.

She dips her head. It feels as if someone has ripped out her heart and stuck it on the end of a blunt stake for all to see, bleeding and mortally wounded but unable to die.

No. Not someone. She has done this to herself. It is a choice that must be made and she must be strong enough to follow through with it, but she can't even begin to know how.

"Thanks for the ride," she whispers, holding the door handle as if it were the only lifeline to the life she wishes she could embrace. She can't seem to force her legs to work.

"Of course," he replies. "See you tomorrow, bright and early."

She grimaces at the thread of excitement lining his voice. "I really don't think it is a good idea for you to meet me at Sadie's car tomorrow. It will just fuel the gossip." She hides her bitter smile, knowing that the whispers would not be too far from the truth. She did make out with him. Painfully brief or not, it is still the best kiss of her entire existence.

"Not the car." He turns to look at her. "The library. Did you forget?"

"You still want to meet there after what happened this morning?"

He reaches across the center console to pull her hand into his. His fingers twine with hers. She closes her eyes to the sight, wishing she could take a snapshot of this moment, of his touch, to carry with her. "Nothing has changed, Rose."

Her eyes fly open wide as her head whips up. She stares back at him, eyes wide with disbelief. "Of course it has. Everything has changed," she cries.

A tremor begins in her hands and works its way through her body. She finds herself standing on the edge of apprehension, teetering precariously toward full-blown panic. Her chest rises and falls rapidly. She pulls her hand out of his grasp. "We can't be together."

"Why not?" he presses, refusing to let her have a second to think. "Because it's too intense for you? Are you scared of what might happen if you get too close to me?"

Roseline nods. Her hair falls in shifting waves of bronze over her face, concealing her tears. "Yes."

"Huh," he mutters. "Okay. I wasn't expecting a straight-out admission."

Roseline groans, burying her head in her hands. Why does this have to be so complicated? If she were normal, or he were immortal, then maybe it could have worked, but she isn't and neither is he. Fate is just not that kind.

When she was planning a life without Vladimir, she never dreamed that she would meet someone else. Why would she? The emotional scars run deep. So deep that only Fane can handle them, or so she thought.

How can she explain how insane the idea of building a relationship would be? Even if she could find the right words, he will think she is crazy, or worse, bound for a mental institute, and rightfully so. Humans are not meant to know about her world.

She draws in a small steadying breath. "There's a lot that you don't know about me. My past is…complicated. I can't drag you in to it."

"Are you in trouble?" Gabriel's eyes darken, like rain clouds on a summer day.

She wants to lie, to tell him that he is way off base, but her emotions are too raw. He will see through her lie in an instant. "There was this guy…he was very abusive and that's why I had to leave. I thought I could run from him, but it was a fool's dream. Sooner or later he will find me, and when he does he will hurt anyone around me. I can't risk him finding out about you."

There, that was the truth. Albeit it a watered-down version, but still true.

Images of Gabriel's face, contorted with pain at the hands of Vladimir, helps to firm her resolve. "I'm so sorry," she says, turning to stare out the window at the empty parking lot. Broken beer bottles and cigarette butts litter the cracked pavement. "I never meant to hurt you."

"Don't do that," he says, tugging at her arm until she turns to face him. The hardness in his eyes softens as tears trail down her cheeks. "I'm not giving up on us and you can't either."

Roseline yanks on the door handle and shoves the door open. She hesitates on the edge of the seat, unable to look back at him. "I don't have that luxury."

She snatches her bag from the backseat and hops out of the car. With a shove hard enough to rock the door on its hinges, Roseline rushes away. The sound of her name being shouted into the wind reaches her. She doesn't stop, doesn't turn back.

"Goodbye," she whispers as she leaps over the chain-link fence at the back of the bar and sprints out of sight.

Eighteen

The physical pain is agony but the mental pain is unbearable. Roseline has a gaping hole in her heart, oozing misery at an alarming rate. The passing days have run together and the pain shows little sign of letting up. On the contrary, it seems to be ramping up with sadistic excitement.

Now she knows why bonded partners are never meant to be separated. Although the bond in invisible, the effects are not. She can't eat, can't drink, and can't think of anything but Gabriel. Every cell, every fiber, longs for him.

She stumbles from the chair by the window back to the bed. The same routine she carries out every hour just to have something to distract her. It doesn't really work, but she feels better just thinking it might sometime. It is pretty pathetic when she thinks about it so she chooses not to.

Cockroaches scatter around her feet, skirting the yellowing floral wallpaper that is peeling from the motel walls. They seem to thrive off the mold growing around the pipes in the bathroom. Who knows what other things lurk in this room.

She made it to somewhere in southern Illinois before running out of gas. Not the crude oil type. Emotionally and physically she had fallen apart. Her legs had given out on her and dumped her off on the front step of this dive, nearly a thirty-minute run from Jimmy's bar and where she left Gabriel behind. One quick stop at her house for a bag of clothes was all the delay she allowed before she ran for it.

Too bad she doesn't have a clue where here really is. All she knows is that it's some backwoods motel with farmland as far the eye can see. Despite the Bates Motel feel about the place, at least it does offer one very appealing thing—privacy.

Flickering static on the TV screen is the only light she allows into the room. The only interaction she has with the outside world is her call to the lobby to pay the sleazy, armpit-stained, tobacco-spitting clerk, who has suggested more than once that he is free after ten each night if she wants some company. She might want to wallow in her degradation but she does still have *some* moral standards.

When the phone rings on the bedside table, Roseline stares blankly at it. The annoying sound wiggles through the haze shrouding her mind. Her hand flops against the sticky tabletop and shoves the old-fashioned corded handset onto the floor. The ringing is replaced by an irritating loop informing that the call has been disconnected.

Rolling back over, she buries her face in the soiled cover. Even the scent of sweat isn't enough for her to move. She wants to die, to do anything to make the pain cease.

With cat-like agility, Roseline leaps from her bed and hovers behind it as the motel room door rocks on its hinges. Someone or something has just slammed against the other side, and it doesn't sound human.

Terror washes over her like a wintry sleet as her gaze sweeps the room. Acid churns in her stomach as she realizes she never planned an escape route. Stupid!

She lunges for her bag, tucks, and silently rolls to her feet beside the door. Whoever is on the other side will know she is braced for attack. It is fight or be taken and she refuses to even consider the second option.

The wall-shaking bang comes again as Roseline crouches low, dropping her bad beside her so her hands are free to fight. There is a pause and a disgruntled curse. Her ears prick at the sound of a key sliding into the lock. She scowls, annoyed with the hotel clerk for royally screwing her over.

Her muscles pull taut as she waits. She stills her breathing and focuses only on the sounds outside—deep breathing and indecipherable, angry muttering.

The door swings open and she dives, slamming the person into the far wall. Plaster rains down around them as Roseline fights for the upper hand. "Ouch!"

119

"Gabriel," she gasps, leaping back from him. She backs away, watching as the figure rises in the dark.

"Nice to see you too, Rose."

"Oh no." She quickly spans the small gap between them and spins him around, scanning for any injuries. "Are you okay? Did I hurt you?"

"I'll be fine," he huffs, holding his bruised side. "Man, you've got a good tackle. Too bad you're a girl." His chuckle sounds forced and edged with a pain that he tries to smooth over. Roseline helps him to the edge of the bed, wincing at the drool-dampened spot where she had just been lying.

She backs away to a safe distance once he is settled. Crossing her arms over her chest, she chews on her lower lip. When he doesn't speak, she is forced to ask the obvious question. "Why are you here?"

"I came for you."

She sinks to her knees as her wobbly legs give way. It is bittersweet to see him. Just the sight of him chases away the sorrow.

Apart from a gash above his eyebrow and probably a few bruised ribs to add to what looks to be one heck of a black eye, Gabriel looks amazing. All warmth and unrelenting love.

"Ugh," he grunts, looking around the room. "This place is disgusting."

Roseline makes a sweep of her own and cringes. "Yeah, well I wasn't going for five-star luxury. I just wanted somewhere secluded."

At the reminder of her sudden disappearance, Gabriel's face droops. "Do you have any idea how worried I was? Sadie's convinced some psycho kidnapped you. William has been putting up signs with your picture on it all over the neighborhood. I wouldn't put it past him to get you plastered on a milk cartoon!"

"I know," she sighs, bowing her head. The tips of her greasy hair brush the cigarette-burned carpet.

"I thought I lost you," he mutters. Roseline closes her eyes to the pain in his voice. It hurts just knowing that he was upset. He drops to the floor before her. "I can't imagine living without you."

A tear escapes through her clenched eyes. "I know."

"Do you?" he asks. His hand reaches out to push back the clumped curtain of hair from her face. "I stopped going to school, stopped going to practice, and royally ticked off Steve, but none of that mattered anymore. You consumed my thoughts and pushed out the rest of the world. I thought I would go crazy if I couldn't find you."

"How did you?" she whispers, staring up into his glorious face through her tears. It is the face of an angel, her guardian angel. Suddenly she wonders why she had ever been foolish enough to leave his side. This is where she belongs. She knew that from the first time she felt the tug toward him, but she fought it. A lot of good that did!

"I felt you," he whispers, gently rubbing his thumb along her cheek. "I can't really explain it without sounding crazy, but I could. I knew you were alive but I didn't know where you were. Then this morning I just couldn't stand it anymore. I got in my car and drove around the city, trying to think, and that's when I felt you. It was faint, almost like a small pulse when I turned onto the interstate but I decided to follow it."

"This pulse led you to my door?" she asks, amazed.

He nods, a smile stretching across his face. "It was the strangest thing, but I knew I would find you. I didn't care how far I would have to drive or how much it would cost me, I was going to see you again. Thankfully you were only a few hours away 'cause I sort of forgot my wallet when I ran out of the house this morning and didn't love the idea of having to thumb a ride when I ran out of gas."

A small laugh escapes her lips. "Somehow I think someone would have given you a lift."

He returns the smile. His hand slips around to the back of her neck. "I found you and I am not letting go this time."

The intensity of his promise stakes Roseline to the ground. The fire in his eyes cannot be denied, nor can the flames burning within her chest. This is right, as incredible as it is, and Roseline doesn't want to fight it anymore.

She had been wrong to assume that he would be able to forget her. By whatever magic that binds them together, Gabriel has become just as in tuned with the bond as she is. The why's and how's will no doubt plague her for many nights to come, but in this moment she feels her resistance falter.

Her fingers curl around his shirt, pulling him toward her. His eyes widen but she only smiles as she brings her lips to within a hairsbreadth of his. Gabriel's hands press firmly on her arms. She frowns, leaning back, annoyed at his rejection.

"No offense," he says, crinkling his nose. "But you kinda reek."

"Oh," she gasps, scrambling to her feet as she realizes the state she is in. "Don't look at me."

She makes a mad dash for the bathroom and slams the door behind her. She slides down the door as Gabriel's chuckle reaches her. "Take all the time you need. I don't want you stinking up my car."

"Be thankful I can't reach you right now," she threatens through the door as she reaches to turn on the shower. Freezing water sprays in erratic squirts as she strips and jumps in. "You never said what your dad did when you stopped going to practice. Did he flip?"

"You could say that," Gabriel responds. "I practically had to sign over my life to him to make up for nearly getting kicked off the team. If it weren't for the fact that they need me to win State, I would be long gone."

"So what did you have to agree to?" Roseline rubs the suds into her hair, sighing with relief as days of filth wash away.

"I'm not allowed to miss any more practice. I have to make up all of my homework that I've missed and I have to wax his car every weekend until I leave for college."

Roseline reaches out to shut off the water. Small wisps of steam rise from her unnaturally warm skin. She yanks down a towel and dries off before tiptoeing to the door. "I'm really sorry, Gabriel."

"It's worth it."

She gazes at his profile through a narrow opening in the door, wishing she could run her finger over his smile. The memory of their kiss in the museum makes her weak in the knees. Heat begins to flame in places best ignored during situations like this, alone, in a grimy motel room.

"Can you throw me that bag by the door?" She holds the bathroom door tightly against her chest to minimize his view.

Gabriel snatches the bag and peeks inside. "You mean this one? The one with all of your clothes?"

Roseline narrows her eyes at his mischievous chuckle. "Don't even think about it."

"What?" he says, grinning from ear to ear. "Would it be my fault if I accidentally threw it just out of reach so you'd have to come get it?"

"Trust me, you will regret it if you do." Her threat falls weak as she bursts into giggles.

Silence fills the room. She leans back against the bathroom wall. "Gabriel?"

"I'm thinking."

Roseline chews on her lip, thinking over her options. She shrugs and gives into her reckless side as she slips out of the bathroom. The towel she is wearing is small, more like a glorified hand towel, but it covers her well enough. Gabriel stands just a few feet away, twirling the bag around his finger. The moment he sees her, his mouth drops open and the bag falls to the floor, forgotten.

His gaze follows the beads of water slowly sliding down her shoulder, dripping from her wet hair. The farther south he looks, the hotter his cheeks grow. All of Roseline's former confidence vanishes as she fidgets under Gabriel's intense scrutiny. For the first time she is struck with low self-confidence. It's a foreign feeling, one that she detests. He gulps, finally returning to meet her gaze.

"Wow," Gabriel says.

Roseline smiles timidly. "Can I have my bag now?" Her fingers dig into the towel's rough material, praying that her trembling hands do not betray her and let go.

Gabriel's Adam's apple bobs as he nods, dipping low to pick up the bag. He steps forward, leaning to hand it to her. His rampaging pulse sounds loud in her ears as he closes the distance. The instant his fingers touch hers, Gabriel jerks back and marches determinedly towards the bed. He flops onto it and plunges his hands through his hair. A heavy sigh escapes his lips.

"Are you okay?" Roseline asks, suddenly unsure. She has never had a guy react like this before but, then again, she has never been with a guy who is physically able to walk away, especially when she presents herself in such an appealing manner.

"Uh…yeah," Gabriel clears his throat, blinking slowly. "I think so. I'm just not sure how much self-control I can manage at the moment."

"Right, well I'll just go get dressed." Roseline slips back into the bathroom. Even through the closed door, she can hear his whispered groan. "Calm down, you idiot. You've just found her so don't mess this up."

Roseline's fists pump in a small surge of triumph. So, Gabriel isn't completely immune to her charms.

Nineteen

The ride back to Chicago is filled with lengthy silences and awkward sideways glances. Neither of them knows what to say after the towel incident but it is obvious by Gabriel's heavy breathing that it lingers in his thoughts.

Roseline takes another bite of the massive burger Gabriel insisted on ordering her from a roadside truck stop with the spare change in his car. Greasy fast food has never tasted so good.

"Is your dad going to force you to play in the State Finals next month?" Her words come out garbled as she chews.

Gabriel casts a worried glance her way. "Rose, the game is this weekend. Don't you realize how long you've been gone?"

The burger loses all taste in her mouth. Three weeks? Was she really gone that long? Roseline lowers the passenger side window and chucks her half-eaten burger out. She can't stomach any more.

"No." She shakes her head. "I guess the days all ran together. I didn't really have the strength to care."

His eyes remain glued to the road ahead, but his concern is nearly palpable. "Will you come to the game?"

Of course she wants to see him play, even though she has decided that she loathes the sport, but is unsure how she should answer.

"Sadie will probably be there," he says.

Roseline nods. Of course, Sadie will be there. She is swept up into football fever along with the rest of the school. "Well, then I should probably go."

Gabriel agrees. "Sure. For Sadie."

"Definitely," Roseline agrees. "For Sadie."

125

As if this agreement has decided how they should move forward with their awkwardly intense relationship, they fall into silence. The miles pass by slowly. Bleak, wintry farmland stretches as far as she can see. Chicago rises on the horizon as the sky begins to darken with a vibrant dusk.

"I know things are confusing right now and I'll admit I'm kinda freaked out by all of this, but I need you to promise me that you won't run away again." Gabriel's voice is strained as they reach the outskirts of the city. His fingers grasp the steering wheel in a death grip. "I can't lose you again, Rose."

I can't lose you either, her mind fills in silently.

She turns in her seat and admires his handsome profile. The ridge of his brow sweeps into a blunt nose; his lips are soft as silk. The memory of their fiery embrace makes her close her eyes as she speaks her heart. "I think we should try to make this work."

"Are you sure?" He flips on his turn signal and pulls off at their exit. His foot adds more pressure to the gas pedal than is necessary to take the ramp. "I thought you were worried about us being well...us."

"I am," she sighs. She has had plenty of time to think it over during the agonizing drive home. "Obviously being apart didn't work out so well for either of us and, to be honest, I'm sick of fighting it. Contrary to what I have said in the past, I really do want to be with you, Gabriel. I'm just...worried."

"About that guy?"

She nods. "Let's just hope the past stays in the past." It is a painfully flippant answer but she is too weary to think beyond this moment. Fighting against the bond that holds them together is too difficult.

Gabriel's silence worries her. What is he thinking? Is she wrong about how he feels about her? No, surely not. He just threw his life out of the window because of her. That has to count for something.

"What are you thinking?" she whispers, too nervous to look at him.

Blowing out a breath, Gabriel shakes his head. "I'm not really sure. A part of me keeps waiting for you to change your mind."

"I won't," she promises, biting down on her lip. "I can't."

"Why not?" Gabriel glances at her as he eases the Range Rover to the side of the road, only a block from his house.

When she looks back at him, she watches his face soften against the tears curling down her cheek. "Because I am bound to you."

Gabriel stretches out his hand and gently brushes back a stray hair from her forehead. Golden highlights in her hair shimmer under the streetlight glowing through the sunroof. His hand pauses as he gently cups her cheek. "That's the way I feel too," he whispers.

Roseline leans into his hand, closing her eyes. Warmth radiates from his palm. It is not the same searing blaze she is used to. This is tender…loving.

"I shouldn't let this happen," she mutters, holding his hand to her, refusing to let him pull back. "But I'm not strong enough to resist you anymore."

"So this is what you want? To be with me?" Gabriel asks, his hope shining through his words.

She nods, pulling Gabriel's hand away from her face. She softly brushes her lips against each of his knuckles before releasing him. "Yes. I want this…but I need time. And I need you to promise me something."

"Anything," Gabriel says as his gaze rises from his knuckles.

"If something were to happen to me…" her voice cracks. "Please don't come after me. I can't bear the thought of you getting hurt."

His thumb tucks under her chin as he raises it to look at him. An intense heat burns in the depths of his eyes. "I found you this time, Rose. I will always come for you."

His altered promise ignites a fire in her chest. Never before has anyone spoken words with such fathomless love. Roseline knows Gabriel would move heaven and earth to find her. "I know. But I had to try."

Gabriel leans across the console. He stops a nose length from her. "I won't let anything happen to you, Rose. Now that I've found you I won't let anyone take you away from me."

She desperately wishes she could believe him, but the reality is that Gabriel would never stand a chance against Vladimir. "I should probably get home."

"You want some company? Your mom might be pretty ticked."

"No. She's away for work. I doubt she even realizes I'm missing." She hates to carry on the lie with him but knows that opening completely up to him will only further endanger his life.

"Lucky you," he smirks as he turns down his street. "Steve's gonna be furious when he sees me."

She reaches out to squeeze his arm. "You'll be fine. I'm not sure so about me," she groans as Sadie barrels out her front door as the Range Rover pulls into the driveway. "Sadie is going to kill me."

Twenty

As odd as it might sound, Roseline is thrilled at Sadie's refusal to speak to her after their initial reunion. She decided that the only fitting punishment for abandoning her without so much as a phone call is to implement the cold shoulder tactic. Roseline walks silently beside her friend, trying desperately to hide her smile. It feels so good to have a friend who cares enough for her to be that put out.

It is Friday afternoon and school ended early in anticipation for tonight's state finals. Roseline is a ball of nerves, excited and leery all at the same time.

"I know you're not talking to me right now, but I was kinda wondering if you were still planning on heading to the game tonight." It is all Sadie talked about before Roseline ran off.

"Of course I'm going," Sadie cries, breaking her vow of silence. "How could you even think I'd miss the biggest game of the year?"

"But aren't you still mad at me?"

Sadie waves her off. "Oh, pish posh. I don't hold grudges," she offers a sheepish smile. "Well, not for too long anyways."

Roseline smiles, letting her eyes linger over Sadie's newest theme. Her hair is dyed black and styled beautifully. Her bangs lay softly across her forehead while the back of her hair falls straight. Gone are the raccoon eyes, spiked jewelry, and flaming pink hair.

Her dress is crimson, which makes her ivory skin glow. Small white-gold hoops hang from her ear lobes and a dainty necklace nestles against the hollow of her neck.

Roseline has never seen Sadie look so good. There is a softness about her that is sadly betrayed the instant her friend opens her mouth. "Don't tell me you're backing out on me now." She yanks Roseline to the side as a group of rowdy football players rush by on their way to the pep rally that should be starting any moment.

Bright posters of varying neon shades line the hall, announcing the highly anticipated victory. It has been nearly twenty years since Rosewood won a state championship and everyone is psyched. Even the teachers have gone easy on the workload for this weekend.

"The bus leaves in an hour and you're not even ready," Sadie moans, looking at Roseline's sapphire blue sweater and jeans. Rosewood's school colors are black and red, which no doubt inspired Sadie's new look. "Where's your school spirit?"

"Right here," a voice calls from behind them. Before she can react, Gabriel wraps his arms tightly around her waist and draws her close. Roseline can't help but laugh. She warned him earlier in the week that they should take things slow but sometimes he gets too excited.

"Put me down," Roseline giggles, batting at him playfully. Gabriel winces and instantly releases her. "Are you okay?"

Gabriel nods, gingerly rubbing his arm. "Yeah. I have been aching a bit the past couple days. Hope I'm not coming down with something."

"Did you pull a muscle in practice?"

"Nah, it's all over. Kinda flu like, ya know. But I'll be fine knowing you're watching me," he grins, pinching her side.

Sadie rolls her eyes. She is not too thrilled with the idea of them pursuing a relationship together, especially since she suspects Gabriel is the reason for her best friend's sudden disappearance. It is a fact that she makes perfectly clear anytime he comes around. "Shouldn't you be at the rally?"

"Yeah, but I wanted to say goodbye first." Gabriel pulls Roseline up close to his side. He tucks his arm around her waist, hooking his finger through her belt loop. "Are you heading to the game with Sadie?"

"And me," William calls, sliding up to his sister. "Thought I should do my brotherly duty and watch over these two. I'd hate for some guy to snatch them away tonight."

Gabriel and William stare each other down. Roseline sighs. Ever since Gabriel had made it known that he was with her, William has been a bit testy. "Weren't you leaving?"

Gabriel's grip around her waist tightens as he grinds his back teeth. "I'll see you tonight, Rose." With a quick peck on the cheek, he turns and is instantly carried away by the swarm of pre-game, adrenaline-laced teens. Roseline acutely feels his departure but quickly covers over her disappointment.

"So, you two seem pretty comfy now," Sadie remarks, slamming her locker shut. She does not even bother to stop and notice her backpack stuck in the door as she pulls Roseline toward the exit.

"Yeah, things are going good," Roseline says noncommittally.

"Have you kissed him yet?" Sadie asks. Even though she has made her views on their relationship very clear, she is apparently not about to give up her chance to get some dirt on Gabriel's famous kissing skills.

Roseline can feel William tense beside her. His expectant gaze makes her bite back a laugh. There is no way she is going to kiss and tell to these two. "We're just trying to get to know each other, Sadie. Stop trying to turn us into one of your smutty TV shows."

"That is high-quality programming, I will have you know." Sadie laughs as she shoves her way through the double doors. A huge bonfire blazes on the edge of the parking lot.

"That's a bit worrying," Roseline mutters as they approach the crowd. A stuffed bull hangs low over the flames. The scent of melting plastic curls in her nose.

"It's all in good fun. I'm sure Claremont is burning our red devil as we speak," William grins, shoving people out of his way.

Sadie giggles behind a gloved hand. "Kinda fitting, huh?"

They eagerly join in with the chants led by Rosewood's cheer squad. Roseline pumps her fists and actually finds herself swept away until she senses a mood change as the head cheerleader's piercing glare finds her among the crowd.

"Yikes. I think Claire's got it in for you," William mutters as he darts a glance her way. Sure enough, the cheerleader's beady little eyes are drilling into Roseline's forehead. People all around begin to follow her gaze. Most nod in understanding, thankful that they are not the one stupid enough to cross Claire. It is social suicide to get on her bad side.

"This is going to be a long night," Roseline sighs.

Twenty-One

Roseline is careful not to bend the metal railing as she jumps and shouts like a mad woman. Rosewood Prep and Claremont High are neck and neck coming up to the final ten minutes of the game. She never dreamed football could be this intense but, then again, it isn't exactly the game that has drawn her attention.

Gabriel has been spectacular throughout the entire night. His throws are longer than she has ever noticed before. He dives in and out of his opponents, taking them out as if they were limp practice dummies. His speed is unmatched, and his accuracy is off-the-charts amazing.

The crowd is going wild. The deafening roar has not faded for over an hour.

"Can you believe him?" Sadie cries. Her face is flushed with excitement. Obviously her frustration with Gabriel disappeared as soon as he threw the first touchdown. "He's a shoo in for MVP."

Even William has to admit Gabriel is in top form. "It's no secret I don't like the guy but, man, does he have an arm. Who knew he could throw so well?"

Their words slowly sink into Roseline's mind and, when they do, she feels sick to her stomach. They are right. Claremont can barely keep up with Gabriel. He is practically a one-man team tonight. She turns and focuses on him as he dives over the end zone with the ball safely cradled in his arms.

"Who does that?" William laughs, hooting right along with the rest of the crowd.

"He's not a man...he's a machine!" Sadie crows, stomping with all her might on the metal bleachers. "I don't know what you've done to him, Rose, but keep it up."

Roseline's face pales and her hands begin to tremble as icy apprehension creeps up her spine. Something is wrong. Gabriel has always been a skilled player but tonight he is spectacular.

She narrows her gaze on his throwing arm as he leaps up to slam the ball into the ground. Dirt cakes his biceps but it does little to hide the evidence that she feared. He has grown.

Not in the sense of gaining an extra pound of muscle or adding a little definition to his already toned body. No, now Gabriel is ripped. There is no way a seventeen-year-old boy can look like that.

"Hey, are you okay?" Sadie asks, noticing Roseline for the first time. Beads of sweat have formed along her brow, despite the plummeting temperatures. She feels weak in the knees. If it were not for her death grip on the railing, she might have passed out completely.

"I'm not sure," Roseline says, shaking her head to clear her frantic thoughts. "I think I need to sit down for a minute."

William leaps over the seat to Roseline's side, easing her down. With his arm wrapped protectively around her shoulders, Roseline begins to breathe easier. Maybe she is wrong. Oh god, she hopes she is!

But there are too many odd things happening to Gabriel. First are the glowing eyes she hasn't completely ruled out. Obviously not a human thing to do. Second, his blood calls in to her in ways that should not be possible for mortal/immortal relationships. Third, his reflexes are spot on and his physique is definitely changing. It is almost as if nature is working to perfect him in ways that defy human logic.

And what about the bond? They have never shared blood or consummated their relationship. Definitely not the second bit! So then why have they entered into a life bond together?

Roseline groans, leaning heavily on William. This is infuriating. Nothing about Gabriel makes sense. How can he be so appealing, so impossibly addicting for her, when he is a mortal? The only thing that even comes close to explaining Gabriel's oddities is that he is an immortal too…but that can't be true either. He should have transformed in one swift and very painful swoop.

No, he can't be immortal. He has human parents and just because they are rudely overbearing certainly does not make them evil immortals. But what else can he be? His human status is certainly up in the air right now. Something strange is going on with him and she needs to figure it out before someone else starts to question it.

"Feeling any better?" William asks, his deep-set eyes filling with concern as they scan her pallid face.

"Yeah, I think so. Thanks for taking care of me." She offers him a weak smile as she eases out of his arms. Although she is touched by his concern, she fears turning to him for comfort. Especially if Gabriel looks up to see her in William's embrace.

She leaps to her feet as the crowd explodes around her. Her gaze locks onto a football Gabriel sent spiraling across the entire length of the field. Rosewood's receiver runs for all he is worth to catch the ball. Claremont falls behind, unable to keep up with their adrenaline pumped opponent.

She watches the ball arc toward the ground in slow motion. The receiver leaps with his hands outstretched. It falls into his hand, teetering precariously on his fingertips before they clamp around the ball. A swatch of grass carves from the ground as he slides to a halt in the end zone. The receiver rolls over and thrusts the ball high into the air, screaming in triumph.

William cups his mouth and joins the roar. "That guy is definitely going pro. Gabriel just broke every record ever set for high school football."

Both sides of the stadium erupt. One side cheers wildly while the other roars with disbelief. The commentators scream over the loudspeaker as the entire Rosewood football team pile on top of Gabriel. College scouts race onto the field, cameras flash wildly, and news reporters fight through the crowd to interview the star quarterback that has just won the state championship almost singlehandedly.

Roseline is too numb to react as Sadie and William's shouts mingle with the roar of the crowd. She does not smile, does not offer anyone a high five. All she can do is stand in horrified silence.

Twenty-Two

"Rose!" Gabriel shouts, shoving his way through the applauding crowd. The camera flashes are blinding. He shields his eyes to see Roseline dash down the stadium stairs, leaving a bewildered Sadie and William behind. "Rose, stop!"

"Gabriel," a shrill cry rings out as a pair of slender arms wrap tightly around his chest. He glances down, instantly annoyed.

"Not now, Claire."

"Oh, come on. Let's celebrate. You won the game," she purrs, curling her finger around a lock of his hair at the nape of his neck. "I'll make it worth your while."

"Not gonna happen, Claire." He unhooks her hands and shoves her aside, ignoring her indignant shrieks as he runs full out toward the bleachers.

"Over here, Gabe." Steve waves him over to a flock of college scouts. "I have some people I'd like you to meet."

"In a minute," he calls over his shoulder as he slips through the crowd descending from the bleachers.

"Where is she?" he shouts up to Sadie from where she hangs over the bleacher. "I can't see her anywhere."

"She's heading toward the entrance. Something really spooked her."

"No kidding," Gabriel grumbles as he flings himself through the crowd, shouting his apologies as he knocks people aside.

"Rose!" he screams, catching a glimpse of her fleeing figure.

She turns. The instant he catches her eye, he knows she is going to run again. "Please don't do this! We need to talk," he yells.

He can see Roseline's tears gleaming under the stadium lights. Pain and confusion jumble on her face but determination quickly replaces it.

"I'm sorry," she mouths as she slips into a yellow cab. The door slams, echoing loudly in his ears as she turns her back on him. He slides to a halt as the taxi disappears into a maze of cars.

Twenty-Three

Roseline shoves her payment through the narrow slot in the window to the cabbie and stumbles out of the car. Once inside, the stairs prove too tricky for her fuddled mind so she takes them on hands and knees. The instant Roseline hits the bed she passes out.

Early morning light soon streams through the grimy windows, warming her face. She groans as she rolls over. Her head feels like it has been kicked in, and her throat burns with lingering acid from the night before. The taste in her mouth and the scent coming from the floor beside her bed tells her that sometime during her night her body expelled the two hot dogs she consumed at the game.

Unwilling to face the day, Roseline throws the covers over her face and falls back into a fitful sleep. Each time she wakes, the computer calls to her, begging her to contact Fane, but she knows an email won't be enough. She needs to speak with him. Hear his voice.

As the sun begins to set, Roseline cleans up the mess beside her bed, opens a window to freshen the air, and pulls on a tank top and shorts. She laces up her running shoes and bounds down the stairs. Running has always helped to clear her thoughts in the past and she really hopes it will work today.

Trapped within the confines of a human world, she is forced into a speed that feels achingly slow, an annoying alternative to the speed her legs long for.

Her heart overrules her mind as her feet pound the pavement leading to a row of shops a few blocks away. She doesn't wake from her haze until the tinkling of a bell on the cell phone company's door snaps her out.   Less than half an hour later, Roseline rushes back home to plug in her new, shiny, electric blue phone.

She paces as the tiny bars cycle through its charging mode. She chides herself for her impulsive purchase, finally convincing herself it will only be used for emergencies.

Isn't this an emergency?

Roseline snatches the phone off the charger and scours the room for the tiny scrap of paper where she jotted down Sadie's number.

"Hey, it's me," she says when the voicemail clicks on. "Look, Sadie, I'm really sorry about bailing on you, again. I know it's becoming a bad habit."

She pauses, running her hands through her wind tangled hair. "I just wanted to let you know I'm okay and that I've got a new phone. The number is…where is it?"

She fumbles through her paperwork and rattles off the number to Sadie's voicemail then hangs up. She releases her breath. "Okay, that wasn't so bad."

Logic reminds her that registering a phone to her name was dangerous, even if it is a pre-paid phone. Paper trails have a way of coming back to bite you. She sits staring at the phone laying in her hands until she jerks upright at the arrival of a new scent. Gabriel has found her!

His fists pound against the front door. She can hear the lock groan in protest as his banging continues. No doubt her neighbors will call the police thinking there is a domestic disturbance on their block.

How does he know where she lives, though? Jimmy's bar is over three miles from here and there is no way Sadie would willingly cough up the information unless…Roseline sighs.

After her last disappearing act, Sadie made it perfectly clear that she would rat her out the moment she sniffed trouble. No doubt her "bat out of hell" act last night sparked Sadie's protective side.

The pounding continues for nearly ten minutes before Gabriel finally gives up and stomps down the porch steps. She tiptoes to the window to watch him slip down the icy sidewalk. He turns just before he climbs into the driver's seat. The grim look on his face nearly convinces Roseline to call attention to herself but she resists the urge.

She walks back across the creaking floor and paces around the center of the room for nearly an hour. The phone feels like an anvil in her hand, dragging her down. She sinks onto the rickety stool with her heart and body weary from exhaustion.

"I shouldn't do it," she mutters, spinning the cell phone in circles on the wooden table. She stares at it, waging an internal war. "Oh crap," she grumbles, flipping the phone open. Her fingers dance over the keys, shaking so badly she wonders if she has gotten the number right.

"Hello?" Roseline bursts into tears at the sound of the deeply masculine voice on the other end of the line. "Roseline?"

She wipes her nose with the back of her hand. "Yeah, it's me, Fane."

"I've been worried sick about you." She can hear a creaking door in the background and remembers how careful she must be. The castle has ears. "Where are you? Why are you crying?"

Her throat catches as she imagines Fane's brow knit with concern. "I've missed you so much," she cries. "I'm so sorry I left you."

"I know," Fane whispers. His hand covers the receiver as he speaks. "I've missed you too."

"I guess you're wondering why I'm calling," Roseline laughs weakly, drying her tears.

She can hear a creak of a chair followed swiftly by a heart thumping bass line. Glancing at the clock, she realizes that she was a fool to forget the time difference. Her family is awake. "Yeah, it must be something pretty important for you to risk exposure. What's up?"

Roseline clamps her eyes shut, wincing at the ache in her heart. She has refused to allow herself to miss him, but now all of her feelings come rushing back in. Fane is her best friend, her only reason for living…until Gabriel.

"I think I'm in trouble."

"Tell me," Fane demands. She can hear a faint sound on the line, a clacking she can't quite place.

"No, it's not like that. I am fine. It's just—" Roseline chews on her lip. "There's this guy."

"Are you kidding me? You drop off the grid without so much as a goodbye and now you want to chat about boys?" She winces at his biting words.

"Yes, please just listen to me—"

Fane cuts off her plea. "No, you listen to me. You need to come home. Vladimir is on a rampage and is taking it out on Brasov. People are dying, Roseline."

"Oh no," she groans, sinking out of the chair and onto the floor. "How bad is it?"

"It's not pretty," Fane growls. "What did you think would happen?"

"I don't know," she snaps back. "I just...I couldn't take it anymore."

Fane sighs heavily on the other end of the line. "I understand, but you know how this will end. He will find you and when he does I'm not sure I can stop him from killing you this time. If you come back, he might be more lenient."

Roseline's fingers begin to tremble. Age-old wounds flare up. Images of blood and pain fill her mind's eye. She clamps her eyes shut, forcing away the memories. "I can't come back."

"You have to. It's the only way to save your life. I can't lose you." Fane's voice chokes off.

Even after all this time, Fane's love for her has never faded. Their secret love affair spanned two centuries, but the amount of time they had managed to snatch together wouldn't even be able to fill one year on a calendar. Vladimir watches her like a hawk and Roseline knew it was only a matter of time before he found out about their relationship. Fane has yet to heal from their breakup nearly fifty years ago.

"Are you going to help me or not?"

She can hear Fane's murmured curses in the background. "You know I will. What's wrong?"

"It's about this boy—"

"Immortal?" he cuts her off.

Here it comes. "No. He's mortal."

Fane blows out a breath. "Oh good, you had me worried for a moment. I'm not understanding why there is a problem."

"There's something weird going on with him. It's starting to worry me." She quickly fills him in on all of the unusual things she has noticed about Gabriel. As the conversation wears on, she begins to sense Fane's tension. "So, what do you think?"

"Never heard anything like it—" he hesitates. "I don't like it, Roseline. He might be dangerous. I think you need to leave, right now."

Roseline sucks in a breath. "I can't do that."

"Why not?" Fane asks. The sharp edge of his confusion makes her wince.

"I just can't, okay?"

His response is delayed far longer than it should have been. Roseline frowns, clutching the phone tightly to her ear as she strains to hear. She detects a faint whirring and stiffens.

"Fine. Then let me come get you," Fane suggests absently. "I don't trust that guy."

Roseline blanches as the pieces of the puzzle come together——the whirring, clacking…he's tracing her call!

"I gotta go, Fane. Thanks for the talk."

"No, Roseline wait." The pause confirms her suspicion. He has probably managed to narrow her down to the United States, perhaps even the Midwest, but has the computer calculated her exact location? "Please don't go just yet."

"I'm sorry," she whispers, truly meaning it. "This was a mistake."

"Roseline—"

"I love you." She disconnects the line to her home, to the only person who has ever truly understood her. Three centuries of memories flood her mind as she launches the phone at the far wall. It bounces off in a rain of shattered bits of plastic. She stares at the lifeless pieces scattered across the wooden floor. She buries her face in her hands. "Just like my life."

Twenty-Four

"So, is this your new thing? Ditching everyone that cares about you?" Sadie growls as she slumps into her usual lunchroom seat the following Monday.

"I'm really sorry about that...but I did call," Roseline says, hoping this tiny act will help to appease her friend but, judging by the firm set of her lips, Roseline knows she will have to try better. "I felt really ill and I couldn't bear the thought of a bus ride home. You know how I hate the smell of those things. Besides, I didn't want to spoil your fun."

Sadie's anger subsides slightly. She pouts for a few minutes more to make sure Roseline gets the message and then smiles. "Oh fine. You're forgiven."

"Thanks," Roseline grins, nibbling on her apple. She subconsciously scans the room for any signs of Gabriel. Thankfully, he is absent. She sinks back into her chair as she chews on her lower lip. What will she say when she sees him? This question tumbles around in her mind. Her talk with Fane left her woefully without answers.

Sadie flips a thick strand of bright red hair back from her face as she takes a massive bite of her hamburger. Roseline grins, admiring her friend's outrageous outfit change. Her delicate dress, simple jewelry, and smooth hair have had been replaced with a red-checked tablecloth.

Her newly dyed hair is done up in tiny pigtails that peek out from under the brim of her straw hat. Brown cowboy boots hug her calves and a jean skirt flares around her knees. "Haven't we already had Halloween?" Roseline quips.

"Oh, not you too," Sadie groans. "Everyone keeps asking me that today. You'd think people would have some appreciation for freedom of dress."

Roseline nods, fighting to hide her smirk. "And what did your mother say when you walked out the door?"

Sadie shrugs and shoves some fries in her mouth. "The usual. It's really starting to get old, you know. My mom thinks she can run my life."

"Yes, how very tragic for you," a deep voice says just behind them.

Roseline cranes her neck around to see Gabriel glaring down at her. How did he sneak up on her? Drat.

Even in the midst of her panic, she notices one major change—Gabriel's voice has deepened over the weekend. It now possesses a husky quality that turns her insides to mush. Double drat.

"I wasn't sure if I would see you," Roseline mutters to the floor, refusing to meet his steely glare.

"Likewise," he retorts. "Can we go somewhere to talk?"

Roseline shoots Sadie a pleading look but she raises her hands in the air. "I'm a lover not a fighter. Don't drag me into this."

"Thanks a lot," Roseline growls as she throws her bag over her shoulder and follows Gabriel out of the dining hall. Eyes glue to them everywhere they go. Some curious, others jealous, but most are outright venomous. Obviously, Claire's new mission to destroy Roseline is already in full swing. Too bad the poor girl doesn't realize how little she actually cares about high school life.

Gabriel grips her hand tightly in his as he shoves through the back door of the school. The metal frame dents along the edge under his abuse. Roseline winces at the reminder of his newfound strength. "Skipping school again?" she asks.

He doesn't say anything as he pulls her along behind him. His fingers clamp around her wrist. She winces, realizing that he is not only strong enough to bruise her but he could actually crush her wrist if he wanted to.

Roseline's stomach twists in knots as he leads them toward the parking lot, toward seclusion. This can't be good.

"You gonna take me out and shoot me?" She forces a laugh as Gabriel pulls her to a stop in front of his passenger side door.

He doesn't speak as he holds the door open, waiting impatiently for her to climb into her seat. As soon as the door slams shut behind her Gabriel whips around the back end of the car and jumps into the driver's seat. He turns the key and revs the engine. With one hand on the wheel and tires squealing, the Range Rover shoots out of the parking lot.

"Where are we going?" Trees rush past as Gabriel drives the gas pedal into the floorboard. They shoot out of the gates before the guard even has a chance to set down his coffee.

"To talk."

"Why can't we do that at school?" She braces herself against the dash as the Rover whips through traffic, creating spaces where none should exist.

"I want to be alone."

"Well, that doesn't sound the least bit ominous," she mutters as she presses back into her seat. She is nervous, no denying that. His erratic driving and death grip on the wheel do little to ease her concerns. Gabriel has every right to be upset with her, but this is a bit excessive.

Instead of heading into the city, Gabriel turns south. His mouth opens and closes as he attempts to discuss the elephant in the room, but each time he clams up to fume a bit longer.

"You came by my house," Roseline says. No sense beating around the bush.

Gabriel nods. "Four times."

He's keeping track. That's not a good sign. "I'm sorry I wasn't there."

"Oh come on, Rose. We both know you were ignoring me. I could hear you upstairs."

She shoots a wary glance his way. "How?"

"I don't know," he growls, yanking the wheel to throw them around a corner. "You've got a lot of answering to do. Who lives in a house that's almost completely empty?"

Roseline's fingers clench tightly against her palms. Dread slows her pulse. She is not ready to answer this question. "Please stop. You're driving like a maniac."

145

"So?" Gabriel challenges. When he turns to meet her gaze she notices his eyes are as cold as a frozen lake.

"Are you so angry that you'd risk killing us?"

Gabriel heaves an annoyed sigh and shakes his head. He swerves to the side of the road and slams on the brakes. The car slides a couple feet before coming to a stop on an ice patch. "Why did you run away from me at the game? I played the best game of my entire life and my girlfriend didn't even stick around to celebrate with me."

Roseline's head jerks up. "I'm your girlfriend?"

His lip curls into a snarl. "Of course you are, Rose, but don't change the subject. Why did you leave? You knew I needed to talk to you."

Even though she has gone over this answer a million times in her head, not a single word of it feels right. She has gone back and forth between daring to tell him the truth and coming up with some harebrained explanation.

"I don't know what to say, Gabriel. I felt sick..." she whispers, staring down at her lap.

"Sick? You think I am going to swallow that excuse? I'm not Sadie, Rose. I know you. You were scared. I could see it in your eyes. I could feel it."

Roseline glances up. "You could feel my fear?"

"Yeah." Gabriel nods as his voice loses some of its intensity. "I was so worried about you. I thought maybe..."

"What?" she presses, placing her hand over his clenched fist.

He turns toward the window. "I thought maybe you were afraid of me."

"Why would I be afraid of you," she hedges.

Gabriel rolls his eyes. "Okay, can we stop the innocent act? We both know what happened Friday night and I think you know more about it then you're letting on."

Reaching out her hand, she gently cups Gabriel's face. His beautiful eyes plead with her. "Please, Rose, do you know what is happening to me?"

What can she say that will not freak him out? She has lived with the unbelievable for three hundred years and yet he is still a mystery to her.

"Gabriel, I'm not sure how much I can…" she cuts off. As one, they turn toward the screeching sound outside the vehicle. The sound of locking brakes fills her mind as she watches a semi-trailer stutter toward them across the icy intersection. Gabriel's face swings slowly toward her; a blue light glows brightly in his eyes as the truck breaches the gap.

In a blur of movement, Roseline shreds Gabriel's seat belt and pulls him into her lap. She wraps her body around him as the semi crashes through the driver's side door. Headlights blind her as she whips around, turning her back to the truck to take the brunt of the impact.

She remains conscious long enough to cocoon Gabriel as they are thrown from the vehicle. Pain radiates through her body as she slams to the ground. Her hands slip from around Gabriel as darkness overtakes her.

The distant wailing of an ambulance siren calls Roseline back from the void. Blood seeps from a deep gash along her hairline. She grits her teeth against the pains stabbing all over her body. She fights to remain conscious as her ribs knit back together and her spine reattaches itself.

Her shattered kneecaps withdraw their pieces as they re-form. Her jaw pops back into its socket. She rolls her head to the side to see her left arm dangling. By the look and feel of it, every bone has been fractured. Her right arm is clearly broken but remains mostly intact.

Gabriel lies unconscious next to her. His legs are completely shattered, his right arm is twisted back at an odd angle and, by the look of the dark bruising along his stomach, he is bleeding internally. She grunts, digging her nails into the road as she drags herself toward him.

"Oh, thank God you're alive," the semi driver cries as he falls to his knees in the bloodstained snow. "I called for an ambulance but they're stuck behind the pile up. The paramedics should be here any minute though." His eyes trail over her broken body. "I wish there was something I could do to help you."

Roseline winces as the thrumming along his neck attracts her attention. Her desperation to save Gabriel makes her resort to the unthinkable. Her right hand slams into the man's temple. He slumps to the ground. "I'm so sorry. I wish I didn't have to do this."

As her teeth pierce the man's soft flesh, warm, tangy blood begins to pool in her mouth. She drinks deep, moaning as healing fires light all over her body. Bones quickly mend and tiny internal fissures seal shut. Tears streams from her eyes as she drinks the forbidden blood. Her guilt finally pulls her away. The pain still lingers but it is more bearable now.

The unconscious man slumps to the side, very much alive but certainly in need of a transfusion. The wounds at his neck have already begun to heal, covering any evidence of her plunder. Roseline wipes the crimson stain from her lips, clamping down on her tears as she leaps to Gabriel's side. "Hold on. I'll save you."

She bends low to brush her lips against his, testing his warmth. She can feel his pulse beating through his tender flesh. Gabriel parts his mouth at her touch, and his tongue licks the final traces of blood from the corner of her mouth. His body flinches. Roseline rears back, staring at him with a mixture of amazement and horror.

Gabriel cries out. Her eyes widen at the sound. It is not a cry of pain but of relief. She lifts his shirt and gasps. The blood bruise has begun to recede. His legs twitch, popping and cracking as his bones begin to rearrange.

"You have got to be kidding," she murmurs, her brain firing on all cylinders to figure out what is happening before her eyes. It should be impossible, but the evidence it staring back at her. Without stopping to think of the consequences, Roseline sinks her teeth into her wrist and applies pressure to the wound. Fresh blood drips into Gabriel's mouth, splattering against his teeth. He gulps it down.

"Oh my god!" she cries, rearing back as his arm snaps into place.

Roseline crab crawls backward, too horrified to move until she hears footsteps approaching at a run. Her first reaction is to turn and fight, to protect him, but she can't be seen. Not while she is healing.

With a heavy heart, she turns and runs.

Twenty-Five

"Dude, you don't look so good," Oliver says as he stares down at the yellowing bruises that cover Gabriel's face.

Gabriel winces as he pushes himself up in bed. Needles in his hands still connect him to various medicines, each one pumping something into his weary system. "The doctors tell me it's a miracle I survived. The Rover was totaled and apparently they found me ten feet from the car."

"And all you ended up with is some internal bruising?"

"Yep," Gabriel coughs, holding his side gingerly. "Amazing, huh?"

Oliver whistles. "No kidding. Thank god this didn't happen before we won state."

Gabriel fights for a convincing nod. "Hey, have you seen Rose? Is she doing okay? No one will tell me anything."

"Oh, not that girl again," Oliver groans. "Dude, when are you going to wake up and realize Claire's claimed you? This fling will never last."

"You don't know what you're talking about," he grunts, shifting in bed. His backside is numb and has been for the past four days of observation. He is sick of the hospital, sick of the nosy nurses and uppity doctors. He is fine but no one will listen to him. All he wants to do is see Rose.

"Can you please just find her room for me?" he asks, pinching the bridge of his nose to stave off his irritation.

"She's not here." Oliver frowns at the bump on his friend's head. "Are you sure you're feeling okay? I can get the doctor if you want." He begins to back out of the room.

"No. She has to be here," he insists. "I need to know that she is okay." Gabriel's voice fades out as his eyes begin to sting. He shoves his fists into his eyes and rubs them, refusing to cry. "I think she saved me."

Oliver blanches. He obviously thinks Gabriel has taken a long walk off a short pier. "Dude, there wasn't anyone in the car with you. The paramedics only found you and the semi driver. That's it."

Gabriel falls silent. Oliver shifts from foot to foot. He has done his job. He has visited Gabriel and now he is ready to split. His friend is acting too freaky for his liking. Without saying a word, Oliver slips from the room. Gabriel doesn't even notice.

As the hall lights begin to kick on, Gabriel blinks, realizing the passage of time. The same questions roll about in his mind like a scrolling digital sign. Where is Rose? How did she manage to escape the wreckage?

There is no doubt in his mind that she was in fact there and that her actions saved him. But there is something more that captures his waking thoughts, a new mystery that sends cold shivers down his spine. Turning his forearms over, Gabriel glances down at the black markings that have appeared on his arm. At first, he was unable to decipher any pattern to them until he brought both arms together. The symbols form a jagged cross.

Where did the markings come from? What is happening to him?

"What am I?" he whispers to the empty room.

Twenty-Six

"Ditched your boyfriend again, huh?"

Roseline turns to find Nicolae lounging against the school bus. She crinkles her nose with disgust. "I am not in the mood right now. I told you to leave me alone."

"Afraid that's not gonna happen." He pushes off from the bus and saunters forward. "Rumor has it that you left with Gabriel on that fateful snowy afternoon. Trouble is no one can account for your whereabouts after you two ditched school. I find that to be very interesting, don't you?"

Anger boils in her belly at his unspoken accusations. "Give it a rest, Nicolae. Gabriel is alive so I obviously didn't hurt him."

His eyebrow arches. "About that…" He grins, picking a fleck of fluff from his cardigan. "It sure is a miracle how a guy like that could survive such a tragic accident. I hear even the doctors are perplexed. It does seem like there are some strange things happening around here."

Roseline stomps up to him. "Have you been snooping around his hospital room?"

He tilts his head, offering an amused smirk. "Should I be? Is there something you're trying to hide?"

She has had about all she can take of his smugness. Glancing around to make sure there aren't any witnesses, Roseline grabs a fistful of Nicolae's coat and slams him against the bus. His feet come off the ground, the back of his head pressing against the glass window. Fear flickers in his eye. "Leave. Gabriel. Alone," she snarls.

With one final shove to rattle the windows of the bus, Roseline lets him drop and stalks away. He picks himself up and stumbles to his feet. "Is that a threat?" he calls.

Glancing back over her shoulder, Roseline drills him with her fierce gaze as she nods. The corner of his eye twitches in response but he says nothing. Nicolae is getting brave. That is not a good thing.

She swings up into the empty bus and storms to the back to wait for Sadie to arrive. Her clomping cowboy boots catch Roseline's attention a few minutes later and she blows out a breath of relief. Sadie throws herself into the seat and eyes Roseline's pale complexion.

"Still avoiding him?" Sadie chucks her backpack into the seat to block a cheerleader from sitting next to them. The girl turns with an exaggerated eye roll and heads back up the aisle.

Roseline blinks, confused by Sadie's take of her mood, and then it hits her. Today is supposed to be Gabriel's first day back. Maybe this is a good thing. It should be easy enough to duck out of sight once they get to the art museum. Fields trips can obviously have more than one positive aspect.

"I just don't know what to say to him," she admits with a genuine sigh. That certainly isn't a lie. She has barely slept since the accident. Images of Gabriel using her blood to heal have haunted her dreams. "I kept meaning to go by the hospital to visit but I thought that might be awkward with his family and all."

"Rumor has it Gabriel *is* officially back at school today but I haven't seen him yet," William says as he plops into the seat next to her. "Maybe this field trip will get your mind off things. Apparently, there is a whole section of Romanian art. Won't that be neat?"

Sadie pops him in the arm. "It's art, doofus. It's boring."

"No, I just meant that it'd be cool to see where Rose is from," William amends, sneaking a glance at Roseline.

"Whatever," Sadie mutters, pressing her nose against the window. "I'm just glad to be out of school."

A little over an hour later, Roseline finds herself inching slowly behind Sadie in a long line at the art gallery. Try as she might, she can't stop herself from comparing the lifeless paintings on the walls to Gabriel's stunning charcoal drawings in his attic. It pains her to think that such amazing talent is kept from the world.

Mrs. Smithton's voice drones on up ahead, informing her students about each artist. From the looks of her classmates, none of them care. Sadie moves on ahead, popping her bubble gum loudly as she goes. Roseline grimaces as her art teacher sends yet another withering glance in her friend's direction.

A hand clasps around her forearm and yanks her backward. She barely has time to adjust to the motion before she slams into Gabriel's broad chest. "What are you doing?"

"Just follow me."

"Like I have any choice," she grunts, struggling to keep up with his fast pace so he doesn't rip her arm out of socket. As soon as Roseline spies his target, she grows nervous. A darkened back hallway is not where she wants to be while he chats with her.

How much does he remember about the accident? Will he confront her right here in front of the entire school? Okay, maybe not the whole school, but enough people to set the rumor lines on fire yet again.

"This is perfect," he says, stopping in the middle of the dark hall. Only one door inhabits the hall at the far end—a nameplate announces the office for the president of the museum.

His brow pinches as he watches Roseline cradle her wrist. "Are you okay?"

"Sure," she shrugs. She eyes him warily. He has gotten stronger since the game but she isn't sure if it is of his own nature or the mingling of their blood. "You've got quite a grip."

Gabriel winces, holding his hand aloft as he flexes his fingers. "Apparently." He lowers his hand to his side. His eyes latch on to hers, pleading. "Do you know what is happening to me?"

She shakes her head. Waves of bronze hair spill over her shoulder, as messy and frazzled as her nerves. "No. I honestly don't."

"But you...you saved me. I saw you."

She drops her gaze. Blood seeps from her face, retracted to her frantically pumping heart. Warmth drains from her body as a disturbing chill attacks her. He knows! "No one will believe you."

"You think that's what this is about?" he growls, anger coloring his voice. "I don't care about exposing you, Rose. I just want to know what is happening to me."

Her fingers clench into fists by her side. She shifts her weight to her other foot. Her first impulse is to run, to flee Gabriel and his questions, to embrace self-preservation. She is a warrior, taught to rely on her instincts, and right now there is an epic battle taking place in her mind that she's sure she can lose.

Flee. Remain. Survive. Take a risk.

A finger pulls her chin up to look at Gabriel. His skin is pale and unnaturally drawn. "Please…"

Roseline shakes her head and clamps her eyes shut. She can't. It is forbidden to tell a human about the existence of immortals. If she allows herself to be weak, both of their lives are forfeit, but he needs to know something. Anything. She can smell his fear.

"I felt you pull me out of my seat. You held me in your arms as the truck…" he gulps, dropping his head. "I saw the truck hit you."

Roseline looks up at him. Tears swim in his eyes as he pulls her close. "When the doctors told me they didn't find you I was sure I had lost you. Sure that they thought I was too fragile to accept your death, but after nearly a week in that place I began to realize that they weren't lying to me. I could see it. I could feel it."

She winces at the awe and frustration mingled in his voice. His gaze trails over her face. "You don't have a scratch on you."

"I heal quickly," she whispers. The feeling of his fingers lightly tracing her cheek makes her weak in the knees.

"How? Why? Please, tell me something."

A shadow passes the entrance to the hall. Roseline stiffens as two brilliant green eyes meet hers for the briefest of moments before moving on. Drat. Nicolae is watching. "We can't talk about this here. It's not safe."

"What the heck does that mean?"

She leans in close, lowering her voice. "It means that I'm asking you to trust me. Give me some time to figure things out."

"Can you? Figure things out, I mean."

Roseline shrugs. "I honestly don't know. Just please don't get your hopes up. You're…different."

Chips of concrete flutter to the floor as Gabriel's fist slams into the wall. His hand buries up to his wrists. Gabriel grunts as he yanks his hand free. No blood. No broken bones. "You see? This is what I'm talking about. It's not normal. I'm not normal."

"I know," Roseline sighs.

"No, you don't," he cries, shoving his hands through his tousled hair. Concrete dust clings to his sandy strands. "You have no clue."

Roseline's chest puffs with indignation. "I've been around a heck of a lot longer than you have."

"Fine. Then tell me what these are." Gabriel wrenches back his sleeves and shoves his forearms into her face.

Instead of the recognition he hoped for, Roseline's brow knits with confusion. "When did you get these tattoos?"

"I didn't." He grits his teeth. "I woke up with them."

She leaps back, bracing against the wall. Her teeth gnash subconsciously. Gabriel flinches, shocked by her reaction. "What is it? Do you know these symbols?"

Unable to take her eyes from the markings, Roseline slowly nods. "It's part of an ancient language, from before man existed."

"Whoa, that's deep," Gabriel blows out a breath. "So what's with this one?" He holds his arms close together, forming the cross.

Roseline blanches. "It's not possible."

Gabriel drops his sleeves. "Rose, tell me what you know."

She shakes. A trembling begins in her feet and travels up her body. "I don't know anything," she insists, struggling to tear her eyes away from his arms.

"Rose…it's me."

Gulping hard, Roseline looks up into his troubled face. "I honestly don't know anything. These markings are sacred. I've seen them before, but I can't read them."

"Then why are you so frightened?" he asks, ducking his head to meet her eyes.

"Because they are forbidden. There are some things that are not meant to be known. That marking is one of them." She closes her eyes, fighting through her memory for a time when she saw this cross. It was in the Bran castle library. During her many years of study, she stumbled across a hidden panel in one of the walls. Inside was a torn page, aged and yellowed with time. Strange markings bordered the page. In the center was Gabriel's cross.

She had never dared to look at it again. When Vladimir discovered her, the punishment was both swift and severe. It was the closest she had ever come to death. That day she learned that some things are better left alone and now it has been thrust back into her life again.

Terror weakens her as she leans back against the wall. What can this mean? How is Gabriel tied to that paper? And why? Is this the reason for his changes? Why his blood calls to her?

Gabriel gently pulls her close. She nestles into his chest, wrapping her arms around his back. Strength and love radiates from him and her trembling slowly abates. "Shh," he soothes, rubbing his hand up and down her spine. "It's okay. We just need to figure out what's going on."

She places her hand on his chest and leans back. "I promise we will try but I can't promise answers."

He nods, raising his hand to cup her cheek. "Can I ask something else?

Her throat closes up. What if he asks her a direct question about her past? Can she really risk answering him?

"Why aren't you afraid of me?"

"I am," she whispers, leaning up on her toes. "But not for the reason you think."

"No?" Gabriel questions softly. He lowers his head to meet her halfway. "Why then?"

Roseline allows him to pull her close, molding his body around hers. "Because I need you too much."

Gabriel's throaty chuckle sends electric shockwaves down her spine. "Good."

The instant his lips touch hers, Roseline's legs go weak. She slumps against the wall, grateful for its solid embrace. His lips move smoothly over hers, his tongue flicking over her lower lip. A contented sigh escapes her lips as Gabriel's fiery kisses trail her jaw line, drifting down to her throat. He pauses over her artery, grinning against the fluttering of her heart just under the thin veil of skin.

"You smell amazing," he coos, nuzzling her neck. "Like cinnamon and vanilla."

Roseline presses up into him as his hands splay across her back, dipping just under the edge of her sweater to touch her bare skin. Her leg curls around his hip as she lifts up on her tiptoes, fighting to get closer. Every touch feels like living fire on her skin, searing the hidden identity from her body, leaving only her essence laid bare for Gabriel to see.

A wolf whistle draws them back to reality. Her cheeks flame brightly as she notices the crowd that has formed at the hall entrance. Guys hoot and holler, cheering Gabriel on. Oliver stands in the back, grinding his teeth as Claire digs her manicured nails into his arm.

"I guess we just confirmed the rumors," Gabriel chuckles deeply, setting Roseline back on her feet. She straightens her top and readjusts the hem of her plaid skirt. Her skin is flushed, leaking hormones at an alarming rate.

"Can we get out of here now?"

Gabriel nods, clearing his throat as he takes her hand in his and leads them through the gawking crowd. As they emerge, Gabriel leans in close. "Oh, there's something else I wanted to say back there."

From the corner of her eye, she notices a fuming Mrs. Smithton closing in on them.

"I love you," he whispers in her ear.

Twenty-Seven

"This is a waste of time," Gabriel grunts, shoving a dusty book across the table. It teeters on the edge before spilling to the floor, crumpling the pages of the ancient text.

"Easy," Roseline hisses as she leaps to the book's rescue. She unfolds the pages and gently sets the book on the pile beside her. "These are really rare."

It has been nearly a week since Gabriel's confession of love and Roseline has yet to acknowledge it. Thankfully, Gabriel's mystery tattoos have kept them busy with research. However, coming across century-old books on spells and myths is not the easiest thing to do in secret. There are only so many antique bookstores in Chicago and Gabriel's anxiety is mounting.

"I don't know," Roseline sighs, rubbing the bridge of her nose. The changes she sees in Gabriel not only worries her, they downright frighten her. She is almost getting desperate enough to try calling Fane again, but logically she knows that will only end up with him swooping in to save the day. Seeing him is the last thing she needs right now. "I told you not to get your hopes up. I wasn't exactly joking around when I said those markings are forbidden. Apparently I'm not the only one who isn't allowed to know about it."

She stretches her arms high over her head, working out the kinks in her lower back. They have been at this far too long.

"We are looking through spell books, mythology, and ancient histories. I'm sorry, but I find this a bit hard to swallow. I think it's time you start coughing up the truth, Rose. What do these books have in common with you?"

Roseline bites her tongue until she can taste blood. "You know I can't say."

"Oh, come on!" He throws up his hands in the air. His voice rises high enough to attract attention from other students in the school library. Roseline glares at him and he has the decency to lower his voice. "Obviously you've seen some pretty wacky stuff while in Romania and I want to know about it."

"Those things are not meant to be known," she snaps. She sucks in a steadying breath as she fights against her anger. Her fingernails dig deep into the flesh of the wooden table. She smudges the indents out with the palm of her hand while Gabriel isn't looking. "Trust me. There are some things you really don't want to know about."

"You know," he presses. His eyes are cold as he turns to look at her again.

"Yes and there's not a day that goes by that I don't wish I could forget it all," she says, reaching out to pull his hand into hers. He flinches but allows her to twine her fingers through his. "I just can't do that to you. There is too much at risk..." she trails off. "I don't want that for you. You deserve a normal life."

She is beginning to wonder if that is even possible for him anymore. How can he hope to live the life he is leading when he is so obviously more than human?

"Whatever," Gabriel huffs, pulling his hand away.

Roseline sinks back into her chair. Fear whispers to her mind. Something is wrong. "What is with you today? You seem really on edge."

She sees the flicker of emotion cross his face before he clamps down on it. "It's nothing," he grunts as he leaps to his feet. His chair flies backward into a bookcase—it rocks, unsettling books. He scowls at the scattered pile and snatches his bag from the table. "I'll see you around."

"But..." Roseline begins but Gabriel flees through the front door of the library. "Great."

She grabs an armful of books and stashes them behind a row of outdated textbooks with an inch of dust coating them like a second skin. No one will ever find them there. As she slips out of the library and heads to class, she can feel eyes watching her every movement. No doubt, she has just birthed another rumor. Lovely.

A few hours later, Roseline slides into her seat next to Sadie. Her friend's welcome falls flat in sight of Roseline's somber expression. "Wow, don't you look glum. What's up?"

"I don't know," she shrugs, letting her bag fall to the floor. She stares at her empty tray, only now realizing that she failed to enter the food line. "Gabriel's been acting really off with me the past couple days."

Sadie frowns. "Is it about the dance?"

"He hasn't even asked me." She knows it's a silly thing to care about a school dance, but Roseline can't help it. Going anywhere with Gabriel should have been a treat, but with his increasing mood swings, she's not so sure now.

"Are you kidding?" Sadie cries. "It's this Saturday night and that scumbag hasn't even asked you?

"Hey," Roseline says, whirling on her friend. "I thought after the State finals you would have started to cut the guy some slack."

Sadie shifts in her chair. "A girl's got a right to be jealous, doesn't she?"

"Jealous?" Roseline snorts. "I didn't peg you for the sort."

"Oh, please! I'm the one that's lived next to the guy most of my life, remember? I was pining over him long before you ever showed up."

"Do I hear a small amount of bitterness in there somewhere?" Roseline asks, leaning in to poke her friend in the side.

"Maybe." Sadie shrugs. "But I don't hold it against you. I'm just ticked that I got stuck taking the loser to the dance."

Oh yeah, she had forgotten about that. Sadie and Nicolae together at a dance? That is a nightmare in the making! "I get that you're bummed, I really do, but you can't let your mom or Nicolae ruin your night. Besides the dance will be the least of your worries. Just think about all of the pictures."

"Oh, gee, thanks," Sadie grumbles, puckering her lips into a pout. "That makes me feel so much better."

"Are things any better between you two?"

Sadie snorts. "Are you kidding? The guy still follows me around all the time. Last night he even tried to sit next to me on the couch while I watched some old re-runs of Friends. He popped a whole bag of popcorn and doused it in my favorite cheese sauce to share. The guy is totally lactose intolerant so what was up with that?" She ducks in low. "You know, if the guy wasn't such a dweeb he'd actually be really sweet, in an annoyingly idiotic way, of course."

Roseline laughs. "So there's still hope for you two."

"Whatever."

Silence falls between them as Sadie attacks the lid of her strawberry yogurt, which seems to be getting the best of her at the moment. The weight of Gabriel's clipped words hangs heavily over her once again. "Maybe I should just assume we are going to the dance together. Isn't that what couples do?"

"Forget that," Sadie shakes her spoon at Roseline. "If he can't ask you properly, then he doesn't deserve you."

Roseline lets her head fall to the table. "Why does this have to be so complicated?"

Sadie grins. "Welcome to high school."

Twenty-Eight

"You will never believe what I just heard," William says, sliding up next to Sadie's locker on Friday afternoon. "Claire Scofield is telling the whole school that she's going with Gabriel to the dance." Sadie stares back at her brother with a look of horror on her face. "What? I thought you'd be happy to see the guy turn out to be such a jerk."

Her gaze shifts as Roseline appears from behind her open locker. "Oh, no, Rose, I'm so sorry." William slaps his palm to his forehead. "I'm such an idiot."

Roseline's hand trembles as she slings her pack over her shoulder. "No, it's okay. I'm glad I finally know why he hasn't asked me." Her voice cracks, betraying the pain Gabriel's betrayal has caused. None of the tortures she has endured at the hands of her husband have ever hurt her so intimately. She was a fool to let herself fall for a mortal, flawed and driven by hormones apparently.

"I was right. He is a scumbag," Sadie spits. Her eyes narrow with anger. "Want me to egg his house tonight? I think mom has a stash of plastic utensils in the pantry if you want me to fork him too."

"No," Roseline sighs. Her emotions are too turbulent to think clearly but somehow forking a guy's yard didn't seem to make up for the ache in her heart. "Can you just take me home?"

"Sure." William tries to offer an understanding smile but it falls flat. Roseline can almost see the words "World's Biggest Loser" stamped across his forehead.

She holds her head up high as she passes by her gawking classmates. Wild whispers fly around the hallway as she allows William to open the door for her. Obviously the rumors are true, and she is the last to hear it. Typical.

The wintry wind feels wonderful on her burning skin. Her tears crystallize as they catch in her eyelashes. She wants to break something. No. Scratch that. She would love to kill something right now. The warrior within is screaming for release. Instead, she plays the part of a heartbroken human and sulks in the backseat of William's car. At least the heartbroken bit isn't hard to fake.

Sadie and William sit in silence, ill at ease, the entire way to Roseline's house. Neither one knows what to say. It's not like they are gurus on the subject of love.

Tears drip endlessly from Roseline's puffy eyes. She refuses to acknowledge her pain as she rapidly builds walls around her heart to stave off the tidal wave of anguish pouring out. How can he do this to her? They are bonded. Doesn't he know how intimate this rejection is for her?

No. Of course not. She hasn't explained any of this to him. If she had, would it have made a difference?

Two blocks from Roseline's house, Sadie breaks the silence. "Alright, I can't take this anymore. The guy is a jerk, end of story, but I'm not going to let him ruin your only school dance here. You're coming with me."

"Oh no. I don't think that's such a good idea," Roseline hedges. She is sure to run into Gabriel and Nicolae will be there waiting for her to rip someone's head off. Judging by the anger boiling in her chest, that idea is starting to sound a heck of a lot more appealing. Besides, there is no way she is going to stick around to be the third wheel. Three strikes, you are so pathetically out.

"Please, Rose," Sadie begs, grabbing hold of her hand across the backseat. "I really need you. You can't leave me all alone with Nicolae."

Roseline groans. Of course, Sadie would hit below the belt. How does she get out of this now? "Isn't it weird for me not to have a date?"

"Of course you'll have a date," Sadie beams, looking far too proud of herself. "You can go with William."

William's eyes bulge as he swerves around the corner. He glances at Roseline through the rearview mirror. "Uh, Sadie, don't you think you should ask before you make assumptions like that. I could have a date, you know."

Sadie rolls her eyes. "Please. We both know you've been hoping Roseline would throw Gabriel's butt to the curb so you could go with her."

William reaches back and knuckles Sadie's leg. "Shut up," he hisses.

Roseline chews on her lower lip. She has to admit that going with William could be fun. He might even be able to cheer her up.

"Oh come on, Rose, you can't miss the last dance of your high school life." Sadie says.

"I'm game if you are," William offers, doing a poor job of hiding his excitement. Oh yeah, this could really come back to kick her in the backside.

Chuckling, Roseline finally shrugs. "Fine, but I have nothing to wear and the dance is tomorrow night."

"No problem. We're going shopping." Sadie grins.

Twenty-Nine

Roseline waves to her friends as William pulls away from the curb. She turns toward the door and freezes as the familiar scent barrels into her stomach, like a wild bull with its horns lowered. "What are you doing here?" she hisses as Gabriel rises from his seated position next to her front door.

She has no idea how long he has been waiting, but despite the red tinting his earlobes, he seems completely unfazed by the cold. "I had to see you. I need to explain—" She cuts him off with a glare. He positions himself between her and the door.

"There's nothing to explain." She tries to push past him but he does not budge. He is like a reinforced steel wall, lined with granite, titanium, and every other immovable metal all rolled into one annoyingly handsome barrier.

"It's Steve."

Roseline juts out her hip and allows him to see every ounce of anger his betrayal has caused. He winces at the vibes coming off her. "I don't care what the reason is, Gabriel. I want you to leave."

"No."

She snarls at him. "If you don't move, I will make you."

Gabriel's laugh is harsh, filled with bitterness. "You think you can?"

"You may be strong but I know a heck of a lot more about fighting than you do." She marches toward him, daring him to test her. Instead, he sighs and steps aside.

"Smart decision," she growls. Her fingers tremble as she digs deep into her back pocket for her keys. Anger clouds her mind as she fights to place the key in the lock. Gabriel sighs and shoves her hand away to unlock the door for her. She snatches the key out of the door and shoves past him into the house.

"I really am sorry," he mutters from outside.

Roseline braces for impact as she turns. The utter misery painted on his face stops her from kicking the door shut in his face. She exhales and fights for calm. Rational is the last thing she wants right now.

"Look, I get it. You have to make your dad happy. Whatever, but don't you dare think you can stand there and give me a sad puppy dog face and think I'm okay with this. You betrayed me, Gabriel."

"Steve's not my dad." He sags against the doorframe. "And I'm not doing it for him. I'm doing it for my mom. She's got this nervous disorder and she can't stand it when Steve and I fight. She had an attack last week and I caved, alright?"

"Back up a second." Roseline pinches her brow. If she were human, she would imagine the pressure building behind her eyes would create one heck of a migraine. "Steve isn't your biological father?"

"No." Gabriel looks away. The muscles in his neck cord as he grinds his teeth. "I don't like to talk about it."

"Well, you're going to. How could you fail to mention this to me before? We've been researching your markings for a week and you never told me that Steve wasn't your dad."

Gabriel's eyes flash; the sheen in them is dangerously close to the blue light she knows can emanate from them. "I didn't think it mattered."

"Of course it does!" she cries. "Do you know who your real father is? Can we track him down?"

His face reddens as he looks fixedly at her. "He is not a part of my life and I'm going to keep it that way."

"You stubborn mule," Roseline growls, pinning him to the doorframe. She rises onto her toes to stare him down. "I don't know what happened to you and to be honest, at the moment, I don't really care. His bloodline is all that matters. He is the missing link we have been looking for."

"Well then maybe you should check your newspapers from back home to find him then," he shouts. "I'm sure he's on the list of most wanted criminals."

Roseline's grip falters as she lowers to the pads of her feet. "What did you say?"

"You heard me. The guy is Romanian." He tugs on his shirt, adjusting the collar. "Happy now?"

She backs up into the opposite doorframe and stares vacantly at him. When she tries to speak again, her voice is muted and croaky. "What happened?"

Gabriel runs his hands through his hair. "I don't know much, only that he messed my mom up real bad. She talks about him from time to time. I think she's still smitten with the bastard."

She waits, holding her breath until her lungs begin to ache from trapped air.

"She was young, stupid. She thought a one-night fling while touring Europe would help her deal with a bad break-up back in America. Boy was she wrong." He grinds out the words. His fingers latch around the doorframe, splintering the wood in his hands. When he looks at Roseline, she can see the bottomless well of pain. "She was in the hospital for nearly two weeks. Broken ribs, shattered right leg, and the scars..." He shudders, falling silent.

"I'm sorry," she whispers, thinking of the countless tortures she has endured. Broken bones heal, burned flesh regenerates, but the mental wounds last a lifetime, or in her case, three lifetimes.

"You want to know the sick part?" he spits out. "She's like one of those battered women on TV. She actually misses the guy. He must've been a real nut job to slice her neck so many times."

"What did you say?" She leaps toward Gabriel, clutching his arms. Please no. There must be a mistake. "How many times did he cut her?"

"I don't know. Fifteen, maybe twenty times. Why? Is he some kind of serial rapist where you live?"

The blood in her veins turns to ice, chilling her. Fear grips her. It can't be. It just can't. "What's his name?" she whispers.

He scrunches up his face as he thinks. "I'm not really sure. It's a funny name. I'd probably butcher it if I tried."

"Do it," she commands.

He flinches back. "What's with you?"

"The name, Gabriel. What is it?" Her fingernails claw into his flesh. He grimaces as blood seeps down his arm. "Lucien something. I think it started with an E."

The room begins to spin. "Lucien Enescue?"

He snaps his fingers. "That's it. I'm sure of it."

Roseline's eyes roll back into her head as she drops to the floor.

Gabriel rushes to her side, tilting her head back. "Rose?" He checks her pulse and finds it strong but erratic. He scoops her into his arms, cradling her head as he carries her into the living room.

Glancing around, he realizes just how empty the house really is. He heads upstairs, careful to protect her head on the narrow stairway. He sniffs, following Roseline's scent until he finds her room. He stands in the doorway and sighs. "Why didn't you tell me?"

She stirs in his arms. "Hold on. I've got you."

He enters the sparse room, curling his lip at the sight of the mattress on the floor. He lowers her gently onto the rumpled covers and places a blanket over her. She moans and rolls to her side. "How could I not have known you were living like this?"

Unsure of what to do, Gabriel crosses the room and sinks down on the stool to wait. It creaks under him but holds his weight. His fingers drum on the wooden table as he watches Roseline stir.

His gaze falls on the spiraling screen saver on her open laptop. She stirs at the tiny beep as the Gabriel brushes his fingertips across the mouse pad, disengaging the screen saver.

Roseline groans as she begins to come out of her haze. She can smell Gabriel's presence nearby but is confused by the change in his scent. There is something masking his masculine aroma.

She presses her face to her pillow as she fights lucidity. There is a reason why she wants to remain in the dark but she can't quite remember it.

Hurried footsteps attract her attention, as does the banging of the bedroom door followed by a final slam of the front door. She pulls herself upright and rubs her eyes.

She can smell the change on the air now—anger. "Gabriel?" she calls to the empty house.

His thundering footsteps race down the front walk. Roseline rises from bed to stand by the window. He disappears around the corner. Less than a minute later, she hears the squealing of his tires. The silver Range Rover slides recklessly around the icy corner and guns away.

Roseline bends at the waist and cradles her head in her hands. The room spins around her as she falls to her knees. Gabriel's scent permeates the room, making her dizzy. What happened to make him so angry?

Her gaze falls on the blinking cursor of her computer screen and her heart plummets into her stomach. She sighs as she sinks down onto the stool to read what Gabriel must have viewed as damning evidence against her.

Dearest Fane,

I miss you so much it hurts to breathe. Speaking with you on the phone was amazing, but I miss seeing the twinkle in your eyes and the warmth of your smile. I miss so much about Romania.

The boy I spoke to you about, Gabriel, is starting to ask too many questions. I don't know what to say to him anymore. How long can I stall him before he finds out my secret?

Should I be afraid of him, Fane? His markings...I cannot understand what they mean. Can he really be a danger to me?

My heart tells me no, but it has been wrong before. Oh Fane, tell me what I should do. I am so lost without you...

"This day can't get any worse," she whimpers, slipping out of the chair to press her flushed face against the cool wooden floor, but she is wrong. Her eyes fly open wide as the memory of Gabriel's revelation hits her all over again. "Lucien."

Thirty

Roseline twirls in front of the floor-length mirror, self-consciously holding the curve of her hips. "If you're trying to make Gabriel jealous I applaud you," Sadie grins. "Then again, I hope Mom has some life insurance on Will cause you're gonna give the dork a heart attack!"

It's amazing how different their two outfits are. Sadie has gone for a black strapless dress with an added paper clip décor. Her knee-high biker boots, black fishnet hose, and heavily applied eyeliner finish off the outfit. It looks like Sadie's love for grunge is not completely gone.

Roseline's deep green corset is low cut, pushing all of her organs together to give her killer curves. Waves of material cascades over her legs, spilling to the floor over her black heels. She is long and lean, yet curvy in all the right areas. Glancing at herself in the hall mirror, she is thankful for immortality's one good gift. Her bronze hair piles in loose curls atop her head and spirals around her face.

"I guess I'm ready. Can we please get this over with?" Roseline begs, wishing the night were already over. Her stomach twists in knots at the thought of seeing Gabriel. The betrayal of his snooping around her computer stings, but not as much as his jumping to conclusions without giving her a chance to explain.

"Not so fast," Sadie's mother calls as she enters from the hall, pushing a rather reluctant Nicolae in front of her. His eyes nearly pop out of their sockets when he notices Roseline standing in the foyer. Apparently, Sadie failed to mention she is joining them. Although it should have been obvious given the dopey grin that has been plastered on William's face since the day before.

"Mom," Sadie groans. "Did you really have to slick down his hair?"

Roseline tries not to laugh but it is hard not to. Nicolae looks like he has just dipped his head in a bucket of oil.

"I think he's dashing," Mrs. Hughes replies. She looks deeply amused by the mortified look on her daughter's face. Judging by the heat rising along Nicolae's collar, this look isn't exactly his idea of dashing.

"I can't believe you're making me do this," Sadie grumbles. She fingers her paperclip necklace with fierce annoyance. "Couldn't you find some other way to destroy the best dance of my life?"

Sadie's mom cocks her head to the side, contemplating. "Nope. This is the best I've got."

Roseline hides her grin behind her hand. She absolutely loves the dynamic in this family. Their pranks might seem cruel to an outsider but in reality, it is all downright good fun. Besides, she has to admit Sadie's mom has found the perfect solution to the after-dance hotel room issue. There is no way Sadie would even consider that one!

"Surely there's a law against this kind of thing," Sadie whines, sounding like a tortured animal.

"Well, just because you're miserable that doesn't mean you have to ruin it for everyone," William calls as he rounds the landing at the top of the first set of stairs. His eyes widen as Roseline comes into view and he trips over the final steps and tumbles into a heap at the bottom.

"Walk much?" Sadie snickers, looking gloriously vindicated.

William rises to his full height. He brushes off his shirt. "Wow, Rose, you look freaking amazing."

"You clean up pretty well yourself," she laughs, giving William an appreciative glance. His shaggy hair has been tamed, waxed, and styled. His tanned skin looks amazing against the white dress shirt, left unbuttoned at the top to hint at the muscles beneath. Khaki pants and brown leather loafers round out the outfit, leaving Roseline slightly taken aback.

"Like what you see?" He grins, twirling so she can get the full view. He pauses to shove out his butt, pulling the material taut.

"I didn't have time to order a tux but I think these pants do justice to my most appealing feature." His eyebrows bob.

Roseline laughs and taps her temple as if in deep thought. "I gotta say, I am really impressed. Who knew you could pull off something other than a ratty t-shirt and jeans," she praises him.

"Amen to that," Mrs. Hughes mutters under her breath.

"I have my moments," William beams, his sapphire eyes twinkling.

"Picture time!" Mrs. Hughes shouts and heads toward the living room.

Sadie groans and yanks Nicolae into the living room. Her tiny hands struggle to fit around Nicolae's arm. "Seriously? You're like a nerd. What's with the muscles, He-Man?"

Nicolae's laugh is strained as he darts a glance at Roseline. "I uh...I used to work out."

"Whatever." She turns to find her mom and dad setting up the video camera, digital camera, and even a webcam so her grandmother can take part. "Is this torture Sadie day?"

Once they are all in place, Sadie leans over toward William. "If you drool all over Rose the entire time, I swear I will kill you."

Snap. The camera light blinds Roseline momentarily. Thirty minutes and what feels like a hundred pictures later, she finally steps back into the foyer.

William shuffles his feet, looking unusually nervous. Even his ears have taken on a red tint. "Sorry I don't have any flowers for you. It was kinda last minute notice and all. I called all of the local florists but they were booked."

Roseline smiles warmly as she tucks her arm through his. "They probably didn't have my favorite anyways." Orange roses would have clashed with her dress, not to mention remind her of someone she really didn't want to think about tonight.

"Can we go now? My feet are killing and we haven't even left the house yet," Sadie whines. Roseline sighs. Yep, this is going to be a long night for everyone.

"Alright, get out of here," Mr. Hughes says as he snatches the camera out of his wife's hand. "You kids have fun."

Sadie grabs Nicolae's hand and yanks him out the door. "Yeah, like that's gonna happen." Roseline follows her out the door, grateful to be released from Nicolae's stare. Is she the only one that noticed?

The cold night air feels amazing on her bare skin. She closes her eyes and allows William to guide her toward his Escalade. A door slams nearby and Roseline freezes. William nearly runs her over. "What's wrong?" he asks, but quickly senses the problem.

Gabriel is rooted in place on the stone path leading to his car. He looks unbelievably handsome in his black tuxedo. His blond hair is spiked in the front and his face is cleanly shaven. Gabriel's eyes shine brightly under the rising moon. Roseline watches as his jaw clenches tightly, his raw pain igniting flames in her belly.

Roseline's head bows. They both feel betrayed. William reaches for Roseline, gently pulling her away. She doesn't look back, doesn't call out to him to explain the letter to Fane. She simply walks away.

As the Escalade backs out of the driveway, she can feel Gabriel's gaze on her. She keeps her eyes fixed on her clenched fists in her lap until they round the corner. She sniffles and shifts so her hair covers her tears.

"You cold?" William asks as he reaches to adjust the heater. Cold air pumps from the vents but she can't bring herself to care. She gives him a half-hearted shrug and turns to look out the window. What does she care about the temperature? Hot or cold? Does it really matter right now when all she feels is numb?

"Thanks for this," William says a few minutes later. The taillights ahead of them cast a red glow on his face.

"For what?" Roseline questions, confused by his words. What on earth has she done to earn his gratitude?

"For going with me to the dance. I know you didn't really want to go…"

"Oh. Yeah. No problem," she replies pathetically.

William frowns at the tremor in her voice. His fingers tap the steering wheel as he darts cautious glances in her direction. His fingers slide over the radio dial and quickly settle on a head-banging Metallica song.

Roseline smiles as she is easily enticed by the rhythmic beats. Her foot taps out the bass. Slowly her funk fades and she shifts to speak to William. "I'm really sorry about all that back there. I just didn't think I'd see him so soon."

"He's gonna be at the dance, you know."

"I do." Her sigh feels weighty. She mentally scolds herself for being such a terrible date. "But I'll have you to cheer me up."

"You bet." William chuckles, ducking in and out of spaces in traffic. Traffic is heavy for a Saturday night as they head into Chicago.

Roseline glances out the window and struggles to get her bearings. "Where is the dance?"

"At one of the fancy hotels in the city. Sadie programmed the directions into the GPS before we left. I'm useless downtown."

Roseline's fingers grip the door tightly as they dart across two lanes of traffic to hit the on ramp. "You always drive like a maniac on the interstate?"

His chuckle fills the car, warming some of the ice coating Roseline's heart. "Yeah, sorry about that. Am I scaring you?"

"Not at all. Just wondering."

William zips to the outer lane and stamps down on the pedal. Roseline grins, thrilled by the deep throaty roar from the engine. She loves the gentle purr of a car when the key turns over, but her heart races at the growl of a throttle fully open.

Her laughter fuels William's need to show off. Although his human reflexes are nowhere near as accurate as her own, Roseline finds herself truly enjoying the time with William. The minutes speed by as quickly as the white lines on the road that William chooses to ignore from time to time.

"I think that's it," William says. She follows his finger toward a glamorous hotel right in the heart of the city. A uniformed door attendant stands waiting for their approach. William jumps out, tosses his keys to the man before taking Roseline's arm, and ushers her inside as if he owns the place.

The plush red carpet whispers under her shoes. "It's gorgeous," she whispers, staring at the high-vaulted ceilings, plush inviting couches, and fashionably dressed guests. Now this is more like it. She is used to splendor and has been sorely missing it. "This place must cost the school a fortune."

"They have it here every year. And I'm sure every year the hotel manager wishes we'd go somewhere else."

Roseline's eyebrows rise. William laughs and tugs her toward the ballroom. Loud bass seeps from under the door, a sharp contrast to the elegance they have left behind. "You sound like you know this from experience."

William shrugs, unable to hide his grin. "It was only one little fire. Honest."

Her laughter is muffled as the doors open. The room beyond is dark. Bright strobe lights twirl around the room, leaving just enough light for the dancers to see. "This is insane," she shouts into William's ear.

Not pausing to respond, William grabs her hand and pulls her onto the crowded dance floor. They have arrived late, thanks to the impromptu photo shoot back at Sadie's house, so they have to fight for position.

"What are you waiting for?" William shouts, twisting and turning in time with the music. Roseline is shocked to find that William is actually a talented dancer. She wants to let go and enjoy herself but she has no clue how to make her body move like his.

"You act like this is your first dance," William says, placing his lips next to her ear.

"It is," she shouts back. At the clubs back home she was required to sit in the private room and watch. No touching and certainly no dancing. Her role was to look ravishing and that was it, but tonight she has every intention of letting go.

William pulls her up against his body. "Just move with me. Don't think about what you are doing. Just let your body move with the beat."

Roseline nods, blushing furiously at his nearness. His firm body presses against her, warm and inviting. He frowns, glancing down at her dress. "Why did you wear something so long? You'll never be able to move in that?"

He is right. As much as she loves the look of the dress, it has got to go. She grabs a fistful of the dress and yanks a new hem. William eyes up the new length. "Yeah, that will work."

She laughs as she tosses the fabric off the dance floor. William pulls her close again and she quickly finds herself wrapped around him, grinding in ways that feel completely inappropriate but she is starting to get the hang of it. The music rises to ear-splitting levels as a new song replaces the old. Hands rise into the air and the tempo increases.

She opens her eyes to see Sadie on the outer ring of the dance floor. Her cheeks are flushed, her eyes alight with excitement. "Is that Nicolae?"

William whips his head around. His mouth drops open as he stares at his sister grinding against Nicolae. "He drugged her. That little bastard."

Roseline places a restraining hand on his arm. "No. Look at her. She's actually having fun."

Never in a million years would she have guessed it, but the evidence was before her. She narrowed her eyes on Nicolae and noticed the slight changes. His hair is tousled, as if he rubbed a towel vigorously over his oil-slicked hair. His shirt is slightly unbuttoned and Sadie's hands are roaming his chest with amazed delight.

"Where are his glasses? I thought the guy can't see without them," William grumbles.

"Apparently he can," Roseline mutters as she stares at his vivid green eyes. His gaze rises from Sadie to meet hers. His pupils dilate as the smile vanishes from his face.

Watch yourself, she mouths silently. He grits his teeth but nods. Message received.

The crowd closes in around them as more and more people arrive. The dance floor is jam-packed and it is getting harder to move. Roseline closes her eyes again and allows herself to be carried away by the bass thumping in her chest. She begins to sway her hips, dipping and grinding. Roseline tosses back her head and laughs, feeling more liberated in this moment than she has ever been before.

She is free of Vladimir. Free of his rules and restrictions. She can finally be herself.

The more she dances the more attention she attracts. Hormones leak from her skin, drawing in the males around her. Their fuming dates gather at the sidelines to watch their guys paw over an oblivious Roseline.

"You're getting it," William shouts as he knocks another guy off her. He glances around, confused by the wall of bodies. "What the heck is going on?" he asks, ramming his shoulder into his chemistry lab partner.

Roseline opens her eyes and gasps, immediately realizing the problem. Even Nicolae has approached but is keeping his distance at the back of the crowd. Sadie glares at him from the deserted edge of the dance floor. Hurt pinches her eyes as she turns to stare at Roseline.

"Oh, crap," she mutters. She had been so lost to the music, to the ecstasy of her careless abandon, that she failed to pay attention to her surroundings. "Let's grab a drink and cool off. All this dancing has worn me out."

She grabs William's hand and pushes her way through the chorus of heartbeats pounding around her. But the harder she pushes, the harder they push back. William clenches his fist and punches Oliver West in the gut as his hand comes to rest on Roseline's backside.

And then it all stops. Her body jolts as if she were stuck by a bolt of lightning. She is nearly knocked off her feet as her hormones snap back into her like a rubber band. Her mind feels fuzzy, her knees weak, as William scoops her into his arm and carries her out of the crowd. This time they are not followed.

"Rose? Are you okay?" he questions, brushing back the sweaty strands of hair from her face after setting her on a chair.

She nods, craning her neck to see around William. She knows Gabriel is there. Somewhere. She can feel him. It's not hard to do when there is a blast of fury aimed right at her. "Oh no."

"What's wrong—" William's question cuts off as Gabriel yanks him backward. He sprawls to the floor, his forehead connecting with the tile.

"Get your hands off her," Gabriel growls, placing himself between Roseline and William.

William rebounds and leaps back to his feet, a bit unsteady but very determined. "Hey! She's with me tonight. Leave her alone."

Roseline clenches her eyes tightly shut. Too many hormones. Too many frantic heartbeats. Too much pumping blood. The smells are nearly impossible to cope with. Roseline feels her control beginning to slip and panics.

"Stop it," she screams, halting both guys in their tracks.

"Rose?" Gabriel questions, shocked by the crazed look in her eyes.

The memory of Gabriel's betrayal winds tightly with the revelation of his ancestry. Gabriel is Lucien's son. No wonder he is special...and extremely dangerous. Fane was right all along. She was too foolish to listen to him. Her heart made her weak and foolish but not anymore.

Roseline turns an icy glare on Gabriel. "You have no right to attack him." She advances, poking him in the chest hard enough to make him wince and to remind him of her brute strength. "I'm with William because you chose Claire, not me, remember?"

Gabriel's jaw clenches. "Your date is waiting for you," she snaps, crossing her arms over her chest. A part of her silently cries out at the raw pain in his eyes, but another part feels vindicated because of his betrayal. No doubt she will hate herself for speaking to him like this later, but right now, it feels good.

Without waiting for him to turn his back on her, she grabs William's arm and leads him away.

"What just happened?" he stammers, fighting to remain upright.

"Nothing," she snaps, carving a path back onto the dance floor. "Let's just dance and forget about him."

"Sounds good to me." He grins and places his hands on her waist to pull her close.

Thirty-One

Not even the pull of the bass can help Roseline forget the look in Gabriel's eyes when she reared on him. She can still feel his pain, even from across the room. It mirrors her own perfectly but she can't give in. She has to prove to Gabriel, and to herself, that she can function without him.

Determined, she slides her arms down William's neck until she is pressed intimately against him. Roseline tries to tune everything out except William's racing heartbeat. As she moves against him, she can smell his mounting desire; she feels his faltering self-control as he struggles to find a place to rest his hands. She wraps herself around his leg and bumps her hips against him. William's heart races like a prize stallion bursting out of the starting gate.

"Oh man," he groans, closing his eyes as he tries to fight off his body's reaction. "What are you doing to me, Rose?"

"Shh," she whispers, placing her finger over his lips as she continues to writhe. She glances across the dance floor, watching as Claire rubs herself up against an uninterested Gabriel. His eyes are locked onto Roseline, face blotchy with anger as he watches her body move against William. She can feel his jealousy and smiles at him coyly. He is getting the hint loud and clear.

Claire follows his gaze. She shoots icy daggers toward Roseline before she pulls the hem of her dress higher to mount Gabriel's leg. Her skimpy dress does little to hide the assets she is trying to pawn off on Gabriel but he doesn't even glance at her.

Just as William's hand moves a bit too close to her cleavage, a hand grabs Roseline's arm and spins her around. William cries out as he tumbles backward. The granite grip instantly sets her nerves on edge. "I told you to leave me alone—" she cuts off as she comes to face to face with someone other than Gabriel.

The man pins her close to his chest. A deep chuckle rumbles in his chest. "Nice to see you too, Roseline."

All fight goes out of her as her mouth gapes open. "Fane? Is it really you?"

"Boy, you sure look pleased to see me," Fane laughs, pulling Roseline into a hug. He molds himself around her, leaving barely an inch of breathing room. "I've missed you so much."

Roseline wants to return the sentiment but her tongue is tied in knots, much like her stomach. "How did you...why are you here?"

Fane frowns. "You knew I'd come."

"But how did you track me?"

Fane holds up his cell phone. "You shouldn't have stayed on so long, Roseline. You know better than that." He turns and stares down at William. "Who's this guy?"

She turns to give William a hand up from the floor. His shirt is rumpled, his hair matted with sweat. The disgruntled look on his face matches the fire in his eyes. "I could ask you the same thing," William bristles. "You know this guy, Rose?"

"I'm sorry, William. This is Fane. He's a friend from back home."

"Yeah." Fane grins, pinching her side. "Roseline and I go way back."

"Roseline?" William glances between them. "What's he talking about?"

Roseline shoves Fane away, turning her attention back to William. "I'm so sorry. He's not normally like this. Can you give us a minute? I really need to catch up with him."

William shoots a wary glance at the stunning man standing before him. Although his face appears to be that of a nineteen-year-old, his muscular physique is that of someone much older. She knows all too well that Fane looks like he personally modeled for one of the Roman statues!

Roseline winces at William's critical stare, knowing exactly what he must be thinking. "Sure," he mutters, finally tearing away his gaze to look at Roseline. "I'll just go grab us something to drink."

"Yeah, you do that." Fane grins, tucking his arm around her waist.

Her smile fades the instant William turns to leave. "Why are you here?" she hisses, shoving Fane into a more secluded section of the ballroom. The shadows are a perfect hiding space for them since human eyes will be hampered by the dark.

"I came for you, of course. I couldn't just leave you with that guy." Fane's head ducks to the side in search of William. His nostrils flare. "I gotta tell you, Roseline, I think your taste in men has really fallen over the last few years. Please tell me he's not the guy."

Roseline rolls her eyes. "Of course he's not. He's just a friend."

"Is that how you treat all your friends?" Fane asks. Roseline flushes, embarrassed by the show she put on for him.

"You were spying on me?"

Fane rolls his eyes. "Oh come on, Roseline. Every male in this room was glued to your little dress." The jealously in his tone is unmistakable.

"Whatever," Roseline snaps. This is exactly what she was afraid of. Fane isn't taking their separation well at all.

"Where's the other guy? The one you called me crying over?" Fane raises his head to scan the room. "I figured he'd be the one you were plastered to."

"We are not talking about this here. You can't just burst into my life and assume I'll be happy to see you."

His eyes soften as his hand gently rises to brush along her jaw. She closes her eyes and her heart to the memories of his touch. "But you are happy to see me."

She sighs, amazed at how odd her native language feels rolling off her tongue. She has spent far too long among the Americans. "Of course I am, but you can be so infuriating at times."

"Of course." Fane grins. "It's one of my better qualities."

She stares up into his eyes, as green as a spring meadow. So beautiful. So tranquil. She used to spend hours staring into them, reading every thought before he could say it. They were inseparable for the first hundred years of her life. He taught her how to protect herself, how to heal, and eventually how to love. She knows him better than anyone else. He has never been able to keep anything from her...and right now he's fighting to hide something from her.

His fingers flicker on her arm, tensing and releasing. His black pupils dilate. The muscle along his jaw twitches. "You're not here to rescue me, are you?" Roseline whispers. She averts her gaze, unable to endure his discomfort. She should have known his shift in mood was a bad sign.

"You always could read my thoughts," Fane says softly, cupping her cheek in his hand. "No, I'm here to take you back."

"You know what he will do to me. I have a chance here. I have friends, a life..."

"And what do you think Vladimir will do to those friends when he tracks you here? Do you think he will spare their lives just because he found you? No. He will tear them apart, piece by piece, to make you suffer. You know this, Roseline."

Tears sting her eyes as she stifles a sob. He is right. She knows he is. She has always known.

"I've been so selfish," she whispers, glancing out at the unsuspecting crowd around her. "I just wanted to be free."

Fane pulls her into his arms and rests his head atop hers. "I know. Trust me, I know. If there was another way...but there isn't. If you love these people you have to come home with me."

She wipes a fallen tear from her cheek. "Does he know where you are?"

"No." He shakes his head. "I covered my tracks. Your friends will be safe."

She closes her eyes to the pain she knows awaits her. Even if she survives Vladimir's brutality, will there be anything left of her soul to carry on?

Can she really live without Gabriel?

This question makes her hesitate far more than the certain pain she faces. The memory of her last escape flashes before her eyes. It was nearly a century ago. She made it all the way to London before Vladimir tracked her. He cornered her in a boat bound for Africa. It took nearly a week to get all of the blood out of her hair after her husband's rampage. There weren't any survivors on the ship. The lifeless eyes of slaughtered men, women, and children had stared blankly up at her, accusing her.

She raises her eyes to see Sadie and William peering in their direction. The firm set of Sadie's lips as she sets down her drink tells Roseline she doesn't have much time. No matter the price she must pay, she cannot ever let Vladimir know of this place. Of these people. Of Sadie and William. She dries her tears and looks to Fane. "He can't come here."

"Then leave with me."

Roseline bristles, sensing the turmoil before she finds him across the room. Gabriel is livid and heading straight for her. His blue eyes pierce through the darkness. "We need to go," she whispers.

Fane glances over his shoulder, noticing the direction of her gaze. His face hardens. "So he's the one that's got you all hot and bothered?" He eyes up the tall boy; a deep rumble builds in his chest as he notes how handsome and self-assured he is. He bares his teeth in response.

"Stop it, Fane," Roseline growls, pulling him away. "That's none of your business." She watches as his mossy green eyes flame to life. He is the last person in the world that should meet Gabriel.

"Not my business?" Fane snarls, pulling her close. "Have you forgotten our time together?" His gaze flits down the curves of her body, the admiring gleam is quickly replaced by something hungrier.

"Of course I haven't." She slaps his hand away. "But that's in the past. Let it go."

She glances back over her shoulder. Gabriel is getting too close. Fury rolls off him in almost visible waves. Roseline's stomach cramps with fear. She has no idea what Gabriel might do with his newfound abilities but one thing is for sure, if he and Fane throw down there is no way Vladimir won't hear about this epic fight once it hits the news channels. "We can talk about this later. Let's go."

Fane smirks, planting his feet firmly on the floor. "Why? Because you think I might hurt your little boyfriend?"

"No." Roseline locks her gaze on Fane so there will be no mistaking her intent. "Because I will hurt you if you try."

Fane flinches, incensed. "You'd fight me over a human?" His fingers dig painfully into her arm when she nods. "What have you been doing while you've been gone, Roseline Dragomir? Did you get yourself a new toy to play with?" Speaking her maiden name is the highest insult he can use against her.

Roseline's hand blurs as she slaps him across the cheek. "That's for being rude. Now let me go or I will rip your freaking arm off."

"You have a lot of explaining to do," he snarls as he sweeps her up into his arms and runs for the door. Fane does not pause when Gabriel bellows at him to stop or when Sadie tries to wrench Roseline from his arms. He shoves her aside. Roseline cries out for her friend as the scent of blood wafts toward her.

Fane races for the exit, past haughty hotel guests, and out through the front door. His fingers close around a pair of keys being tossed through the air to the valet. In one fluid motion, he shoves Roseline into the passenger seat and leaps over the roof of the car, landing next to the open driver's side door.

"What the..." the middle-aged man in a pricey tuxedo cries as Fane pushes him to the ground.

"Fane!" Roseline cries.

Ignoring her call, he shoves the Mercedes into gear and tears out into the street. Car horns blare and tires screech as he swerves dangerously out into traffic.

Her piercing scream bounces around the car as Fane yanks the wheel, barely missing the front bumper of an oncoming car. "Are you insane?" she shrieks, gripping the door handle tightly. The thin metal bends into the shape of her hand.

Fane throws back his head and laughs as he plays chicken with a semi. "Someone has spent too much time around the humans. Did you forget you're an immortal, Roseline?"

"Even if we can't die from a car crash that doesn't mean we don't feel the pain, you idiot."

His smile fades as he throws the car up onto the sidewalk, sending pedestrians sprawling to the ground. The tires squeal as he rounds the corner, finally exiting the one-way street. He melds into traffic and slows to a more reasonable speed.

"Where are you taking me?" she asks, trying to sound bolder than she feels. She is furious that he practically kidnapped her in front of the entire school, but fear of being presented to Vladimir has begun to worm its way into her mind.

"Your house. You need to pack." He glances over at her to find her watching the buildings pass by. "Are you gonna tell me about him now?"

"He's just a guy," Roseline mutters, pressing her nose against the cold window. Her warm breath creates a fog that she rubs out with her hand. "He doesn't matter anymore."

"Just a guy, huh? I am not buying it, Roseline. You've never threatened me before," he says, keeping watch over her from the corner of his eye as he winds through the heavy city traffic.

"You never gave me a reason to."

Fane growls with frustration. "You call me out of the blue, crying over this guy and his crazy abilities, and now you won't open up after you've just threatened me? Has he done something to you?"

"No," she cries, shaking her head. "It's nothing like that."

His sigh is weighty. "I've been your best friend for three centuries, Roseline, and sometimes more than that. You know you can tell me anything."

"That's why I can't tell you about him. You're too involved."

"You got me involved, remember?"

She runs her finger along the fogged window, drawing random patterns as she feigns indifference. "I really don't want to talk about it."

"Tough." He clenches the steering wheel so hard Roseline fears he will snap it off the column. "I saw how you were dancing and it wasn't for that friend of yours. It was for that boy, wasn't it? You were trying to make him jealous."

Roseline pulls the bobby pins from her hair. Her loose curls spill around her shoulders as she sighs. "I was trying to prove a point."

"What? That you're open for business?"

Her hand flashes out and strikes Fane's cheek, still red from the last pass. "Don't ever speak to me that way again."

185

He groans and presses back into his seat. "I'm sorry. You know I didn't mean….it's just that I've never seen you like that before with a human. It was almost sickening to watch."

"*You* never complained before." She closes her eyes to the memories of stolen moments long ago. A passionate kiss, a stolen touch, a whispered promise.

"I know, but it's different now. We're different."

"Exactly. We are not together anymore, Fane. You have to accept that. Just like Gabriel has to accept that he has no place in my life. It's forbidden."

"So you two never…" Fane trails off, taking his eyes off the road to observe her reaction.

Roseline stuffs down the sob rising in her throat. "No. Never."

"Good." Fane releases his breath. He winces at the fury blazing in Roseline's eyes and adds to his words. "If Vladimir were to smell him on you he'd be a dead man."

She knows all too well the pain Vladimir would inflict on Gabriel if he ever found him. Maybe this is for the best. If she leaves with Fane, she will be the only one punished. Gabriel will be safe. "Take me home."

"I am."

"No. I mean to him. I'm ready."

Fane snarls as he yanks the car to a stop. Horns blare as the car behind swerves to miss their back bumper. Fane's gaze drills a hole into the side of Roseline's head, but she refuses to look at him.

"You are in love with him!" If Fane had been free of the car, Roseline is sure he would have yanked off a mailbox and hurled it like a javelin or maybe he would have settled for a pine tree. Instead, he settles for clamping his fingers over his kneecap until his bones groan in protest.

When she finally looks up at him, the depth of misery seeping from her tear-dampened eyes shocks him. "Does it really matter now? I'm leaving and will never see him again."

Roseline fights back the sob that aches to be released. She dams up the floodgates that threaten to spill over. She can't lose control in front of Fane, it would only jab the knife in deeper.

"You'd choose a human over me?" His strangled whisper wrenches at her heart.

Hurting Fane is the last thing she wants to do. *Oh, why didn't he stay in Romania where he belongs?* Roseline slides her hand across the gap, resting it gently on his forearm. "I never had a choice, Fane. It just happened."

Enraged, he slams his hand against the steering wheel. "What's that supposed to mean?"

Roseline pulls back from his anger. Why did he have to ask the one question she is terrified of answering? Fane waits, unrelenting. He wants an answer. Sighing, Roseline glances out of the window, noticing for the first time that it has begun to frost over again. Her warm breath has faded, just like her life here in Chicago. "We're bound together."

Fane sucks in a breath. The bond between immortals is far stronger than any romantic feelings a human can experience. For Roseline to be bound to this boy it would mean...

"How? You said you've never..."

"I know!" Roseline cries, plunging her hands into her hair as she bends at the waist. "Don't you think I know that? I can't explain it. That's why I called you, but you weren't exactly much help. And then later I had to save his life and we shared blood...but the bond was already intact before that," she rambles.

Immortal bound to a human. Such a thing is unheard of. It is forbidden by the immortal community to even care for a human, let alone be bound to one. It is impossible. Isn't it?

"You didn't tell me you were bound to him," Fane protests, grinding his teeth at the thought. "If I'd have known..." he trails off.

Would it have changed anything? No. This is one of those unspoken rules that are passed down through the ages. You never break a bond. She has already proven that you can't outrun it.

Her tears well up in the corners of her eyes. "He's just a boy."

"Exactly," Fane says, his voice softer now. "He doesn't know what love is. But I do." He gently pulls her hands into his. "Roseline, we've been together through wars, plagues, tortures, and so much more. I know you in and out. That boy could never know you as well as I do. I am the one that should be by your side. You know how much I love you."

Turning to look at him, Roseline manages a weak smile. It is true. They have shared several lifetimes together…but it changes nothing. He is her best friend and former lover, but he is not the one meant for her. No matter how hard he fights it, Roseline hopes deep down he knows it too. "I've always known, Fane," she whispers, glittering tears flowing like a moonlit river down her cheeks.

Fane's head bows low, his long blond hair falling into his eyes, loosed from the leather thong that held it back. He sighs deeply before straightening his shoulders. With the gentlest of touches, Fane clasps her delicate hands to his chest. "Run away with me."

Despair turns every nerve ending into ice. The creeping freeze steals all the way from her toes, locking her heart into a crystallized glacier. "Even if I could, I wouldn't. Vladimir would kill you."

Breaching the invisible barrier between them, Fane leans across the console. He brushes back the hair that curls around her jaw. His thumb glides over the silky smooth curve of her cheek. "I'm willing to take that risk to be with you. We can make it. I know we can."

"You're wrong. It's just your foolish heart talking right now. We both know that Vladimir would never give up. He'd hunt us to the ends of the earth just to hurt me."

"Is that the only reason you won't go?"

Roseline glances away, unwilling to look at him as she speaks the words that she knows will crush him. "I can't, not now that I am bound to Gabriel. You know how it works."

"But what if you're wrong?" he presses, grasping at the tiniest straw of hope. "Maybe it's just an infatuation."

She laughs bitterly. "Do you have any idea how much I wish I were? I know what this means. My life, his life, is forfeit now. We can't live apart but there is no way for us to be together."

A single tear escapes from his eye. "So I really have lost you."

He pulls back from her, withdrawing into himself. Roseline can't bear to look at him, to see the misery that she has caused.

Instead, she fixes her gaze on the taillights in front of them as Fane pulls back out into the traffic flow.

Thirty-Two

Gabriel prowls like a caged lion in the deserted corridor outside the dance hall. "Are you completely insane?" he rages at William. "How could you leave Rose with a stranger?"

The longer she goes missing the more panicked he becomes. Why did she act like she knew this guy? He had sensed her turmoil, felt it spilling over into his own veins. She had been angry, very angry, and then it all stopped and he had felt her mood shift. The "why" question is nearly enough to drive him insane.

"Stop ranting!" Sadie cries. "It's making my head ache."

She holds an ice pack against the large bump forming on her head. The bleeding has stopped but the pounding is getting worse. Gabriel's shouting is not helping anything.

William shoves Gabriel back as he rounds on Sadie. "Back off. I get that you are worried, we all are, but attacking my sister is the last thing you should be thinking about right now."

Gabriel's fingers clench into a fist at his side. The idea of smashing William's face in is a bit too tempting. "Fine," he says, sinking onto the plush couch. Laughter and music spill down the hall as the double doors open and close. Their classmates' carefree banter makes him nauseous. Don't they know Rose is missing? Shouldn't the dance be stopped to find her?

Of course not. No one in that room is as intimately aware of Rose as he is. When he went to tell the teachers, they laughed it off as a classic prank. Since Roseline didn't scream or make a scene, it made his case that much harder to prove. Even the hotel management didn't seem concerned about a missing girl since one of their hotel guest's vehicles have been stolen. Gabriel tried to tell them she was probably in the car but they had already turned him away to wait for the police.

He leans his head back against the cushion. "You're right. I'm sorry, Sadie. I just don't know what to do. No one will listen to me."

"Well, duh. You're running around like a raving lunatic. I wouldn't listen to you either," she snorts. "But he does have a point, Will. Why'd you leave her with that guy?"

William shrugs. "She said she knew him. They seemed pretty friendly to me so I didn't think anything of it until I heard Gabriel yell."

"But how did she know him?" Sadie asks, settling on the couch next to Gabriel, moaning as she slips her boots off.

"He said they go way back."

Sadie chews on her lower lip. "If he is from Romania too, I wonder if Nicolae might know him. Hang on a second. Where'd he go?"

Gabriel growls. "Is that really important right now? I thought you didn't even like the guy."

"I don't," Sadie snaps. "Well, I mean I guess he has his moments. He was okay tonight, actually, but I think he disappeared around the same time Rose did. He went to the bathroom and never came back. Do you think he went with them? I mean, he is from the same country and all. Maybe he knows the guy."

William thinks it over. "I guess it's possible."

"No, it's not." Gabriel adamantly shakes his head. "Nicolae wouldn't go anywhere with Rose unless he had to. You both know how weirded out he gets around her."

"I've been wondering about that..." William trails off, scratching the back of his head. The styling wax has begun to lose its effect from all of the sweating on the dance floor and his usual scruffiness has returned. "Everyone seems to like Rose, right? I mean, she is the sweetest person I've ever met. So why does he always seem so intense around her? There's definitely a bad vibe between them."

Gabriel rubs his jaw. His brain hurts as he fights to remember any clues to explain Nicolae's strange behavior. "I don't know. When we find him, we can ask. Right now all I want to do is find Rose."

"You mean Roseline," William mutters.

191

"What's that?" Gabriel asks, sitting up straighter.

"That guy...he called her Roseline. I've never heard anyone call her that before."

Sadie rolls her eyes. "She probably changed it when she moved here. It's not exactly a popular name, is it?"

Gabriel frowns. Something doesn't feel right. He saw Rose and the stranger talking, laughing, and then everything changed. The man's face had darkened and he looked furious with her. What if Roseline was in danger? "I can't take this anymore. I'm getting out of here."

"What about Claire?" William asks, glancing at the sequined figure racing toward them from the ballroom.

"I don't care about her. Let her find a friend to give her a ride home," Gabriel says, surging to his feet. "I've got to find Rose."

Sadie nods, rising too. She clutches her biker boots under her arm and stares at her brother with firm resolve. "I'm going with Gabriel. He can drop me off once we find Rose."

"What about your car?" William protests. Sadie rolls her eyes. There is no way he cares about her car. Besides, it was sure to be safe in valet parking overnight. He's just trying to cover his backside.

"Just deal with Mom and Dad, alright? I'll owe you."

"You're darn right, you will!" he calls as Sadie runs to catch up. Gabriel ignores Claire's furious shouts as he slams through the front door, startling the door attendant. Instead of waiting for the car to be brought around, he grabs his keys and rushes into the parking garage, frantically searching for his car.

"Try the alarm," Sadie suggests, struggling to catch her breath. She might be slender but she is far from fit. Working out is for jocks and cheerleaders and she certainly is not one of those.

Gabriel pushes the alarm and rushes toward the end of the row where his silver Range Rover is parked between a Hummer and a Lincoln Navigator. He pushes the alarm button again and deafening silence fills the concrete prison. "Get in," he commands, unlocking her door.

Sadie leaps inside and tosses her boots into the backseat. She shoves her seatbelt into the lock just before Gabriel throws his car into gear and races out of the garage on squealing tires. The SUV slides wildly on the ice before righting itself. "Where are you going? She could be anywhere."

White knuckles grip the steering wheel as Gabriel winds in and out of traffic. He is too focused on his mission to answer Sadie. There is only one place that he can think of to look.

The drive to Roseline's house is tense with an oppressive silence blanketing the car. When they arrive, the two-story bungalow stands dark. There is no sign of movement. The driveway is empty apart from a fresh set of tracks are ground into the snow.

"She's not here." Gabriel roars, slamming his hand against the steering wheel. Tingling numbness races up his forearm but he refuses to acknowledge it. "I was sure she'd still be here."

"Yeah, well, it looks like you were wrong," Sadie snaps. Her anger and concern for Rose is making her very irritable. "Where to now, Sherlock?"

Gabriel yanks on the door handle and spills out into the snow. His dress shoes slip underneath him as he races for the porch. Gabriel works his way up the icy steps with far more ease than Sadie could have managed.

"What are you doing?" Sadie calls. There is no way she is going to leave the warm comfort of Gabriel's car to go bang on an empty house in the middle of the night.

Gabriel pounds on the door until his fists go numb. Tears of frustration slip from his eyes as he cups his face to look through the window. The same bleak emptiness stares back at him as he saw the day before, but there is something new this time.

Leaning closer to the windowpane, Gabriel breathes in deep. The scent burns as it slides through his nose and down his throat. Cinnamon and vanilla mingles with pine and dirt—the stranger.

"She's not home," Sadie calls again, leaving only enough room for her head to fit through the raised window. She shivers against the frosty night air. The windshield is slowly freezing over, courtesy of the sleet that began falling not long after they left the dance.

Gabriel rushes back to his car, annoyed with Sadie's lack of help. "Thanks for stating the obvious," he snaps as he clicks his seat belt in place. "Is that all you're good at?"

"Don't yell at me," Sadie snaps. "I'm not the one that pushed her into some stranger's arms."

Gabriel's mouth drops open. "I didn't…it's not my fault," he stammers.

"Oh no? We both know how you betrayed her. Rose was crushed."

"Right," Gabriel growls, backing down the drive. "Did she also tell you about the email to her boyfriend back home?"

Sadie frowns. "Boyfriend? What the heck are you talking about?"

"Fane. The guy she's in love with," Gabriel spits out the words. Even now they feel like poison on his lips.

"Are you insane? You're all Rose has been able to talk about since the first time she met you. No way is there another guy," Sadie protests.

"You didn't read the letter."

Sadie's eyes bulge. "And you did? You actually violated her privacy?"

Gabriel winces. "Yes, but I never meant to…she's been lying to me, Sadie, and I needed to know why."

"So you think that gives you the right to go snooping? Un-freaking-believable. I was so right about you. You are a jerk!"

"Hey," Gabriel objects. "I'm not the one with secrets."

"Well, maybe she had a good reason for keeping her secrets. Ever think about that?"

Gabriel sighs. Of course, he has thought of that, but the idea of Rose trying to protect him doesn't allow him to excuse away his anger. Gabriel blows out a breath, imagining the anger flowing out of his body, riding on the ripples of heat flooding from the vents. "I'm sorry. I shouldn't have yelled at you. I'm just worried about Rose."

Sadie begrudgingly agrees, crossing her arms over her chest. "So what's the plan now?"

Gabriel shrugs, feeling a heaviness settle over his heart. "What about a phone? Did she ever give you a cell number?"

Her squeal drives Gabriel's foot into the brake. They lurch forward and slam back into their seats. Sadie scowls at him. "Smooth, genius. Real smooth."

"Well why the heck did you scream?"

"Because she bought a phone not too long ago. She called once to give me the number. Said it was for emergencies only."

Hope flares to life. "Great. Give her a call."

Sadie rolls her eyes. "Do I look like I have a purse?"

Gabriel glances at her form-fitting dress. He really did not want to guess where she would have to hide a phone in that. "Where is it?"

"My house."

Thirty-Three

"Wake up!" a shrill voice screams in Gabriel's ear. He groans and bats it away, worried that his eardrum might burst. "My mom's gonna kill me if she finds you here."

Gabriel jerks upright, confused by the room around him. A purple lava lamp glows on the desk nearby, red converse sneakers poke out from under an untidy bed, and a bright pink neon beanbag sits under a window. Various rock band posters cover the ceiling. Gabriel rubs his eyes as he tries to remember where he is. A girl shoves her face over his. "Argh."

Sadie stands up, rolling her eyes as Gabriel picks himself up off the floor. "Oh please, like it's such a shock to wake up here. You spent the entire night running up my phone bill trying to reach Rose, remember?"

Sleep's haze quickly dissipates as Gabriel brushes his fingers through his tangled hair. The events of the previous night begin to come back to him. "Rose? Did she call?" A withering glance from his neighbor is enough of an answer. "I had to ask."

Sadie shrugs. "So what do we do now? Go back to her house?"

Gabriel nods and grabs his car keys off the floor before racing for the door. Sadie blocks his path. "Hold on there, bucko. You can't just go waltzing through my house at six in the morning. My mom will have both our heads."

"Then what do you suggest?" he asks, annoyed with the delay.

Sadie smiles and points to the window. Gabriel groans. "Oh, you have got to be kidding me."

"Nope. There is a tree not too far from the ledge. Just swing on over and do your best Tarzan impression, but for goodness' sake, be quiet."

Gabriel grabs his tuxedo jacket and lifts the window. He glances down and gulps. "Don't tell me a big guy like you is afraid of heights."

"No. I'm afraid of falling. Big difference," Gabriel corrects her tersely as he swings his leg over the ledge. His mind races through all of the crazy things that have happened since he met Rose. Super strength, increased speed, amazing hearing, freaky tattoo…but can he trust that he will survive this fall?

Glancing over the edge, Gabriel's fingers hook tightly around the window ledge. His knees lock down and he goes pale with fright. After a minute with zero headway, Sadie sticks her head out next to his legs. Her mocking humor vanishes. "You really are scared, aren't you?"

All Gabriel can do is nod. His eyes are riveted to the ground, his breathing shallow as he fights to control the churning contents of his stomach. There is nothing in the world that frightens him more than heights. No, that's not true anymore. The fear of losing Rose is far worse.

"You don't have to do this," Sadie says softly. "Come back in and we can head out in an hour when mom has left for her aerobics class."

Gabriel shakes his head. "No, I can't wait that long. Rose needs me."

Sadie observes the firm set of his mouth and the waves of determination flooding off him. "You really love her, don't you?"

His wide eyes flit her way. "More than you can imagine." Despite his fear, his voice does not waver.

She tugs on his hand and slowly helps him back inside. "Fine. Then let's get this over with."

"Wait, you're gonna go now?"

Sadie offers him a wry smile. "Who am I to stand in love's way?"

With her brave face firmly in place, Sadie opens the door and leads Gabriel into the hall. She stops short as William's door cracks open. "You sneaking snake," she hisses as she shoves the door open, knocking Nicolae flat on his back. She rears back and kicks his shin. "When did you get home?"

Nicolae clamps his hands around his throbbing leg. "Last night. Before you two got back," he groans.

"Why did you disappear from the dance?" Sadie snaps, winding up for another blow to his shin.

"I just needed some fresh air."

She rolls her eyes. "Sure you did. At the exact moment Rose was kidnapped."

"You think she was kidnapped?" Nicolae's laugh grates on Gabriel's frayed nerves. "Why would Fane kidnap her?"

Liquid ice freezes him in place. "Fane? That's who took her?"

Green eyes flicker over Gabriel and suspicion pinches Nicolae's features. "How do you know about Fane?"

"I read an email."

Nicolae's face relaxes. He rolls over and sweeps up to his feet. "Yeah, well then you already know they're best friends so it makes sense that she'd leave with him."

"Friends?" Gabriel chokes out. He has a bad feeling about this.

"I thought you knew." Nicolae frowns, darting a glance between Sadie and Gabriel. "What's going on?"

Sadie rolls her eyes and plants her hands firmly on her hips. "He thought Rose was in love with Fane. Stupid jealous fool."

Gabriel swallows down his bitter guilt. "I didn't know."

"Of course you didn't," she snaps. "You decided it was easier to think she'd betrayed you than to just ask. It's guys like you that drive girls to romance novels!"

A groan rises from a tangled pile of sheets on a bed. William rubs his eyes as he sits up. He is still wearing his rumpled dress clothes. His hair is plastered on the side of his face. "I didn't realize we were having a slumber party," he grumbles.

"We're not," Sadie snaps. "Rose is still missing."

William looks crestfallen. Nicolae backs away. "Where do you think you're going?" Sadie cries, yanking him back.

"We don't have time for this, Sadie. Just let him go," Gabriel says, heading toward the door. "Rose needs us."

Reluctantly, Sadie turns, motioning for William to follow. She shoots a threatening glare toward Nicolae. "Don't move. I'll be back for you."

Thirty-Four

T he instant they hear the coffee mug hit the granite countertop they know they are busted. Gabriel winces as he rounds the corner. Mrs. Hughes glares at him first before turning to glare at each of her children in turn.

"You've got a lot of explaining to do," she says as the trio shuffles into the kitchen.

"It's really not what it looks like," Sadie says, nervously tugging on a stand of her hair.

"Oh no?" her mother questions as her lips purse. "'Cause it sure looks like the three of you crashed upstairs after a long night of partying."

"Oh," William snickers, fighting to straighten the wrinkles from his shirt. "Then it is what it looks like."

"Uh-huh. So that explains why Gabriel's father has been calling us nonstop for the past three hours."

Gabriel groans. "I'm so sorry, Mrs. Hughes. I never meant to disturb you."

"I understand that, Gabriel, but what I do not understand is why you are here. Your father is under the impression that you should be with Claire."

"Yes, ma'am." He sends a warning glare at Sadie as she opens her mouth. She instantly clams up and passes on the look to her yawning brother. "I got a ride home from Sadie last night but forgot my house key. I tried to wake my parents but I guess they couldn't hear me. Sadie was kind enough to let me crash here."

"In her bedroom?" Mrs. Hughes glares.

"Nah, he was with me," William covers smoothly. "He crashed on the floor. Looks terrible, doesn't he?"

Gabriel swallows down his cutting remark. If it weren't for William's quick thinking, his tail might be skinned by the butcher's knife beside Mrs. Hughes hand. For a moment, she looks like she is contemplating using it but finally her face sags with exhaustion. "I don't know how you kids slept through all that racket. I swear all that ringing has spawned a migraine from Hell!"

"We haven't had a land line in our rooms since we were eight. How on earth would we have heard the phone?" William rolls his eyes. "Get with the times, Mom."

"Yeah, yeah," she yawns. "Well now that I know you're not dead in a ditch somewhere I can get some sleep. But you and I are gonna have a little chat this afternoon, Sadie Marie Hughes."

Sadie winces at the dreaded middle name. "I'll be here." She forces a smile.

Mrs. Hughes glares one final time before heading back up the stairs. Gabriel breathes a sigh of relief. They wait until her bedroom door closes before dashing to the hall to collect their coats and bustle outside.

"Where's your car?" William asks. The street and drive in front of Gabriel's house is vacant.

"We parked around the corner so my parents wouldn't know where I was." Gabriel sets off at a quick pace, unfazed by the sheen of ice covering the path. Sadie grips William's forearm to remain upright.

"Good thinking, except for the part where you shacked up with my sister for the night," William growls. "What were you thinking?"

"I wasn't," Gabriel replies, as he races ahead to his car. He presses the key fob and dives into the driver's seat. William and Sadie quickly follow, moaning about how cold it is. Gabriel frowns. He hadn't even noticed the temperature.

"This is taking too long," he mutters as he cranks the defrost on full force.

"Patience is a virtue and I think it really sucks." Sadie rubs her hands together. The tingling numbness has turned into agonizing pain. "I hate winter."

William glances between his sister and Gabriel in the front seat. "So, is anyone going to fill me in?"

201

Gabriel looks back over his shoulder. "We're going to Rose's house again."

"Looking for clues?"

"Something like that," Gabriel nods. He flicks the windshield wipers and watches as they clear a small streak. "Good enough for me." He ignores the worried glance the siblings share as he pulls out onto the road.

Five minutes later, Gabriel slides to a stop in front of Rose's deserted house. "Everyone coming?" he asks as he jumps out of the car.

He doesn't wait to see if they will follow him as he hurries up the path. His shoes crunch heavily on the ice-glazed grass as he crouches.

"What are you looking for?" Sadie calls, wrapping her arms tightly around her waist. Her black ski jacket does little to keep out the biting chill of the arctic air that whips down the street.

"A rock."

Spotting a large, jagged gray stone half buried under the bushes, Gabriel digs it out and tosses it in the air, getting a feel for its weight. Before Sadie can protest, Gabriel chucks it right through the glass panel edging the door. "Are you insane?"

"You got a better idea?" he grunts as he slips his arm through the broken glass, turning the lock. "Got it."

The door swings open but no one moves to walk through. "This is so illegal," William mutters, staring into the dark space.

"It's Rose. Do you think she will press charges?" Gabriel asks, stepping over the threshold.

"What the…" Sadie exclaims, turning around. "Where is everything?"

"Was she robbed?" William ducks his head into the kitchen. The counters are empty, cupboards bare, and the fridge door is open. "Man, they took everything."

"No." Gabriel shakes his head as he moves toward the stairs. "This is how it's always been."

"But that can't be," Sadie protests, hurrying to follow Gabriel up the stairs. Her gaze flickers over the empty room on the right. Its sole occupant is the largest, hairiest spider she has ever seen.

"Gross!" she squeals, slamming the door closed. Gabriel stops in front of a partially open door, his hand pressed against the splintered frame.

"What's wrong?" William appears from the bottom floor.

"It's her room," Gabriel responds with a hushed voice and pushes the door open. The room has not changed much. The same lumpy mattress sits in the corner with its sheets falling haphazardly onto the floor. The room is just as barren and bleak as he remembers it, but one thing has changed—Rose's laptop lies lifeless on the floor with a fist-sized hole punched through it.

"Wow, what do you think did this?" William asks, bending to poke the machine.

Gabriel's lips thin out. He knows exactly what happened but feels too guilty to offer a false explanation. Another pile of plastic bits lies off to his left. "I guess we know why she's not answering her phone."

Sadie groans as she reaches down to sift the shattered phone parts through her fingers. "Now we have no way of reaching her."

"Maybe that's not true," William mutters, staring out the window.

Gabriel turns. "Meaning?"

William picks up a photo from the end of the table. Gabriel and Sadie move in closer to take a better look. Gabriel rears back, shocked by the evidence before him. "I think we need to have a little chat with Nicolae."

Thirty-Five

S adie throws up her hands. "No, Mom, I'm not joking. Will you please just put him on the phone?" She covers the speaker with her hand and turns on Gabriel. "This had better help Rose."

"It will," he assures her as he returns his focus to the slick roads. "Tell him to meet us at the community building at the park on Travertine Street."

Gabriel knows the instant Nicolae picks up because Sadie's face clouds over. Apparently their fiasco at the dance has placed Sadie right back to where she used to be—deep loathing of all things Nicolae. She quickly gives him the directions and hangs up. "He'll be there in five minutes."

"Good." Gabriel nods, pressing harder on the accelerator. His left leg bobs up and down, unable to control the nervous tension any longer.

The Range Rover's tires stutter over the ice as he slides into the deserted parking lot a few minutes later. No one in their right mind would be out on a day like this. It is windy, icy, and downright miserable.

A lone figure stands huddled against the tall wooden community building. "Let's go," Gabriel says as he hops out of the car.

The grass crunches underfoot as the three friends hurry toward shelter. Nicolae turns and enters the abandoned building as they approach. Sadie rushes inside, not waiting for either of the guys to open the door for her. "It must be ten degrees out there," she groans through chattering teeth.

A cold draft filters down from above since the roof is not completely covered. The building is used as a semi-outdoor movie theater in the summer but at least it offers a slight reprieve from the brutal winds, as well as some privacy.

"Why am I here?" Nicolae asks, pushing his glasses up the bridge of his nose. He looks away, wary of meeting anyone's glance.

Gabriel is not fooled. "You have answers. We want them."

Nicolae's callous laugh echoes from wall to wall. "I don't have anything that can help you."

"What about this?" Gabriel snarls, shoving the incriminating picture into Nicolae's face. "Recognize anyone?"

Nicolae's stony exterior crumbles as he shoots a worried glance at Sadie. "Alright, I admit it. I sent that picture to Rose. So what?"

"You were threatening her with this, weren't you?" William challenges, stepping closer to Gabriel's side to provide a strong front.

"No," Nicolae protests lamely. "It is nothing. Just a picture."

"I'm not buying it," Gabriel huffs, stomping forward. "You knew exactly what you were doing. Funny thing though…this picture was not in Rose's room the night before the dance. So you must have slipped into her house after I left, or yesterday when you knew she'd be out dress shopping with Sadie."

Backed into a wall, Nicolae has nowhere to run. Sadie and William flank Gabriel. "Is this some kind of sick joke?" Sadie questions. "Why did you take a picture of Roseline's ancestor at the art museum?"

Nicolae's meek demeanor shifts. He laughs as his shoulders straighten out of their slight hunch. The skin around his eyes release the squinty look he always portrays. "Is that what you think I did?"

Gabriel's eyes narrows at the faint increase in Nicolae's pulse that thumps in his ears. Why can he hear it? He shakes his head, trying to clear his thoughts. He has to focus. "I want the truth, Nicolae. No more lies. Rose is in danger and I need to help her before she gets hurt."

Nicolae startles everyone with a bitter snort. "Trust me, she's fine. Nothing can hurt her."

"What's that supposed to mean?" Sadie presses. She spins a lock of her short hair around her finger as if needing something to occupy her hands while she plots to throttle him.

"You wouldn't believe me even if I did tell you," he responds, averting his gaze. He doesn't even try to hide his disgust now.

Gabriel narrows his eyes as he leans in closer. A strange warmth builds along his neck and up into his cheeks as he stares Nicolae down. "Try me."

Nicolae pales as a faint blue glow emits from Gabriel's eyes. "Holy crap," he gasps, jerking back against the wall. "You're one of them!"

"What the heck are you talking about?" William paces back and forth.

Nicolae turns to look squarely at William. "A vampire."

"See? I knew this was going to be a waste of time," Sadie grumbles as she crosses her arms over her chest. "He's full of crap, Gabriel. We're wasting time."

Gabriel does not break eye contact with Nicolae. Something about the word vampire resonates with him. Nicolae doesn't flinch, his voice doesn't tremble, and there is no hint of anything beyond revulsion when he spoke the word.

"You know something," he says, stepping closer.

Nicolae's gaze sharpens instead of darting to the side like normal. He meets Gabriel's glare head on. No hint of fear. No backing down. Gabriel can see the fire in his eyes and realizes he has seriously underestimated Nicolae.

"Think about it," he says, leaning forward. Gabriel stiffens but doesn't back away. "Have you ever wondered why all of the guys want her? I'm not just talking guys our age. Ever see Mr. Robert's stalking her down the hall? It's creepy but proves my point."

"Go on," Gabriel growls. The thought of that old tweed-loving fart following Rose sets his blood to boil.

"What about how she talks? Surely you noticed that it took her a while to pick up on your speech patterns."

Sadie frowns. "She was pretty formal in the beginning, but that doesn't mean she's a freaking vampire!"

"Any other proof you'd like to share, Nicolae?" William's question drips with sarcasm.

Nicolae scowls. "What about her house? Didn't you think it was odd that the mom she claims to exist doesn't even have a bedroom in that house? No food in the cabinets. No pictures of family or anything? What mom do you know would be willing to live in a dump like that?"

Sadie and William exchange a glance. Gabriel doesn't have to ask what they are thinking to know there is no way their mother, Mrs. Homemaker of the Year, would step foot in a home like that. "So?"

Nicolae's eyes widen. "So? So she's a vampire. Have you all forgotten that she's from Romania? Brasov, to be exact."

He pauses for theatrical effect but it doesn't hit like he had hoped. He rolls his eyes. "Seriously? Nothing?" He sighs. "Ever heard of Bran castle?"

William's face lights up. "Sure. Dracula's home."

"Exactly. Do I need to give you three guesses as to what her address is?"

Gabriel shoves Nicolae back into the wall. "That place is a museum for tourists."

Nicolae laughs around Gabriel's arm. "Of course it is...during the day. It's all a ruse. Tourists are only allowed in certain sections of the castle. Why do you think that is?"

Sadie's brow furrows. "You seem to know an awful lot about someone who you apparently only met when you came here."

For the first time, Nicolae averts his gaze. His lips curl into a partial scowl. "When you live in Romania, you hear things."

"Myths and legends, you mean," Gabriel says, pressing his forearm into Nicolae's windpipe.

Nicolae's eyes darken as he pushes back against Gabriel's hold. "Where do you think they came from? These aren't just stories to scare children at bedtime or make Hollywood rich. The stories are true."

"So what are you saying then? Roseline is a descendent of Dracula or something?"

"No, not a descendent." He turns to meet Gabriel's gaze. "His wife."

Nicolae gasps for breath as he falls to the floor. Gabriel staggers back, rocked by his claim. It can't be true. It just can't.

"Okay, that's it," Sadie cries, stalking forward. "Are one of you gonna hit him or do I have to?"

No one answers her. William leans back against the wall, his shocked gaze flitting back and forth between Nicolae's wariness and Gabriel's intense scrutiny. "Don't tell me you actually believe this guy," she scoffs, pacing back and forth, itching to rearrange Nicolae's face.

"I get that your country is riddled with tales of vampires or whatever, but to stand there and claim something that ludicrous about Rose is just plain wrong," William scolds, crossing his arms over his chest. "Not cool, man."

Gabriel says nothing as he straightens to observe Nicolae. He watches every facial tic, every blink of his eye, and the way he grits his teeth. There is no doubt in his mind that Nicolae believes what he says.

Something begins to stir in Gabriel's soul, like a long-awaited answer is brewing and he is about to get his hands on it.

"Come on, Gabriel. We're wasting time." William tries to pull him away but he easily shakes William off.

"I want to hear what else he thinks he knows." He tosses his keys toward William. "Why don't you two go get warmed up? We'll meet you back at your place in fifteen minutes, but make sure you hide my car again. I don't want you to have to deal with Steve."

"If you want to stay here and listen to his lies, then fine, whatever." Sadie grabs William's arm and heads for the door. "Just make sure you hurt him a bit for what he said about Rose."

Gabriel's lip curls into a smile at Sadie's protective hostility. He can't blame her, but, unlike Sadie, he has something vested in this. The instant the door closes he snatches a fistful of Nicolae's shirt and slams him against the wall. "Talk."

"So you're taking Sadie's request seriously, I see," Nicolae smirks. His chest muscles ripple in response but he doesn't attack.

Gabriel grins. "Smart move. If I were you, I wouldn't push me today. You know I can make it hurt."

Nicolae leans forward. "So can I, but lucky for you I'm in a talkative mood."

"So talk then."

He tilts his head to the side to observe Gabriel. "First I want to know more about you."

"That's what you're gonna tell me. And stop with the vampire crap. I'm not in the mood for your tall tales," Gabriel growls.

Nicolae's bitter laughter fills the room. "Ah, Gabriel, I thought you of all people would be willing to listen to a history lesson."

The impulse to smash in Nicolae's face is strong as he begrudgingly sets Nicolae on the ground. He crosses his arms over his broad chest. "I'm listening."

Nicolae nods as he smoothes out his sweater. "Good, because I'm only going to say this once. You are not human and neither is Roseline."

"You mean Rose."

"No," he corrects forcefully. "Her name is Roseline. She shortened it when she came here but changing your name doesn't change who you really are."

"Whatever."

Nicolae holds up the photo in his hand. "What do you see?"

Gabriel stares at the image. "I see you standing in front of a painting. I'm assuming you took this on our field trip to the art museum." Nicolae nods and waits for him to continue. "It's a girl who looks like she could be Rose's twin."

"Not a twin. Take a look at the bottom of the painting."

Gabriel's gaze drifts again to the photograph. Even though the wording is small it is still legible. "Roseline Enescue." His blood runs cold.

"Name ring a bell?"

"Oh, god," Gabriel gasps, holding his stomach as the contents churn violently. "She's my step-mother?"

"What?" Nicolae exclaims, rushing to Gabriel's side, weaving with him. "What did you just say?"

"Enescue. Lucien Enescue. He's my biological father. Oh God, that's why she passed out yesterday."

Nicolae's fingers clamp down on Gabriel's arm but he barely notices as Nicolae's next words bring sweet relief to his tortured soul. "She isn't your step-mother, Gabriel. Lucien is her brother-in-law."

The relief vanishes only to be followed by crippling grief. Gabriel falls to his knees, choking on the sobs that rise in his throat. "She really is married?"

"Yes. To the man you would call Dracula. He has gone by many names in many cultures but his real name is Vladimir Enescue."

"This isn't possible," Gabriel groans as he rolls onto his back. He shoves his fists into his eyes and fights for control. "She can't be married."

"It gets better," Nicolae whispers next to his ear. "She's over three hundred years old."

Gabriel's howl shakes the rafters, sending nesting birds into the sky. Nicolae sits next to Gabriel, confused by his grief. "You honestly didn't know?"

"No," he gasps, fighting for breath.

"But you're one of them..." Nicolae trails off. His brow furrows deeply as he leans in close, sniffing the air around Gabriel. "Your scent is human...so that must mean Lucien is your father and your mother is a human?"

"You say that as if it's an odd thing," Gabriel snorts. He rises to his knees and run his hands through his hair. This is too much to take in. His brain feels as if it will explode. Heat burrows into his chest as sweat clings to his body. He pushes up his sleeves to release the sauna within.

"What the heck is happening to me?" he asks, dropping his arms with exasperation. They slam into his knees, like stone against stone.

Nicolae's eyes widen with shock as he leaps toward Gabriel. His shoves Gabriel's forearms together and blanches. "It can't be," he whispers, backing away. His gaze is riveted to the jagged cross before it rises to meet Gabriel's. "You've got to be kidding. *You're* the one?"

Gabriel frowns. "What are you talking about?"

"The prophecy." He slaps his forehead. "How could I have been so stupid?"

Nicolae flips open his phone. His fingers blur over the buttons and then he waits. The instant someone picks up the line, a strange, beautiful language rolls off Nicolae's tongue. Gabriel stares down at his arms, shocked to find the tattoo symbols glowing bright blue.

"What the heck is going on?" he demands, rising to his feet. "What is happening to me, Nicolae?"

Waving him off, Nicolae speaks a few more unintelligible sentences before snapping his phone shut. "I need you to come with me."

"Not until you tell me what you know," Gabriel growls, unconsciously baring his teeth.

Nicolae doesn't back away from Gabriel's threat. "I promise you will get your answers, but I need you to come with me, now."

"Where?" he asks, forcing steel into his wobbly legs. He feels like every ounce of the amazing strength he has been gifted with has been sucked from the marrow in his bones.

"Romania."

Thirty-Six

Gabriel holds the phone away from his ear as he and Nicolae march rapidly down the deserted street. His boots punch through the ice with ease. Nicolae only shows slight signs of difficulty, causing Gabriel to once again question who he really is.

"Have you completely lost your mind?" Sadie screams at him down the line. "You're actually going to get on a plane with that lunatic?"

"What choice do I have?" he says back, fighting to keep the anger from his voice. He has to remember that she cares about Rose too. "He knows where Rose is. I have to go after her, Sadie."

There is an extended pause. Gabriel can hear the clacking of fingernails on a wooden surface. "Sadie?"

"I'm thinking," she snaps. Gabriel sighs as they cross the road. They are getting close to his home and he needs to be planning out what to pack, not fighting with Sadie.

"Fine," she finally says, "but I'm coming with you."

Nicolae blows up when Gabriel relays the message. Sadie's screechy voice mingles with the ringing in his ears. Nicolae snatches the phone from Gabriel's hand and immediately leaps into the fray. "Out of the question. I will not allow you to put your life in danger."

"It's my life and you have no right to tell me what I can and cannot do with it," Sadie explodes.

Gabriel grimaces, almost feeling sorry for the guy. "Bad move, man," he mutters in Nicolae's ear.

After five more minutes of fighting, standing one block from Gabriel's house, Nicolae finally concedes to not only allowing Sadie to join in, but William as well.

"Fools. They have no idea what they're walking into." Nicolae hands the phone back to Gabriel.

"We good, Sadie?" Gabriel asks.

"Yeah, the idiot actually thought he could use not having a passport against me. I've got that baby sitting in my top drawer from our summer vacation to Jamaica."

"That figures," Gabriel mutters, unwilling to start another brawl over his own concerns. Going with Nicolae is one thing but bringing along Sadie and William will slow them down. "Meet us at my car in twenty minutes. You still got my keys?"

"Duh." She hangs up on him.

"I've got a bad feeling about this." Gabriel sighs. "Look, I've gotta grab some stuff and try to avoid Steve. Pack a bag and sneak out with Sadie. I'll meet you there."

"Fine, but make it quick," Nicolae growls, obviously in a bad mood.

Nicolae's scowl falters as Gabriel's hand catches his. "You're wrong about her. I know Rose. She would never hurt anyone."

Nicolae's eyes frost over. "When I was a little boy, I saw her for the first time. My parents had gone to a party that night and made me stay home with my nanny. I was angry they wouldn't let me go, so I snuck out and ran across the town square to the main hall." Nicolae closes his eyes against the tears that threaten to spill over. "By the time I arrived, the doors were locked. Their screams still haunt me."

"What happened?" Gabriel asks, letting his hand drop away.

"Every single person inside was slaughtered. It took weeks to clean the blood from the floors," he chokes out. "My mother, father, and two sisters were found among the carnage…in pieces."

"Oh, god." Gabriel grimaces at his loss. "I'm so sorry."

Nicolae straightens his shoulders and pushes away the memories. "Vladimir is a sadistic monster, Gabriel, but he doesn't even come close to comparing to your father."

"And Rose was with them?"

Nicolae nods. "She was."

"And you think she was a part of this massacre?" Gabriel's mind refuses to accept it. Rose is gentle and kind. She could never be a killer.

"I know she was." Nicolae takes a few steps but turns back. "She's not who you think she is, Gabriel. Or maybe you already know that. Maybe you're keeping a few secrets of your own."

Gabriel is shocked by the urge to rip out Nicolae's throat for speaking such things. Unsettled by the sudden desire, he stands his ground. "I don't know who, or what, I am. All I know is that I love Rose and I'm going to save her."

"Even if she's a blood-sucking monster?"

Gabriel nods. "Even then…but I know you're wrong. Can you honestly tell me that she's the same person today that you think she was then?"

Nicolae thinks for a moment, considering his words. "She is different than my Uncle Sorin has led me to believe. I have not seen her kill or maim anyone during my time here."

"Then maybe she isn't as evil as you think she is," Gabriel says.

"No. I think she is exactly as evil as I have been told." He meets Gabriel's gaze. "She plays on people's emotions. Look at how she has captured your heart and those of William and Sadie. No," he shakes his head, "she is a master at deception. Nothing more."

"Make no mistake, Roseline is evil in its purest form. She's far more dangerous than you can ever imagine, especially since this evil is masked behind such exquisite beauty."

Struggling to breathe, Gabriel forces his shoulders to rise in a shrug. "It changes nothing. I am still going after her. I won't let Vladimir kill her."

A faint gleam flashes across Nicolae's eye. "Trust me, there are things far worse than death for a vampire."

Thirty-Seven

Two hours later, Gabriel sits impatiently in the first class lounge. He rubs his temples as he tries in vain to block out the loud voices next to him. Sadie and William are still arguing with Nicolae over the tickets.

"Look, it's no big deal. The tickets weren't that unreasonable," Nicolae insists, obviously wishing they would just drop it.

"You just bought four first class tickets to Romania and you want us to believe that they are cheap?" Sadie cries. "Do I have LOSER written across my forehead?"

Nicolae sighs. "Fine. The tickets were seven thousand apiece. Happy now?"

William jerks upright, spilling his fancy espresso. "Good night! Where did you come up with that kind of cash?"

"My parents. Just trust me, the money will never be missed." Nicolae folds his hands over his lap and leans back to get some rest. Gabriel hopes Sadie will take the hint, but that just isn't in her nature.

"So your family is, like, rich or something?"

Nicolae groans as he opens his eyes. "I'm a foreign exchange student. Do you think that's cheap?"

"Huh," William mutters, scratching his jaw. "You know, I never really thought about that."

"Well, there you go," Nicolae says. "End of story."

Gabriel frowns at his answer. "What about your visa? Are you allowed to come back?"

Nicolae sighs, resigned to playing twenty questions. "No. It's a one-time deal. I hop on that plane and goodbye America. At least that should make *one* of you very happy," he says, staring pointedly at Sadie.

She squirms. It's no secret that she has spent the past couple months loathing the guy but now, as Gabriel watches the emotions shifting over her features, he realizes she might actually miss Nicolae. Girls! They are all screwed up.

"I feel weird sitting here," William says, sinking lower in his seat as gawking travelers pass by, peering in at the four teenagers who must have found a way to sneak into the private lounge.

"Don't worry about it. Your ticket says you're first class and that's all the flight attendant's care about."

"I'm still jumpy," Sadie says, rubbing her arms as she darts a glance around the empty space. "Mom and Dad are going to flip when they figure out we aren't coming home tonight."

William waves her off. "It's couples dancing at the country club. You know Mom. She'll have a few too many drinks and come home tipsy. Dad will carry her up to bed and probably pass out too. They won't even know we are gone until morning."

"Maybe," Sadie frowns, "but Mom was pretty ticked about Gabriel sleeping over. She's probably pacing the kitchen right now waiting to tear me a new one."

"At least you'll still be alive when she gets done with you. I was supposed to be heading to Notre Dame this week to view the school," Gabriel mutters, fingering his ticket. "There won't be anything left of me when Steve's done."

Nicolae gives him a curious stare but says nothing.

"Now boarding: Flight forty-six to London Heathrow. All first class passengers are welcome to board at this time," a robotic voice calls over the loud speaker.

"London?" Sadie questions, looking down at her boarding pass. "I thought we were going to Romania."

Nicolae smirks as he offers to help her to her feet. "That's just the first stop, love."

Thirty-Eight

The flight into London was eventless, apart from William's loud snoring. Even the flight attendants were annoyed by all of the racket. After a lengthy visit with Heathrow's immigration, the four friends made it to their connecting flight with five hours to spare. Not exactly ideal when you're facing another long flight.

William and Nicolae passed the time shopping. Sadie tried to sneakily browse the teen magazine rack while Gabriel paced around their pile of carry-ons. The closer he got to Rose, the more anxious he became. Is she okay? Will she confirm Nicolae's crazy story? Will she be happy to see him?

Now that their flight into Romania is nearly complete, he is bursting with anticipation. Sadie stretches her arms high overhead, working out the kinks in her sore body. "What time is it?"

"It's nearly four. We're about to land," Nicolae answers her as William yawns, waking from another catnap. Gabriel hasn't slept. He is sure that will come back to bite him later.

He glances over at Nicolae and instantly notes the shift in his appearance. His glasses met their untimely end with the on-flight bathroom not long after the seat belt sign went off. Sometime during Gabriel's obsessive musings, Nicolae discarded his baggy clothes for a designer sweater that hugs his muscular frame, faded jeans, and expensive leather slip-ons. His hair is waxed and styled in a messy look. All evidence of his former façade has been erased.

"What's with the new look?" Gabriel whispers across the aisle.

"I'm home." Although that is all he says, those two words feel like the answer to a million questions.

Gabriel leans back, smirking at the cautious glances Sadie shoots toward Nicolae. He appears to be completely oblivious, too tormented by his own demons, but Gabriel has no doubt that when he finally does notice he will be intrigued by her budding interest.

"Will your parents be glad to see you?" Sadie asks. Her eyes can barely believe the transformation before her—annoying nerd to confident model. How did he hide it so well?

Gabriel tenses, sure that Nicolae will find some way around telling her the truth, but the newly transformed boy surprises him. "They died a long time ago."

"Then who paid for our flights?" William leans forward to join the conversation.

"They did. Or at least my trust fund did." Nicolae's face contorts with pain. "After my parents died I was sent to live with my uncle. He lives on a large estate just outside of Brasov. When I turned sixteen, I was given full access to my parent's wealth. To be honest, I never knew they had so much money."

Sadie smirks. "So *you're* the one that's rich."

"Not in comparison with my uncle, but he has a highly sought-after job. I guess you could say it's a rare commodity." He pauses to think over the irony of his words. "My uncle is a hunter."

"That doesn't sound so rare to me…" William cuts off as a flight attendant rushes forward to shush him. She manages to scold them to put on their seatbelts before rushing back to her seat only moments before the wheels touch down.

After a manic rush to get off the plane and through customs, Nicolae leads them to their next gate. "Are you serious?" Sadie moans, rubbing her lower back. "I don't think I can stomach another flight."

Nicolae nods, beginning to betray signs of his own weariness. "Otopeni Airport doesn't get us close enough to Brasov. We have to take a flight over to Bucharest."

After the brief internal flight, the weary group of friends departs their final plane. "I really don't want to get on another plane any time soon," William groans, stretching out the kinks in his body.

"Not to worry. It's only a car ride now," Nicolae calls over his shoulder as he opens the door leading outside. Parked next to the curb is a sleek, blacked-out limo.

"This is yours?" Sadie gasps, clinging to her brother. It is frightfully cold, with winds gusting wildly, tossing snow in their faces. Her short-cropped hair waves madly in the wind.

"It's my uncle's," Nicolae corrects, his ears tinged with red. Gabriel seriously doubts the color has anything to do with the frosty air. "Hop in."

Sadie practically dives inside, desperate for warmth. She completely ignores the guys as she wallows on the soft, luxurious leather seat. "This is what I dream heaven will be like."

Nicolae seems pleased with her comment, but quickly looks away to share strange words with the driver. As soon as the doors close, Nicolae settles back and closes his eyes.

"I take it this will be a long journey?" Gabriel grumbles, rubbing the sore muscles in his thighs. How is he supposed to rescue Rose when he can barely walk without a darn muscle cramp?

"Yes. About three-and-a-half hours, depending on the snow."

"Lovely." Gabriel glances out the window at Romania. He has visited parts of Europe with his family over the years, so he is familiar with the narrow streets and stone buildings. Numerous people walk the stone paths, braving the frigid temperatures instead of simply driving to the store. Europe has always held a sense of wonder for him.

"You never finished telling us about your uncle," William says, more out of boredom than real interest.

Nicolae glances at the driver before flicking the privacy button. As the blacked-out screen rises, Gabriel's eyebrows mirror their movement. Apparently, what he has to say is best not overhead. Even Sadie stops petting the leather long enough to listen.

"I told you that my uncle is a hunter…but I failed to mention what he hunts." Nicolae's voice comes out barely above a whisper as he glances warily at Gabriel.

Seconds tick by before the meaning behind Nicolae's gaze hits him. "Oh no," Gabriel moans, gripping his stomach tightly as he bends over. How could Nicolae keep this from him? What if he is too late? What if Rose has someone *more* than her husband to fear?

Thirty-Nine

Nicolae watches Gabriel like a hawk as his chest rises and falls, his eyes darkening with fury. "Look, Gabriel, it's for the best."

"I'll kill you!" Gabriel roars, hurling himself across the narrow carpeted aisle. His fingers tighten around Nicolae's throat. Strangled gasps dribble from his mouth as Nicolae's fingers claw at Gabriel's grasp.

Sadie screams as the car swerves off the road. William picks himself up off the floorboard, as the back door is yanked open. A tall, hulking man dives through the door and starts pounding on Gabriel's back.

He howls but tightens his grip, ignoring Sadie's shrieks and William's pleading. He ignores the iron-clad fists beating his back. He stares into Nicolae's bulging eyes and snarls. "You did this. It's your fault!"

Nicolae's lips part; shaky words inch between his lips. "You...need...me."

The lights go out as a final blow lands at the base of his neck. Gabriel slumps and passes out.

When he comes to, William has Sadie cradled in his arms. They stare at him with a mixture of fear and awe. Gabriel winces as he rubs his head.

"No," Nicolae shouts from somewhere behind him. He slips fluidly into his native tongue. The man protests but Nicolae cuts him off with a stern glare.

Gabriel cranes his head back to meet the livid glare of the driver. He dodges the spitball the man shoots at him before slamming the car door closed.

"What the heck is going on?" Sadie trembles, staring at Nicolae then turning on Gabriel. "Have you both lost your mind?"

Gabriel rises slowly, refusing to look away from Nicolae. "Why don't you ask him? I'm sure you'd like to know why Nicolae was sent to Chicago to hunt Rose."

Sadie's eyes widen. William's arms tighten around her. Nicolae bows his head under their weighty stares. "It was my job."

"What's that supposed to mean?" William asks.

"Nicolae isn't a normal exchange student, Will. He's a hunter, just like his uncle, and he's after Rose."

Nicolae raises his gaze to meet Sadie. "I never knew she would be your friend. When I realized that you cared about her, I did everything I could to protect you. I'm not actually a creepy stalker." He offers a weak smile.

Sadie isn't buying it. "So all this time you've been watching her for what exactly? To drink someone's blood? To raise someone from the dead?" The more ludicrous her statements become, the higher her voice rises.

"Something like that." He looks away.

"This is insane," she growls, crossing her arms over her chest. "Vampires don't exist."

Nicolae turns to look back at Sadie. His gaze is haunted, intense. "Just because you choose not to believe something doesn't make it the truth. Rose is a killer, born and bred."

"A creature of the night?" William scoffs.

Nicolae's anger singes William. "Mock all you want, but she killed my parents. That is not something you easily forget."

Sadie's gasp draws his attention. He winces at the blood draining from her face. She wavers as William pulls her close. "Smooth move, idiot," Gabriel says as he moves closer to Sadie.

William turns to survey Gabriel. "You don't seem surprised by Nicolae's words."

"No," he says, pulling Sadie's hand into his own. He awkwardly gives it a pat. "I already know."

"How?" she whispers. Her fingers flinch in his palm.

"I stuck around to listen to the full story at the park, remember?" He smiles weakly.

"Yes, it's a shame they didn't get to hear *your* story, Gabriel." Nicolae's gaze is icy but it softens when he looks past Gabriel to Sadie.

"Okay, I want to know what the heck is going on, and I want to know right this instant!" She is losing control but really does not care. Her freaked-out state totally vindicates her tantrum.

William stares out the window at the landscape flying past. "Why are we here?" he whispers.

"Because Rose needs us. That's why," Gabriel responds.

"Does she?" William shoots a wary glance at him. "If what Nicolae says is even possible, and at this point I'm assuming we might believe that it is, then what can she possibly need us for?"

Gabriel opens his mouth to answer, but he doesn't know how to respond. What can he say to that when he doesn't even really know why he came? Only that he had to. "I don't know, William. I don't know anything right now."

"But he does," Sadie murmurs, glaring at Nicolae. She pulls out of William's grasp. Her pale skin blotches with anger. "So what are we? Bait for Rose?"

Nicolae closes his eyes. "No. I'd never risk your—" he clams up, shaking his head. "I tried to warn you, but you are so stubborn."

"Then why did you give in?" Sadie pounces, getting right up in Nicolae's face. His eyes widen; his Adam's apple bobs as he fights to swallow. Nicolae gently pushes her back before he answers. "Because she means so much to you."

"So? Why do you even care?" she retorts, practically spitting in his face.

Nicolae looks away. "Because I can't help it. What you care about, I care about. What you like, I like. I can't get you out of my mind!"

Sadie sits back, shocked. William grinds his teeth. "Oh, no you don't. You don't get to sound like the noble hero in all of this, Nicolae. I don't know what kind of crazy fling you have for my sister, but it's not gonna happen."

"Says who?" Sadie snaps, rounding on her brother. "Who are you to tell me who I can and can't like?"

William blinks. "Are you telling me you like this guy now? All I've heard for the past two months was how annoying he is."

Sadie doesn't even bat an eye. "Yeah, and I meant it. But he's obviously risking a lot for Rose...so I gotta appreciate that."

She glances back at Nicolae, surprised to find him staring frankly at her. Gone is the meek, pimply-faced boy that dogged her every step, annoying her like a younger brother that refused take a hint. "He's changed."

"Yeah," Gabriel growls. "He's real good at acting, isn't he?"

Sadie begins to protest but Nicolae cuts her off. "You're right, Gabriel. I was acting. It's what I've been trained to do."

"By your uncle?" William asks.

Nicolae leans back in his seat and rubs his thumb against the palm of his right hand with enough force to bruise the skin. "My uncle made it his mission to hunt down vampires after my parents died. Most kids went to a normal school to learn normal things. Not me. I had to learn kill shots and master weapons training."

"I didn't have friends growing up. I had sparring partners. Instead of a summer break, I was sent on vampire raids all over the continent. My uncle was brutal, working me from dawn until long after dusk. Always preparing me."

"For what?" Sadie asks with eyes widened in awe.

"To take down a vampire."

"So you're a real vampire slayer? Like that old TV show with Sarah Michelle Geller?" William laughs. "At least she was hot!"

Nicolae shrugs. "If she killed vampires, then yes. I guess that's what I am."

Sadie leans forward, engrossed in the tale. For the first time since meeting him, she finds him completely irresistible. There is a new strength to his words, a confidence that calls to her wild side. "That's actually kinda cool...if you believe in this sort of thing, I mean. And I most certainly do not."

"Are you even listening to yourself, Sadie?" Gabriel growls, pulling her back. "He is hunting Rose, your best friend, remember?"

Sadie's sappy grin instantly vanishes and a new wariness takes its place. "You're right." She glares at Nicolae once more. "Why didn't you kill her when you had the chance?"

Nicolae scratches the back of his head, embarrassed. "Well, I've never...um...I've never actually killed one before."

Gabriel snickers, rolling his eyes. "Typical. You claim to be this badass vampire killer and it's all a joke."

Nicolae's eyes darken as his fists clench against his thighs. "It's not a joke. People are dead because of her!"

"No," Gabriel snarls. "She isn't a killer. Her husband and my father are."

William has to pick his jaw up off the floor. "I'm sorry. Did you just say your father?"

Gabriel nods, grimly. "Yeah, sorry. I forgot you didn't know. Rose's brother-in-law is my biological father." He hates to speak of the man, if he can even be considered a man. Gabriel highly doubts it. Surely, Lucien is more monster than anything, but no matter how hard he tries, Gabriel can't put his precious Rose in the same category.

Sadie blows out a breath. "Man, this just gets better and better. So Rose is actually married?"

Nicolae nods, ignoring Gabriel's groan. "Yes."

"And she really is Dracula's wife?" William asks, struggling to wrap his mind around the conversation.

"I'm afraid so," Nicolae speaks softly.

Sadie shakes her head. "No. I can't believe it. She doesn't hold up to any of the myths. She comes out during the day, she's not afraid to go inside a church, and she doesn't seem particularly afraid of sticks. Plus, she eats normal food and her teeth are perfect. I haven't seen any sign of fangs."

Nicolae agrees. "You're right. Her family does seem to defy all of the normal vampire laws. I've questioned my uncle on this very thing but he just tells me to mind my own business and get back to training."

"So, you could be wrong then," William says, turning his back on the window. "Maybe she's not a vampire after all."

"No. She has to be. Roseline is over three hundred years old. That's not human."

Gabriel is desperate to find something that will prove Rose isn't evil. "Tell them how your parents were killed." Maybe if his friends hear the gruesome tale they can help him fight against the lies.

Sadie winces. "Oh, come on. I'm sure that's not something Nicolae wants to talk about."

"No. It's okay." He smiles wanly at Sadie. "I want you to know."

He clears his throat and eyes the blacked-out privacy window. Judging by the earlier intervention of their driver, it isn't completely private. Nicolae leans close but keeps his voice low. "As I told Gabriel before, they attended a masquerade ball on Halloween night."

"I thought vampires didn't go out on Halloween," Sadie says.

Nicolae laughs bitterly. "That must be Hollywood's version of vampire fiction. Here in Romania, Halloween is the Devil's night. Anyone who has any sense stays home."

"So what happened?" Gabriel presses.

"They were slaughtered, along with every other living soul in the room. Over two hundred people were murdered that night."

"And they found...teeth marks?" Gabriel said, grimacing on the last bit. He simply can't imagine Rose sinking her teeth into anyone's neck.

Nicolae shifts uncomfortably. "Well....no. My uncle said they didn't have much luck finding any evidence."

"Why not?" Sadie buries her chin into her knees. She would never admit that she is afraid, but she is. Very much so.

"There wasn't much left." Nicolae's voice sounds almost monotone, as if he were reading a very boring report instead of speaking of his parent's deaths.

"Is that normal?" William asks, gulping as he grips his sister's hand.

"No. Not normally. Most vampires just drain their victim and leave. They do not like any publicity. They don't want the rest of the world knowing they exist."

Gabriel taps his temple, feeling like he is missing something. Suddenly the light bulb flickers on. "Has Rose ever acted in a normal vampire fashion? Has anyone ever seen her bite a person?"

Once again, Nicolae looks deeply uncomfortable. "Not to my knowledge."

"So, you're just assuming that she's a vampire then," Gabriel grins, sure that he is getting close to vindicating her.

"I don't know, Gabriel. It sounds pretty gruesome to me." Sadie's eyes are rounded with fear. Her lower lip trembles. "What if we are wrong? Is it really possible that all of this is true?"

"Not you too," Gabriel groans. "So, now you think she's a blood sucker, too?"

Sadie buries her head in her hands. "I don't know what to think. The only thing we know is that Rose's family sounds really dangerous and we're headed straight for them."

A heavy silence falls over the small space. No one dares to verbalize his or her fears. Even if Rose is not a vampire, her family obviously gets off on sadistic mass murders. Gabriel can't help but wonder what they are getting themselves into.

Forty

"My uncle will know what to do." Nicolae finally breaks the silence. The dark undertone of his voice makes Gabriel glance up. The limo slows at it approaches a towering wrought-iron gate. Just beyond, down a winding lane, stands a large stone estate covered with snowy ivy.

Gabriel shivers. "We're here already?" He isn't sure he is quite ready to face what lies beyond.

"Time flies by when you're scared to death," William mutters, pressing his nose against the tinted glass to get a better look.

Nicolae pokes his head out of the window to speak to the man guarding the entrance. The gates groan as they shift open. The sound reverberates through Gabriel with a sense of evil foreboding. The tires crunch on the gravel path as they creep along at a snail's pace.

Gabriel feels like pulling out his hair or screaming as the driver inches toward the mansion. The irrational need to escape is overwhelming but as the gates slam shut behind them, Gabriel knows he is trapped.

Once the limo has come to a complete stop, the driver comes around to open the door. Each of them is met by his enormous, broad chest and short-cropped hair as they rise from the vehicle. A jagged scar runs from his temple to his throat, disappearing inside his black uniform.

"Well, that's not creepy," Sadie mutters as Nicolae shifts to offer her a hand out of the car.

Gabriel glowers back at the chauffeur as he turns to lead them up the steps. They incline sharply and end at the base of an enormous door.

"Who lives here? Giants?" William jokes weakly as he leans back to stare at the top of the door that towers fifteen feet above them.

"It's just for show," Nicolae chuckles, grasping a nearly invisible door handle. A normal-sized door opens inward to reveal a dark hall beyond.

"I can't believe you live here." Sadie clings to Nicolae's side.

He smiles down at her and squeezes her hand tightly. "Pretty depressing, huh?"

"No kidding," William follows closely behind his sister.

Gabriel brings up the rear. He nearly jumps out of his skin as the door slams behind him without anyone there to push it closed. "Okay, now *that's* creepy."

Footsteps echo from up ahead. Nicolae goes rigid. He ducks out of Sadie's grasp as he stands to attention like a soldier in the military. "Uncle." He bows low as an imposing figure emerges from the shadows.

The man is tall, though not nearly as tall as their chauffer. His face is rugged, lined with scratches that Gabriel guesses to be fingernail marks. His black hair is slicked back and a trim goatee clings to his broad chin. He wears a tight-fitting black uniform under a heavy cloak, identical to the chauffeurs. The man walks with rigid determination.

"Nicolae." His booming voice echoes around the vast hall as he formally greets his nephew in Romanian. He doesn't sound the least bit pleased to see his kin.

"Yes, Uncle. She has returned, as I informed you," Nicolae says in English.

Gabriel glances at Nicolae. It is disconcerting to hear such a strong voice coming from the nerdy boy he has grown to dislike over the past couple months. The transformation is now complete.

"You've brought unexpected guests." This announcement is tinted with anger as his uncle concedes to the language change.

"Yes, Uncle. They are…friends."

Nicolae's uncle eyes each of them, sniffing the air. His beady eyes drill into Gabriel. Two guards, armed with heavy black guns, emerge from behind tall marble pillars on either side of the room.

Gabriel's heart is in the center of their targets. "You were not supposed to bring him here."

That doesn't sound good. He looks toward his friends and see the same thoughts mirrored on their faces—they made a big mistake coming here.

"He has come looking for Roseline, Uncle." Nicolae steps forward. His voice drops so low Gabriel strains to hear him. "He is unaware of the prophecy."

The sudden gleam in the imposing man's gaze unsettles Gabriel as he is regarded with new interest. Nicolae's uncle does not relax his tense stance as he speaks around Nicolae. "You know what she is?"

"I know what you think she is," Gabriel corrects.

Nicolae stares at him in amazement. Never in a million years would he have spoken so boldly to his uncle, but then again Gabriel doesn't know what his uncle is capable of.

The older man strokes his goatee, staring at Gabriel with a hint of admiration. "And yet you still come?"

"Yes, sir," Gabriel nods. "I love her."

Sadie bristles at the man's boisterous laugh. "You can't help who you fall in love with," she retorts.

His laughter fades as he glances at Sadie for the first time. "Spunky," he mutters, noting how his nephew stiffens. "I can see why you like her."

Sadie blushes but does not look away. "You are right though, my dear. When it comes to vampires, your friend never stood a chance. He will love her until the day she sucks him dry."

Gabriel isn't sure if he said the words so bluntly to scare them or because he believes it to be true. Either way, it has quite an effect on everyone in the darkened entry room.

"I supposed I should introduce myself. My name is Sorin Funar. I welcome you to my home."

Without a sound, the two guards vanish into the shadows and Sorin heads back down the hall without another word.

"Well, that was odd," Sadie mutters under her breath.

"You have no idea," Nicolae says as he moves to follow his uncle's lead.

Forty-One

Gabriel is beginning to get a distinct feeling about this house. Everywhere they look, floor-to-ceiling velvet curtains block out the sun. The only sunlight they have seen since entering comes from glass windows lining the vaulted ceilings above. The cheery glow does little to ease the somber mood of Sorin's study.

"How much do you know about your girlfriend?" Sorin asks, snickering on the last word as he sinks into a black leather armchair. A roaring fire casts an eerie halo around his head.

Towering bookcases, filled with ancient leather bound books, run the perimeter of the room. Medieval-style swords hang from the walls. One in particular is encased in glass. Light from above highlights a dried bloodstain on the tip of the sword.

Gabriel struggles to pull his attention away as Sorin clears his throat impatiently. "I'm sorry. I was just admiring your décor." He returns to the conversation at hand. "The only thing I know about Rose, apart from what Nicolae has briefly told me, is from the times that I've spent with her at school."

Sorin sits forward, his gaze is intense, face rigid. "And did you spend any time alone with her?"

Gabriel frowns. "Of course I did."

"And yet you're still alive," Sorin mutters, stroking his goatee. "Interesting."

"Not really," he counters. "Not if she isn't what you accuse her to be."

Sorin's booming laughter echoes into the recesses of the room. "You're feisty, I'll give you that." He smiles. It is not a nice smile. It is dark and sinister and makes Gabriel's skin crawl. "But you're the biggest idiot that I've ever met."

Gabriel's jaw clamps down hard. His fingers wrap painfully around his kneecaps as he bites his tongue against the abuse he wants to sling back. However, he is painfully aware of all of the weaponry scattered around the room and knows he would be useless against this war-hardened man. Strength or not, Sorin Funar is obviously a skilled killer.

"Now that I've got your attention," Sorin's voice rumbles as he rises to his feet, "I'd like to show you a bit of our history to convince the halfwit about his precious Roseline."

Sadie sits forward, aching to hear more, even if it does come from a creepy, old man. William looks sick as he slinks farther down into his chair while Nicolae remains rigid by the door.

"Have you ever heard of The Black Church?" he asks, pointing to a picture hanging over the fireplace. The stone building looks tarnished, as if by soot or dirt.

"Of course not," Sadie rolls her eyes. "They don't exactly teach Romanian history in our country."

William hisses at her to be quiet but Sorin simply smiles. "Well, my dear, your friend Roseline was born in that church."

Sadie glances at the picture again, confused. "In a church?"

Sorin returns to his seat. His fingers form a steeple before his eyes. "Not as a baby. As a seventeen-year-old girl."

"You mean that's where she was raised from the dead?" Gabriel snorts. Sorin's indifferent shrug angers him. Why is he so focused on Roseline? It's not as if he can prove she is the one that murdered Nicolae's parents.

"The girl you know as Rose was born Roseline Dragomir, an English name given after her mother's side of the family, I believe. Her father was a man whose lust for wealth and prestige drove his lovely daughter into the arms of Vladimir Enescue. Poor Roseline knew the man was vile, but she had no idea he was a vampire." Sorin's eyes gleam with a fervor that makes Gabriel's skin prickle with alarm. This man is obsessed.

"So, then what happened?" Sadie asks, drawn into the story.

"Vladimir killed all of the wedding guests." His voice is monotone, uninterested with the gruesome details. Of course he probably is. A tale like this has become legend in Romania, passed down from parent to child as a warning against speaking to strangers or breaking nighttime curfews.

Sadie scrunches up her nose. "How awful!"

Sorin's grin shifts into a leer. "You haven't heard the best part." He motions to another picture, this one of a young girl with snowy skin and pale pink lips. Her blonde hair is a startling contrast with her sparkling, baby blue eyes. "This is a likeness of Roseline's younger sister, Adela Dragomir. She was the last to die."

Gabriel stares at the portrait, drawn in by the doe eyes that hold him captive. Although her coloring greatly differs from Roseline, she has the same warmth radiating out of her. There is no doubting her connection to the girl he loves.

"I'm sure you're telling us this for a reason." Gabriel's heart thunders in his chest. "Just get on with it."

Sorin nods, returning his gaze to the three friends seated precariously on his leather couch. "Adela's blood was the tool used to damn her sister." Gabriel snorts with disgust. Sorin's bushy eyebrow rose. "You don't believe me?"

"Why should I? You have no proof. And apart from a picture hanging in some art gallery, Nicolae doesn't have any real proof either. How do you even know she is the same girl? Rose could be a descendant," Gabriel roars, his chest heaving with exertion. He is getting annoyed. All he wants to do is speak to Rose. She will clear this up.

Nicolae flinches, unsure of how his uncle will react to Gabriel's blatant disregard. His rigid stance nearly falters completely when Sorin settles back into his chair instead of smacking the smirk from Gabriel's face.

"Did you happen to notice the soot on the church?" Gabriel's eyes flickers to the picture over Sorin's head. "This church dates all the way back to 1477, but its name, The Black Church, wasn't chosen until after a fire in 1689 that left the church blackened from smoke."

"Great history lesson," Sadie grumbles. "But what's this got to do with our friend?"

"The fire occurred on the night of dear Roseline's wedding...and her rebirth." Sorin fixes his eyes on Gabriel, weighing out his reaction. "And that, my stupid boy, is recorded in our history books."

"Wait a second," William gasps, speaking for the first time since he entered the gloomy room. "You're saying Rose is...three hundred and twenty-two years old?"

Sorin nods. "Yes, that's exactly what I'm saying."

He rises and moves toward the far wall. Placing his hand on one of the dark wooden panels, a hidden chamber appears. He motions for them to follow him. "Come...if you seek further proof."

Gabriel hangs back with William and Sadie as Nicolae follows directly behind Sorin. "I've got a bad feeling about this," he mutters under his breath. Nicolae darts a glance over his shoulder but says nothing. Gabriel would bet his brand-new Range Rover on the fact that Nicolae is hiding his own concern.

"Stick close to me," he whispers as he ducks inside the hidden passage.

Sadie wedges herself between Gabriel and William as they descend a drafty spiral staircase. They walk on and on, burrowing deeper into the heart of Sorin's lair. Flickering torch light struggles to illuminate the narrow space.

"How much further?" Gabriel calls ahead to Nicolae, but there is no response. This worries him even more. Surely, they are miles underground by now. If things go bad for them their screams will never be heard.

"Ah. Here we are," Sorin's voice wafts up past Nicolae. By the stiffness of Nicolae's shoulders, Gabriel prepares for the worst.

When his foot finally reaches solid ground, Gabriel is not the least bit surprised to find himself standing in a medieval torture chamber. Rusted chains hang from the walls and some of the manacles still show signs of dried blood from their prisoners. The scent of aged urine and feces lingers on the air, soaked into the grout lines of the uneven stone lining the floor. Gabriel frowns at the scratches in the walls—claw marks.

The skeletal remains of those who resided here are strewn about the floor. Most have been pushed against the outer walls. The ceiling is vast, towering nearly thirty feet overhead. The walls curve, no doubt to reflect the screams of the victims around the room. Gabriel shudders.

"What's that?" Sadie gasps, clinging to Gabriel's arm.

"That, my dear, is called a *Strappado*." A wide grin stretches across Sorin's face. Nicolae shudders and averts his gaze. "This device is used much like a rack. A person's hands are tied behind their back and raised by this pulley system. Their feet are attached to this weight."

"How dreadful," Sadie pales.

"On the contrary." Sorin shakes his head. "It is quite useful."

"To interrogate?" William gulps.

Sorin's smile makes Gabriel's blood congeal. "Oh, no, this is just for fun."

Sadie's gasp wrenches at Gabriel's heart. He reaches back to clench her hand in his. "Why have you brought us here?"

Sorin's black cloak billows as he whirls around. "Why, to give you the proof you need, of course. Put the other two in the cell," Sorin orders Nicolae as he stares Gabriel down. His lip curls with anger at his nephew's hesitation. "Now!"

"I don't think so." Gabriel pushes Sadie back and charges at Sorin.

Despite appearing to be well into his fifties, Sorin moves as gracefully as a cat, easily side stepping Gabriel's charge. With the flick of his wrist, a small dagger appears and slices cleanly through Gabriel's upper arm.

He gasps and clenches his hand over the stinging wound. "Don't make this any harder than it has to be, boy." Sorin flips the dagger into his right hand. His knees bend as he crouches to attack.

"Somehow, I think that is exactly how you like it." Gabriel charges again. His shoulders hunch over like he's going in for a football tackle but his newfound strength only throws him off balance. He sees the glint of metal a second before pain slashes through his chest.

Sorin laughs as Gabriel tumbles to the stone floor. It feels cold against his feverish skin. His chest heaves, sucking in the damp air. "Dumb and slow. What did Roseline ever see you in?"

Gabriel's hand trembles as he holds his palm to his wound. Blood seeps between his fingers. His head is woozy but is alert enough to know the wound isn't deep. Judging by the maniacal grin on Sorin's face, he won't be so lucky the next time.

Gabriel struggles to rise to his feet but his legs give out on him. Sorin twists the knife in his hand as he stalks closer

"Stop!" Sadie screams as she thrusts her hand into the air in surrender. "We'll go."

"Good girl," Sorin grins. "At least she's smart enough to know it will be safer locked behind bars than it will be for you, foolish boy."

Nicolae remains rooted in place. He watches as Sadie pulls her brother into the cell. "What will happen to them?"

Sorin charges across the room to grab Nicolae by the throat. He doesn't struggle. He knows better than that. "I will excuse your insolence because of the girl, but do not make the same mistake twice. Do you understand me?"

"Yes, Uncle," he wheezes. He drops to his knees as his uncle turns away. Finger marks appear on his neck as he rises and walks to the cage. "I'm sorry," he whispers through the aged iron bars.

Gabriel notices the sag of Nicolae's shoulders. His desperation makes Gabriel wonder if his friends will be safer locked away. Are those rusted bars really strong enough to keep a vampire out or have they just been placed in a feeding trough?

"What do you want with me?" Gabriel asks, turning toward Sorin as the lock falls into place.

"You are simply a means to an end. You want proof that Roseline is a vampire and I want her dead. It's a win-win situation."

The dagger pierces his skin before he even realizes Sorin moved. A deep gash runs the length of his arm. Warm blood soaks into the tattered remains of his sleeve, dripping from his fingers onto the floor.

Sadie screams as Sorin appears behind him. The knife tip digs dangerously close to the artery in his neck. "Tie him up."

Nicolae shifts to obey. Sorin releases him as Nicolae drags Gabriel up onto a platform in the middle of the room. A wooden table lies horizontally across the raised area. Well-worn straps hang lifelessly over the edge, dried bloodstains clinging to the leather. Gabriel's eyes widen with fear as he struggles against Nicolae but his strength is waning.

"How can you do this to us?" He spits in Nicolae's face. "Traitor!"

"Now, now, Gabriel. According to you there's nothing to fear…unless I'm right," Sorin grins wickedly before turning to head back up the stairs. "Make sure you leave his scent trail for her to find. I don't want to take any chances tonight." The small dagger spirals through the air. Nicolae's hand catches the bloody weapon with ease.

Gabriel howls as Sorin disappears into the darkness. He bucks against the straps Nicolae has fastened across his chest. "I'm really sorry about this," Nicolae whispers, lowering the blade to his flesh. "Trust me, this will hurt a lot less if I do it."

Sadie burrows her head into William's chest as Gabriel's screams echo in her ears. The frenzy fades over several moments; his cries deepen to a guttural moan as his body begins to twitch on the platform. When silence finally reigns, Nicolae stumbles backward. The dagger clatters from his bloodstained hands.

Nicolae buries his head in his hands. "Oh, god. What have I done?"

Forty-Two

Fane slips through the arched wooden door. He gently presses it closed, wincing as the latch falls into place. He turns, steeling himself for what he fears he will see. A strangled cry rises from his throat as his gaze falls on Roseline.

"Oh, god," he cries, racing to the side of the bed. A bloodstain seeps down the white sheets from the streams of blood running down her sides. Strips of flesh have been scourged from her back so deeply that Fane can see glimpses of her ribs.

His hands tremble as they hover over her body, unsure of where to touch her. The rise and fall of her chest is shallow. A raspy wheeze escapes from between her lips.

"Roseline? Can you hear me?" He crouches next to her ear. His fingers sweep back bloody strands of hair to reveal a broken and swollen face. When she doesn't respond, Fane lifts her eyelid and winces at the ring of burst blood vessels around her pupils.

Tears stream freely down his face. "Please, say something." His hands wind around her shoulders as he tries to hold her close.

A pained groan gives him hope. He holds his breath as Roseline's eyelid flutters. "Oh, my love, what has he done to you?"

Never before has her beating been so brutal. Never have her injuries been so extensive. If she had been human, she wouldn't have made it through the first few minutes of this horrific punishment. Fane clenches his fist against the urge to hit the wall. He can't risk someone hearing him but he allows a guilt-driven moan to escape.

"I'm sorry but I have to roll you over," he whispers in her ear as he cradles her to his body and shifts. Her whimper tears at his heart as he slides her onto her side. She lies in his arms, as limp as a rag doll. Most of the bones in her body have been shattered. Fane's eyes roam the length of her arms and neck and he grits his teeth at the evidence before him. Vladimir waited for her to begin healing before he broke her bones again and again.

Fane had been beside himself as he listened to her screams echo through the corridors of the castle for endless hours. From sunup until long after the sun had disappeared from the horizon. Then he had to wait an unbearable length of time until she was finally returned to her room.

Blood seeps from Roseline's mouth as she tries to speak.

"Shh, it's okay," Fane whispers. "I'm getting you out of here."

"No," she croaks. "Leave me."

Fane clenches his eyes shut. He never should have brought her back. He knew Vladimir would be furious with her rebellion, but Fane had hoped that his obsession with his new mistress, Lavinia Ardelean, would ease some of his anger. Fane was wrong. Oh, so wrong.

Roseline's frantic screams will haunt him for centuries to come. "I'm not leaving you here," he whispers, brushing his lips against her forehead, the only place that still seems intact. "I won't ever let him touch you again."

A single tear slides down her cheek. Fane can't tell if it is acceptance, hope, or sorrow, but he decides not to stick around long enough to find out. Rising from her bed, Fane loops Roseline's arm around his neck. It hangs there limply before falling free again.

His eyes roam the stone walls, searching for the hidden latch he knows must exist. His free hand flutters along the wall nearest her bookcase. "I know it's here somewhere," he grunts. A click sounds softly from behind the wall. Dust filters down onto the plush rug.

"Got it." Fane shoves the panel aside.

Only three people know of this passage. Fane discovered it not long after Vladimir tore apart the entire castle in search of Roseline, but try as he might to hide his discovery, Lucien found it as well. His only hope this night is that Lucien remains enchanted with the human girl he bewitched away from a tour group earlier in the night.

"Don't," Roseline gurgles.

Fane glances down. A tender smile stretches across his lips. "I love you too much to let you stay."

"You'll die," she rasps, another tear escaping.

Fane nods solemnly, his love for her burning in his eyes. There is no denying his devotion. He will save her tonight even if that means his life is forfeit. "Then so be it."

Roseline is too weak to protest further. Her head lolls to the side as Fane ducks low and hurries through the wall. The door slides shut behind him with a soft hiss.

Fane twists and turns, racing through the passage as fast as he is able. His eyes narrow to pierce the dark. Fane holds her close as the tunnel thins out up ahead.

When he reaches an impasse in the tunnel, he is forced to lower Roseline through a narrow hole and then shimmy down next to her. At other places, he is forced to pull Roseline behind him when the ceiling drops off dramatically. Thankfully, she passed out from pain after the first drop and feels no pain now. Finally he detects light up ahead.

"We're almost there," he whispers. "Hold on just a little longer. I can see the well up ahead."

As he approaches the light, Fane presses back against the stone wall as voices filter down from above. He places his hand over Roseline's mouth to muffle her raspy breath.

"You seem to be in a good mood," a low husky feminine voice coos overhead. Fane struggles to hold back his snarl when he realizes who stands less than six feet away.

"She learned her lesson," Vladimir responds indifferently.

"Oh, don't even try to act like you didn't enjoy it," the woman purrs. "You know you enjoy a good torture." A grunt of affirmation is all Lavinia is afforded. "Perhaps you'd like to work off some of that pent-up frustration on me, my Lord."

Fane clamps down on his jaw, sickened by the teasing voice of Vladimir's mistress. He has always assumed the woman must possess a blackened heart in order to capture and retain Vladimir's attention, but to actually hear her in action is revolting.

"What did you have in mind?" Vladimir asks. His interest is piqued.

Fane is grateful that he can't hear the whispers and is disgusted by the quickening of Vladimir's pulse. Whatever Lavinia has suggested must be sadistic enough to excite him. With a high-pitched giggle and a rustle of silk, the couple rushes off.

When they are far enough away, Fane blows out the breath he has been holding. He glances down at the beaten face of the angel he holds in his arms and feels his rage surge. From the moment he first met Roseline she captured his heart. And now, over three hundred years later, his love for her has never dwindled.

The few brief moments they have shared are what have kept him going all this time. Without her, Fane's life would be meaningless. He has to save her, no matter the cost.

Roseline needs blood to rejuvenate to normal strength. Taking another's lifeblood has serious consequences, but he has to risk it. His stomach twists at the knowledge that this blood can't come from him. He will need his strength if they hope to make it out of the country. If there were any other way, he would never put a human's life in danger.

"Hold on, my love." Fane pushes the grate out of the way. He pauses, listening for any signs that their escape has been discovered, before poking his head up through the hole.

The old stone well stands in the middle of the courtyard. A gothic cross dangles from the top, hindering his view. Deciding it is now or never, Fane leaps out of the small space and crouches low as he scans the deserted area.

The moon shines full overhead, lighting the snow kissed ground. Frost hangs in the cloudless night sky. Fane pulls Roseline into his arms and races across the grounds and out of sight.

Vladimir roars with outrage as the door to his chamber swings open mere seconds after the pounding ceased. "This had better be good," he growls, pushing Lavinia away. She scurries back under the covers. Lucien ducks as she pulls a dagger from under the blanket and aims it right at his head.

"Easy, pet. Lucien deserves a chance to explain."

Lucien yanks the curved dagger from the wood molding behind him. "She's gone," he hisses as he tucks the blade into his belt. The muscles of his waxy cheeks pulsate.

Vladimir leaps from the bed, unashamed of his state of undress. "How?"

Lucien averts his eyes as he tosses his brother a robe. "There's a passage in her room that leads to the courtyard. That's how she escaped before."

"And you never cared to tell me about it before now?" Vladimir shouts. His black eyes gleam with murderous intent.

"I felt she was in no condition to escape again," he replies, sounding bored.

Vladimir snatches a pair of pants off the floor and shoves his legs in. "There's no way she could have healed so quickly. I beat her within an inch of death."

Lucien's lips curls into a snarl at Lavinia's giggle. "She had help."

"Who?" Vladimir growls. His hand clamps around his brother's arm.

Lucien glares at the offending hand but doesn't pull away. "Who do you think?

Vladimir's lips pull back over his teeth. They glisten like mother of pearl in the candlelight. "Fane."

Forty-Three

Fane ducks behind a grove of trees as he skirts the castle walls. His pulse pounds in his ears, making it nearly impossible to detect anyone following them. He is desperate and because of this, his risk of making a mistake rises exponentially.

"Hold on just a little longer. I'll find somewhere safe for us," he whispers, more for his own benefit than Roseline's. She hangs unconscious in his arms.

If they don't escape they are both dead. Vladimir will probably tear her limb from limb while Fane watches just to torture him. The image of her dismembered body drives him over the wall and out into the open.

Reaching the road doesn't offer any help. No one in Romania is dumb enough to be out on a full moon night. Too many superstitions have been created around such an evening. He is on his own.

With the greatest of care, Fane adjusts Roseline in his arms and leaves the castle behind. He heads farther into the countryside, away from town. If he leads Vladimir into the heart of Brasov, he will set the town ablaze until he flushes them out. Too many innocent lives will be lost.

Dogs howl in the distance. Fane stops, gripping Roseline to his chest. "Oh no."

His desperation mounts. Vladimir knows they have escaped. Fane looks to the sky and whispers a prayer for the heavy snow that has begun to fall. It will help to slow Vladimir down, but he is no fool. Nothing will stop Vladimir now.

Fane races through the woods, ignoring the branches that lash against his skin. He cuddles Roseline, shielding her as best he can.

A scent hits him only a few miles from town. It is bold and mouthwatering. He slides to a stop and sniffs the air. It is blood...fresh human blood.

Fane shifts his course without thinking. All that matters is healing Roseline. If she can feed, they might stand a chance. He follows the scent into unfamiliar territory. If he had been thinking rationally, Fane would have instantly realized why he has never been in this part of the woods before, but his terror overrides sanity.

The stone wall before him poses little challenge as he scales over it. His feet land with a soft whisper on the snowy grass. His is racing ahead before his mind even realizes he is on the ground.

A small, darkened hole appears and Fane races right into it. His feet plod on the hard dirt floor. The scent is getting stronger as he pushes forward, calling on energy reserves that he hasn't been forced to use in ages.

The second he steps into the light, he knows it's a trap. A glint of steel shoots out from the dark and narrowly misses his neck. Fane dives to the right, curling his body around Roseline as he rolls back to his feet.

A sword wedges into the stone overhead, deep enough that a human would struggle to pull it free. It's a good thing that won't be a problem for him.

"I'm sorry, my love." Fane kisses Roseline's feverish forehead and lays her on the bare floor. He hates to leave her, fearful that she might be attacked while she is helpless, but he has little choice. He must keep his attacker's gaze fixed on him until he can dispose of the human. At least blood will readily be available for Roseline.

An arrow whizzes past his ear as he yanks the sword from the wall and spins back out of sight. A narrow miss to be sure.

"I didn't expect *you* to come," a deep voice calls from the shadows.

Fane searches for the source of the voice. The sword and arrow came from two different directions, which means he has at least two attackers to draw out. "I thought I'd take a midnight stroll." He rolls along the ground to a nearby pillar. Each movement is visible for only a split second. He hopes it is enough to distract them away from Roseline.

"You were a fool to come, but I guess it is just as well. She will come for both of you."

Scrunching up his brow, Fane ponders the man's words. He knows the voice. Sorin has made it his life's mission to kill Fane and his family after that little Halloween incident ten years ago.

But what does he mean about both of them? Has another of his family been captured? He can't smell anyone. No big surprise since the human blood is overloading his senses. It is cool and refreshing, like the smell of a golf course after a spring rain. The mouthwatering aroma turns his stomach.

He refuses to become a monster like Vladimir or Lucien. The pull of human blood will not sway him, but it will give healing life to Roseline once he deals with Sorin.

"Don't you want to come out and play?" the throaty voice taunts.

Fane cocks his head. He can hear a heartbeat, but it is not alone. He listens and singles out five distinct heartbeats. One is to his right, perched up in the rafters of the dungeon. A second, racing rather quickly, is hiding just off to his left, tucked behind a half wall. His fear teases Fane's nose with its enticing scent. The animalistic predator in him rises to the surface but he instantly squelches it back down.

Two other heartbeats huddle together across the room. Fane risks a glance to see two kids locked in a cell. He doesn't stop to wonder why they are caged as he throws himself to the side, kicking off the stone wall. Fane flips over the half wall, startling its young occupant. An arrow spirals toward him but flies wide as Fane lands on his toes and scales the pillar before him.

Once he is in position high above Sorin, Fane gets a view of the room. Twenty feet below him is the last heartbeat. Now he can understand why it is slowly fading. A boy, his face rolled away, is slowly bleeding out. His body is a mass of small incisions to allow a slow trickle of blood to pool on the ground below.

Fane grits his teeth, angered by the waste of the boy's precious blood. Roseline desperately needs it. Then it hits him. Fury curls like a venomous snake in the pit of his stomach. The boy is the trap meant for Roseline.

He gnashes his teeth at Sorin's cruelty. If he had not been so desperate to heal Roseline, he never would have followed the scent. How could he have been so stupid?

"Do you like my little party favor?" Sorin asks.

A whimper below catches Fane's attention. His gaze drills into the girl trapped in the cell. She clings desperately to a boy whose facial features greatly resemble her own. The girl's frightened eyes are locked onto the bleeding boy on the platform. Something flickers in the back of his mind. Recognition? Perhaps. She does look oddly familiar.

"Come now." Sorin shifts in his perch. He searches for his enemy but can't find any trace of him. This makes Sorin visibly ill at ease. "Don't you want a taste? Just one little bite."

Fane licks his lips, struggling against the sudden urge to do just that. He shakes his head and silently scolds himself for being so weak. "It won't work, Sorin. The boy doesn't entice me."

"Then why are you here?" he taunts back. "Surely you smell something you like."

Yes. He likes it all right. Far more than he should.

Rising to see over the half wall, Fane spies Roseline's pale form. Blood has begun to seep out from beneath her. It won't be long until it trails into Sorin's line of sight. He must move quickly.

"So what do you propose?" Fane asks, leaping down from his perch. He stretches out his hand, letting his fingers graze Sorin's cheek as he passes.

Sorin jerks back so violently that he nearly topples from his perch. Foul curses drift down from above as he motions frantically.

An audible gasp nearby shakes Fane's concentration. He glances to the side only to meet the girl's furious gaze. "You," she shrieks, rising to her feet. "What have you done with Rose?"

That is all it takes for Sorin and the boy to attack. Fane ducks as arrows fly. One plants firmly in his calf as he dives out of the way. He howls with pain as he rips the metal tip from his leg. He rolls back to his feet but favors his injured leg. This will even out the odds far more than he would have liked.

"Not quite so fast now, are you?" Sorin crows.

The boy is on the move. Fane listens as his heartbeat drums loudly, masking the sound of his feet on the stone floor.

"Watch out." The boy in the cell yells just as Sorin launches himself from his perch.

Fane waits until the last second before ducking to the right. Sorin screams as his ankle crunches under his weight. The boy darts from his hiding place but slides to a halt as he watches his uncle stumble.

"Did you forget that you're human?" Fane laughs, approaching Sorin slowly. The older man backs up, wincing as his ankle buckles beneath him. "That's the nice thing about being me," he laughs, jumping on both of his feet. "I heal quickly."

Sorin's eyes blaze with fury. "You won't when I cut off your head."

Fane cocks his head to the side, tapping his lips as he pretends to think it over. "Well, no. That might ruin my day."

The boy starts to inch forward but jerks back when Fane glances at him. "If you want to live, I'd stay right where you are."

"Don't listen to him," Sorin roars. "Kill him."

Fane glances back at the boy, his eyes narrowing. "Hey. Don't I know you?" The boy pales. Fane snaps his fingers. "You're that boy I ran into at that stupid dance. I thought you looked familiar."

"So, you're the one he sent to spy on Roseline." Fane's eyes darken with anger as the truth washes over him. His pulse rises as he braces for a fight. "I should kill you where you stand."

"No!" the girl in the cell screams. "He's not like his uncle."

Fane glances behind him. Now he begins to understand why she looks familiar. "You're the girl from the dance, the one I pushed aside," he says, more to himself than anyone else. His eyes flicker toward William and a shadow of anger drapes over his face. Oh yes, this one he remembers.

"Yeah and I've still got the bump to prove it," Sadie grumbles, unconsciously rubbing the sore spot. The swelling has mostly gone down but the bruise will linger for days. "Where's Rose? What have you done with her?"

Fane blinks, shocked by the concern he hears in the young girl's voice. "I didn't do anything to her."

"You kidnapped her!" she cries shrilly.

Sadly, Fane shakes his head. "No. I mean...I went to find her...but she wanted to come back."

Her shock hits him like a battering ram in his gut. "But her husband...she must have known he would be furious."

"Of course she did," Fane spits, disliking the way his guilt tastes on his tongue. He could have done things different...should have. "But she wouldn't risk that human's life."

The boy rises to stand next to his sister. "Gabriel?"

Fane nods. His stomach churns with acid. "Yeah. That's the one she was trying to protect."

Sorin's nephew shifts around to Fane's front, his eyes searching for some sign of trickery. His crossbow lowers slightly. "Roseline was trying to save Gabriel?"

Fane laughs bitterly. "You act like that surprises you. Didn't you spend any time with her? She's the most selfless person to ever walk this earth—" he trails off as his gaze flickers to where Roseline lies. "And now she's dying."

The girl cries out, covering her mouth with trembling hands. Her brother embraces his sister but is helpless to do anything. The nephew, on the other hand, follow Fane's gaze and notices a pale slip of white. "She's here?"

Fane nods reluctantly. His eyes mark Sorin's every breath, every twitch. If he takes one step toward Roseline, Fane will rip his throat out.

"What is wrong with her?" the boy asks, rising on his toes to try to see her.

"She was punished, as she knew she would be, but she went anyways. She was trying to save you." Fane looks to the brother and sister in the cage. "Vladimir would have come after you if he ever knew you existed. This was her way of saving you."

The green-eyed boy mulls this over. His crossbow slips lower. "Bring her out here," he commands.

Shooting a warning glare in Sorin's direction, Fane reaches Roseline in two bounds. He walks carefully with her out into the light. The girl wails at the sight of Roseline's broken body.

"What have you done to her?" the boy gasps, horrified at the sight before him.

"That is what a vampire does, Nicolae. Remember your training. Kill him while he's distracted," Sorin orders as he hops toward the nearest wall. His ankle is swelling at an alarming rate.

Sorin's nephew looks torn. The evidence is right in front of him and yet the grief shining from Fane's eyes belay that proof. "Can you help her?"

Fane's tormented gaze meets his and a flicker of hope flares to life. "Yes. She needs blood." His gaze darts to the platform where the shirtless boy's blood drips uselessly onto the floor. "Without it she will die."

Nicolae blanches. He raises his crossbow, aiming it directly into Fane's heart. "So you are a vampire."

Sadly, Fane shakes his head. "No, I'm not a vampire. I'm not evil enough to live up to that myth."

"Well, what the heck is that supposed to mean?" the girl cries, pressing against the bars. Fane can see that it is killing her to be in there, locked away, unable to help her friend.

"It means I'm not the sadistic murderer Sorin assumes I am," Fane snarls, glaring at the man in mention. Sorin rolls his eyes, clenching his teeth against the pain. The bone is pressing tightly against the skin of his ankle. A bad break, but he will live.

"Then what are you?" the brother asks, growing bold behind the bars.

"I'm an immortal."

Nicolae frowns. "If you're immortal then why is Roseline dying? Her wounds—" he breaks off as his stomach rolls. He has seen death and more than enough blood to fill a thousand horror films, but he has never seen such a mangled body. Roseline's flesh is actually hanging from her body, bloody strips clinging to Fane's hands. It is a miracle that she is still alive, if death really is an option.

"Blood is life...even for us. She has lost too much. She needs more."

"Take mine."

Fane's gaze follows the hoarse whispers to the boy atop the platform. It is the first time he has spoken. With great effort, the boy rolls his head and locks his glazed eyes on Fane. "Save her. Please."

"You," Fane gasps. "This is a trap."

He curls Roseline into his chest and crouches low, preparing to fight his way out. He scans the dark recesses of the room, sure that others must lie in wait to ambush him, but he hears nothing. Sorin's greed and pride have blinded him to his need for his hunters on this night.

"No," Nicolae cries, stretching out a hand toward Fane. "Wait. It's not what you think."

Sorin's harsh laughter echoes throughout the room. "It's exactly what you think, vampire. You have been set up. Elaborate, eh?"

Fane vision shifts into red hues as his blood boils. "Before this night is through, I will have your head."

Sorin grins, leaning heavily on the sword in his hand. "Why wait? I'm right here."

Fane's arms flinches, desperate to pummel Sorin, but he still holds Roseline in his arms. Nicolae shifts, pulling Fane's attention away.

"Whose side are you on, boy? Choose now," Fane growls.

Nicolae casts a worried glance at the girl in the cage. Her lips tremble as she looks back. "Help her, Nicolae."

His shoulders straighten as he faces off with Fane. "Will you let Sadie live?"

"You fool," Sorin sneers. "You're making a deal with the devil. He'll rip her throat open as soon as he's done with us."

Nicolae refuses to look at his uncle. He takes a stand for the first time in his life. "Well?"

Fane nods. "You will all go free except Sorin. He's mine."

"Please," Gabriel begs. His voice is barely above a whisper. "There isn't much time."

"Will she kill him?" Sadie asks, glancing at her best friend. Roseline's blood drips onto the floor, pooling around Fane's feet.

"More than likely," Fane replies evenly. He doesn't try to hide his remorse at the thought. No one knows the effects his death will have on Roseline more than him. Saving her life by taking his might destroy her, but at least she will be alive.

"Do it," Gabriel croaks, struggling to lift his arm to Fane. "Save her."

Glancing to make sure Sorin cannot reach him, Fane leaps onto the platform. He lowers Roseline's head to place her open mouth directly under the blood dripping down the leather straps but it's much too slow. Gabriel's life is waning too quickly.

"What's happening?" Sadie cries, desperate to know the details. Her head cranes as far as it will go but she can't see anything.

Nicolae swallows back his revulsion. "He's feeding her."

William gulps down the bile rising in his throat. He clenches Sadie tightly to his side. "Is it working?"

Nicolae shakes his head, unable to look away from Roseline. "No. She's not moving."

Fane shakes her unconscious form, his desperation mounting as her pulse dips to comatose levels. "Please, Roseline...don't leave me."

"How touching," a sinister voice snakes out from the darkness. All eyes turn toward the tunnel entrance, each one widening in terror at the sight of Vladimir and Lucien. "It looks like the party has already started," Vladimir croons, stroking the sword hilt at his side. His eyes gleam black, maniacal and bloodthirsty.

"Let's have some fun, brother," Lucien grins.

Forty-Four

" Take her," Fane roars as he shoves Roseline's limp body into Nicolae's arms. He doesn't take time to pray that he has made the right decision in trusting the boy as he leaps from the platform. Soaring high into the air, Fane arches his back and lands just out of reach of Vladimir's sword.

"Fane," he snarls. "I believe you took something tonight that belongs to me."

With his hand curled tightly around the hilt of his sword, Fane's lips peel back into a triumphant grin. "I think you're mistaken. I took Roseline many years ago."

Vladimir's eyes darken and a jolt of dread washes down Fane's spine. Maybe that wasn't the best thing to say. "How dare you touch what's mine!"

The clash of swords shakes Nicolae out of his paralysis. It is hard to tear his gaze away from the man Sorin has called Dracula ever since he was a young schoolboy. This man brutalized his parents. Nicolae's blood begins to boil.

"Watch out!" Sadie screams.

Nicolae ducks as his years of training kick in. He whirls out of the way of the oncoming sword. It whistles past as it grazes his ear. A tuft of hair slices away from his head, evidence of how close he came to losing his life.

"Behind you!" William shouts

Without thinking, Nicolae lunges to the side. He lets Roseline slip from his arms as he cartwheels away. Lucien growls in frustration as Nicolae flips over his head, snatching the crossbow as he goes. As soon as his feet touch the ground, Nicolae ducks behind a pillar.

He tries to squelch out his desperation as he fights to remember everything Sorin taught him—speed, agility, cunning. Nicolae knows he is no match for Lucien but he has to try to avenge his parents' death. Hopefully Fane won't kill Vladimir before he gets a chance at him as well.

Sadie burrows into William's embrace as she watches Nicolae's dance with death. She has never seen anything so mesmerizing before. Lucien's eyes are the purest evil she has ever seen. If Satan became flesh and blood, his name would be Lucien Enescue. And to think he is Gabriel's father!

"Nicolae, the keys!" she cries as she reaches her hand through the bars.

Three arrows streak through the air toward Lucien, each aimed perfectly to force him behind a pillar. Nicolae tucks his crossbow close and dives for the key ring that was knocked loose from his belt during the fighting.

Kicking off the wall, Nicolae spins and chucks the keys toward Sadie. He barely has a chance to appreciate William's skillful catch when a sword flashes in front of him, slicing through his shirt to leave a shallow line from sternum to waist.

He grimaces as he pushes the pain aside and aims an arrow for Lucien's heart. With a grunt, Lucien spins away but comes face to face with Sorin. For all the old man's bluster, he doesn't hesitate as he engages Lucien.

Sounds of the battle ring out around the room. The clanging of steel is nearly deafening. Fane fights to keep up with Vladimir's flashing sword while Sorin finds himself backed into a corner. The instant he is free from attack, Nicolae leaps onto the platform and grabs a dagger from his boot, slicing through the bindings that hold Gabriel to the table.

Sadie slides to a stop at his side. Her jeans quickly soak up Gabriel's blood from the floor. "Help me get him into the cell."

Gabriel's pained cry is weak as they drag him across the room. Fane catches a glimpse of their progress but instantly regrets his lack of concentration. Vladimir crows with pleasure as his sword plants itself firmly in Fane's side. Fane staggers backward, clutching his wound.

William rushes out of the cell. He stoops to cradle Rose in his arms. He tries not to think about the feel of her raw flesh against his skin as he rushes back into their safe haven. Sadie and Nicolae pass by him and lay a nearly unconscious Gabriel on the ground beside her.

"Take care of them," Nicolae shouts as he races back to the cell door.

"No!" Sadie lunges for him but comes up short as he slams the door in her face. Her fingers cling to his shirt. Blood stains her hands. She peels back his shirt to reveal his wound. "You're hurt."

"I'm fine." Keeping the pain from his voice isn't easy but he refuses to let her know how much it hurts.

"Let me help you," Sadie pleads. "I'll claw their eyes out."

Nicolae smiles sadly. "I know you would, but Roseline needs you."

Sadie's lower lip began to tremble. "But we need you. I…I need you," she whimpers as tears well up.

"Did you just say—" Nicolae's eyes widen in surprise as he grasps her hand. "We will talk about this later."

He squeezes her hand before rushing off to join the fray. Sorin yelps as Lucien's blade slices through his arm. His sword clatters to the stone floor. A wicked grin stretches along Lucien's lips as he kicks the weapon out of reach.

Nicolae frantically searches for another sword and spies a glint of steel poking out of the shadows. "Yes!" He dives to the side of the room and clasps the sword in hand. It is weighty, much heavier than the swords he uses in practice. Upon closer inspection, Nicolae realizes this is the blood-tipped sword from Sorin's wall. He must have gone back for it. That's why he left Nicolae to leave the blood trail.

He doesn't take the time to ponder why the sword made its way to the dungeon when he tosses it to his uncle. "Sorin, catch!"

His uncle's fingers latch onto the familiar weapon. He bellows as he leaps at his enemy. Lucien twists and twirls, ducking and dodging as he fights Sorin blade and Nicolae's crossbow.

Fane grits his teeth as he pushes Vladimir past Nicolae. The fighting is intense as he struggles to remain focused. The pain in his side is agonizing, his strength weakening as blood seeps from his wound. He has no chance of winning this fight. Vladimir is too skilled, too quick, and he knows it.

"I should kill you slowly," Vladimir snarls, lunging once more. Fane parries and whirls just out of reach. "I will settle for having your head mounted on my bedroom wall so you can watch as I reclaim your precious Roseline over and over again."

Fane waits for Vladimir's advance before he grasps a chain overhead and swings through the air. His legs lock, braced for impact. Vladimir realizes Fane's intentions too late to stop his forward momentum as his sword slices the air just under Fane.

Vladimir grunts as Fane's feet slams into his chest, toppling him end over end.

"Fane!" Sadie shrieks. He spins around and launches himself toward the cell. He nearly faints with relief when he sees Roseline safely locked away, but his joy is short lived. "I think Gabriel is dead."

Vladimir roars like a rampaging lion as he shoots across the room, sword lowered and aimed directly at the betrayer's heart. Fane spins out of the way with a second to spare. His ears train on the cell, desperate to hear four heartbeats. Two of them race madly, pumping blood with dizzying intensity. One is slow but definitely there. The fourth is horrifyingly weak.

"He's alive...but only just," Fane grunts, knocking Vladimir's sword to the side then instantly whirls around to parry his next blow. "You have to wake Roseline up. She has to drink directly from his artery."

Sadie meets William's terrified gaze. They look down at their friends; both appear lifeless on the cold stone floor. "Help me!" Sadie screeches, yanking William down next to her.

"How do we wake her up?" William asks. How is he supposed to know how to save a vampire, an immortal, or whatever the heck she is?

"I don't know." Her desperation is beginning to melt into sheer panic. "Slap her." William hesitates, horrified at the idea of hitting any girl, let alone a dying one. "Oh, move over, you big lug."

Sadie pulls her arm back and brings it down with more force than she knew she possessed. Her hand smacks against Roseline's head, tossing it forcefully to the side.

"Easy, Sadie," William hisses. "I think her neck is already broken."

Rose groans but doesn't wake. "Should I do it again?" Sadie asks hesitantly. She doesn't want to hit Rose but she will if that's what it takes to save her life.

Without waiting for William's response, Sadie slaps her again. This time Rose's eyes flutter open.

"Oh, thank god." Sadie exclaims, shaking her shoulders. "Rose, you need to eat."

Her mending arm feebly tries to push Sadie away, but she is too weak to fight. William grabs Gabriel and whispers a prayer of thanks that he is unconscious for what comes next. He places Gabriel's arm over Rose's mouth and waits.

The scent of fresh blood hits her hard. She sniffs the air as saliva pools in her mouth. Her lips close around the wound, sucking deeply. A contented sigh escapes her lips as blood slowly trickles into her mouth.

"Is it working?" Fane shouts, narrowly missing another precision lunge. He throws himself horizontally down the length of the solid oak slab. The maneuver gives him a couple seconds to breathe before Vladimir is on top of him again.

"She's drinking…I think," William calls.

Vladimir casts a murderous glare at William. He shrinks back. "Sadie, are you sure these bars will hold?"

She looks up to find Vladimir's gaze on her. She stares evil in the eye and shudders. "I don't know. That looks like one really ticked-off dude."

"Hurry," Fane shouts, launching himself at Vladimir.

Sadie bounces up and down next to Rose, finding it freakishly odd that she is cheering on her friend. She's going to need years of therapy over this one.

Roseline grunts in disgust, weakly tossing Gabriel's arm away. A trickle of blood seeps from her mouth as she cries out in pain. Her body shakes as a spasm hit her. Bones splinter, cracking loudly in the small space. William doubles over, losing every ounce of the pretzels he devoured earlier on the plane.

Sadie holds her friend as Rose shrieks in agony. "Fane, something is wrong!"

"Gabriel's barely breathing." William wipes his mouth. He moves forward and cradles Gabriel's limp form under his arm. William tears the bottom of his shirt and uses it to stanch the blood flow from Gabriel's arm, noticing for the first time the tattoo running along his arm, but it's a bit too late for first aid. "I think he's almost dead."

Fane grunts as he hurls a torch at Vladimir. The ashes light Vladimir's cloak on fire. He dances about, beating his clothes as Fane pauses to survey the room. Sorin's arm is shattered and Nicolae's thigh and chest sport nasty gashes. This is not going well. Vladimir and Lucien are outmaneuvering them.

And then…everything stops. Fane whirls around, sniffing the air. Vladimir and Lucien lower their swords, their eyes light with bloodlust.

"No!" Fane cries as the two brothers rush the cage. Their battle with Fane and Sorin is long forgotten as the scent of newly spilled blood drives them into a frenzy. With fresh wounds lining their bodies, the brothers are desperate to rejuvenate their strength.

Sadie grimaces as she drops the dagger she grabbed from the platform. It clatters to the floor, splattering blood on her leg. Sound echoes in her ear, as if she is in a tunnel. Fresh blood pours from her neck, staining her shirt. She is barely aware of the guttural screams nearby or William's desperate cries.

Rose appears before her with pained eyes filled with need. Sadie rolls her neck to the side and waits. Her breath hitches as Rose's lips surround the wound. She expects pain but instead feels an odd tugging sensation. Then the floodgates open and Sadie sags. Her energy drains quickly.

"Let her go," William cries, dropping Gabriel to the floor as he tries desperately to pull his sister away from Rose, but it was too late. The bloodlust has taken over.

Rose hisses at William, her aqua eyes blazing with fierce possessiveness. "William, back away, now!" Fane shouts, racing across the room. "Don't try to stop her while she's feeding. She'll kill you."

William backs away in horror. Pain flares on his neck and he whips around. Lucien grins as he pulls back a bloody fingernail. He sniffs William's blood, closing his eyes as he the aromatic scent curls in his nose. Lucien's head lolls to the side as he licks Vladimir's finger, savoring the taste.

Using his hand to staunch the blood, William backs away and trips over Gabriel. His gaze locks onto Lucien, horrified as he watches Vladimir fight his brother for a taste of William's blood. "Oh, that's just wrong," he groans, feeling his stomach flip flop again.

William spies a glint of silver just before the bloodlust in Lucien's eyes is replaced by disbelief as a thin red line appears on his neck. A tiny trail of blood slips from the line, dropping onto his bright white shirt. Glazed eyes stare at William as Lucien's legs give out on him. His body slumps to the ground. Vladimir's piercing screams rise in intensity as his brother's head separates from his body and rolls across the grimy floor. It halts at the base of the platform in the remnants of Gabriel's blood.

Sorin stands a foot beyond, grinning triumphantly at his fallen foe. "That's for my sister," he shouts, spitting into Lucien's lifeless face. Blood seeps freely from the horrid neck wound. A thick pool of crimson blood stains the stone, seeping into the ancient cracks, mixing with Gabriel's shed lifeblood.

"You're a dead man," Vladimir rages as he attacks Sorin with lightning quick reflexes. Sorin barely has time to think before Vladimir chops down at him from overhead. Sorin fumbles backward, sure this will be his last moment on Earth, but Nicolae snatches up Lucien's fallen sword and parries the blow.

Fane watches in amazement as the humans fight against Vladimir. Lucien is gone, leaving only one vengeful immortal left, but rage makes him twice as lethal. "Let me in," Fane cries to William as he arrives at the cell door in one bound.

William looks at him with distrust. "How do I know you won't bite me?" he asks, cradling his wounded neck in his hand. Fane has to admit William does smell good, but his concern for Roseline overrules his discomfort.

"If you don't let me in your sister will die."

Sadie's face is ashen and her eyes have rolled back into her head. Roseline clings to her neck, desperate to take the blood she needs to live. Survival has tossed sanity out the window.

"Please. I can save both of them," Fane pleads. He glances over his shoulder to make sure Vladimir is still busy. Sorin and Nicolae have skillfully backed him into the far corner, but Fane has no doubt Vladimir will rebound. He always does.

William stumbles forward and shoves the key through the bars. Fane quickly inserts the skeleton key and yanks open the door. He throws himself at Roseline's feet. "Roseline, listen to me. You have to stop now. You are killing your friend."

Roseline growls at Fane, unwilling to let go. William paces behind him, terrified of losing his sister. Fane tries again. "Roseline, my love...I don't want to hurt you."

She yanks Sadie around, nearly pulling the girl's hips out of socket as she fights to keep her prey from Fane. Roseline is not going to share.

"Hand me that torch," Fane orders, holding out his hand.

William finds a metal sconce on the wall and yanks the torch free. He tosses it into Fane's waiting hands.

"I'm really sorry," Fane whispers as he brings the torch down over Roseline's head. She retracts her teeth from Sadie's neck as she turns to fight.

Fane catches her attack in his midsection and rolls with her. Roseline rises up and claws at Fane's face and bare arms. Her eyes are blackened with thirst. "Roseline...it's me."

She snarls at him, gnashing her teeth as she goes for his throat. Fane knocks her aside, holding out his hands to keep her at bay. A shrill scream jerks their attention off each other.

"Uncle," Nicolae cries, rushing to Sorin's side.

Vladimir shouts in triumph as Sorin falls to the ground. Lifeless eyes stare at the ceiling above. A sword lies buried in his side, nearly cleaving him in half. Nicolae howls in agony.

"One down," Vladimir taunts.

Rising to his feet, Nicolae grasps the sword firmly in his hands. His attack is swift and brutal, forcing Vladimir to retreat in search of another weapon. He dives for Sorin's fallen weapon and leaps to his feet to prepare for Nicolae's attack.

"Fane?" Roseline whispers, blinking rapidly as she glances around her. "Where am I?"

He takes her in his arms, cradling her as she weeps. Most of her wounds have sealed over; internal tears have begun to knit back together, but there are some wounds blood cannot fix.

"Shh. It's okay, I'm here," he soothes. "I won't let anyone hurt you."

Roseline sinks into his embrace and lets the world fall away, even if only for a moment.

Forty-Five

Nicolae grunts as the tip of Vladimir's sword buries deep into his arm. He grits his teeth, summoning the waning strength in his right arm, and tosses his sword into the other hand. Vladimir's triumphant grin melts away as Nicolae confidently approaches. With a clash of steel, Nicolae not only holds his own, he sets Vladimir on the run.

"Oh, my gosh. Sadie!" Roseline screams, diving for her friend the instant she sees her.

"Back off," William snarls as he shoves Roseline.

She rears back, shocked by the venom in his voice. "William...what's wrong?"

"You. You're what's wrong." He shakes his head, disgusted with everything. Sadie knew what she was getting into the moment she sliced her neck. "You needed blood and she was stupid enough to offer it."

"No. Oh no," she wails as she hangs her head. "Oh, Sadie, you stupid girl. I could have killed you."

"You probably have," William mutters as he strokes the damp hair from Sadie's face.

"Fane?" She is too panicked to concentrate. Her mind too fuzzy. Her body is still buzzing from the fresh blood that races through her veins-Sadie's blood.

"She will be fine. You stopped soon enough."

"Really?" William growls at Fane. "'Cause it sure looks like she's dead to me."

He has a point. Sadie has lost all color in her face. Her breathing is so shallow it's hard to tell if her chest is moving.

"Her pulse is slow but strong. I promise she will recover," Fane assures him. "Her neck wound is already healing from Roseline's saliva."

Roseline closes her eyes. Tears flow freely as she strokes her friend's hand. She never wanted this. She thought by leaving she would save her friends the pain of discovering her secret. Now look where they have ended up.

A clash of swords catches her attention. She gasps, noticing for the first time who is fighting her husband. "Is that…Nicolae?"

"Yeah. Guess you're not the only one with secrets," William says coldly.

She watches in amazement as Nicolae twirls out of Vladimir's grip with ease. She glances over at Fane and sees that his thoughts mirror her own—he is good, deadly good.

"So he finally came out then," Roseline mutters.

"You knew?" William gasps. Fane's brow furrows at this development.

"Of course I did," Roseline says. "Do you honestly think he'd let a monster like me around your sister?"

William glances down at Sadie, his tears fall onto her pasty cheek. "I think he loves her."

Roseline nods. "He always has. He's been trying to protect her all this time…from me." Her voice cracks as she looks away.

"Oh, no!" She throws herself onto her knees as she crawls to Gabriel's side. Her hands flit over his face. His scarred chest and gaping wounds fuels a fire deep within her soul. "What happened to him?"

"He was bait," Fane replies without emotion.

Heat floods her body as she turns a fierce glare onto Fane. "For me?"

He nods and looks away. Her enraged howl curls his lips into a smile. Sorin was a fool to awaken the warrior within Roseline. Vladimir created her to be lethal, a killing machine that once turned on will not stop. Fane has no idea what she is capable of. No one does.

She holds Gabriel to her chest, fighting to calm the rage swirling within. Like an acid cloud, it poisons her mind and spills over into her nerves. She closes her eyes, fighting to still her wrath long enough to find Gabriel's heartbeat. Her eyes pop open.

"How is he still alive?" she asks Fane. "He should have been dead hours ago."

Fane shrugs, completely at a loss for an answer. He has been wondering the same thing. No human can lose that much blood and survive but, then again, Gabriel isn't entirely human. He is Lucien's son, after all.

Unable to bear the pain in Roseline's tortured gaze, he rises. "I should probably go help—" his words cut off as blood gurgles from his lips. A crimson stream stains his pale skin as it drips from his chin and splatters onto his shoes.

"No!" Roseline cries out as a sword pierces through Fane's chest. In a hacking motion, it rises dangerously close to his heart.

Fane jerks to the right when the sword pulls back and changes its deadly course. Vladimir appears over his shoulder and he shoves the blade deep. The new angle splinters his sternum but saves his heart. A sickening gurgle erupts from Fane's throat as a bubble of blood bursts, splattering Roseline and William.

William cries out as he frantically wipes his face, smearing the blood more than he manages to remove it. The sword jerks to a halt as Nicolae attacks from behind, forcing Vladimir to retreat to find a new weapon. Roseline must release Gabriel to help Fane. She sets Gabriel gently back on the ground and backs away. Her vision tints red around the edges as she steps up to Fane. "Are you okay?"

"I will be—" he chokes, and his knees buckle and he falls to the floor. Roseline grasps his arm in time to ease him onto his side before sword connects with the ground. She kneels by his side and places her hand behind his back. "Just get it over with," he grunts.

Without hesitation, she yanks the sword from his chest. Fane's scream wrenches at her heart but she clamps off her emotions. She eases him onto his back and turns to William. "When I leave you need to lock that door. No matter what happens, don't open it."

William's eyes are as wide as saucers; his mouth fills with the foul taste from a second wave of bile rising in his throat. "What about Fane?"

"Keep him comfortable till I get back," she replies in a clipped tone

"You mean he's not going to die?" William gasps, horrified at the reality of how much it takes to kill an immortal.

"No, but I bet he wishes he could." She slips off her bloodied cloak and tosses it to William. "Use this to stop the bleeding. I'll be back soon."

She crouches low and leaps through the opening. She spins in midair and slams the door shut. The lock clangs into place before her feet touch the ground.

"Holy crap," William gasps. "I didn't know she could do that."

"You should see her when she's really angry," Fane wheezes sarcastically. He winces at the burning in his lungs.

Roseline ignores their quips and she focuses only on Vladimir. He has yet to realize she has joined the fight. That's good. She still has the advantage.

Blood drips from her matted hair, splattering her shredded dress. It hangs in strips along her body, revealing her gruesome wounds. Bruises bloom along her stomach and abdomen as the internal bleeding recedes; strips of skin regenerate as the old sloughs off.

She rocks onto the balls of her feet as she watches the battle unfold. The sword swings back and forth like a pendulum, counting down the seconds until she will engage her husband for the first time ever.

Vladimir is the stronger of the two; Nicolae has speed on his side, but even this is starting to betray him. His forehead drips with sweat as he lunges and parries. Blood seeps from several wounds. He is forced to favor the one on his right leg, which leaves him at a disadvantage, one that Vladimir is skillfully playing to. It is only a matter of time before Nicolae makes a mistake.

"Vladimir!" she screams, planting her feet as she raises the sword her husband carved Fane with.

Her husband bashes the hilt of his sword into Nicolae's face. He doesn't even pause to enjoy the spray of blood that flies from Nicolae's nose as he turns to face her. "Ah, I see you are whole again…and looking as lovely as ever." Vladimir's frosty voice sends chills racing up her spine.

"No thanks to you," she hisses, clasping the sword tightly in her hand. Her knuckles turn white as they pop under the strain. This is a battle she refuses to lose.

"This is all your fault, you know," he says, waving his hands around the room. His gaze flickers toward the cell. "Your friends and your lover are all in pretty bad shape because of you."

"You're poisonous words won't work on me this time, Vladimir," Roseline growls. She won't let them.

He tsks, shaking his head. "That's no way to speak to your husband."

Roseline snarls at him, raising her sword into the air. "I want a divorce."

Vladimir's cold black eyes narrow. "You belong to me, Roseline Enescue."

Her aqua eyes flame with rage. "My name is Roseline Dragomir!" she screams, launching herself across the room. Her lips peel back from her teeth as she strikes. The muscles in her arms quiver as their swords clash. Sparks fly as she grinds her sword against his, running it all the way to the hilt. She snarls, spitting in Vladimir's face before she dips and knocks his feet out from under him.

His enraged cry follows her as she drops her sword and leaps onto the wall. Her fingers latch onto a pair of manacles. She runs up the wall, coiling the chains loosely around her arm.

"Get down here!" Vladimir roars from below.

"Coming, dear," she growls as she launches off the wall. Roseline arcs around the center of the room and spins back toward him. He braces, his sword ready to cut her down, but Roseline releases her hold on the chains at the last second and flips over his head.

Vladimir cries out as the heavy chains uncoil and slam into him, knocking him off his feet. Roseline sprints for her sword as Vladimir rises. His gaze is murderous as he spits out teeth and blood. "You will pay for that."

For years, she balked at her training, shied away from embracing the anger that always seethes just under the surface, but for the first time, she latches hold of it.

"But I thought you like it rough."

With a wild scream, Vladimir attacks. Roseline bends backward, narrowly missing his first lunge, but is ready for the second. She spins, in a whirlwind of blood, and slices clean through

Vladimir's sword. The pieces of his sword clatter uselessly to the floor.

"How did you—" Vladimir flips backward to the middle of the room, in search of another weapon. Roseline has to move fast. She crouches low and shoots up into the air, whirling over Vladimir's head. The bottom of her dress grazes his face, obscuring his vision for a split second, but it is enough.

"Roseline," Nicolae shouts, tossing his crossbow high into the air.

The instant her fingers wrap around the weapon, Roseline's foot smashes into Vladimir's face. Blood spews from his lips as his four front teeth are ground into dust. He sprawls on his back, head smashing against the stone floor. The sharp crack of his skull fracturing fuels Roseline's rage.

She kneels above him, trapping him with her knee on his chest. "This is for my sister," she says with air of calm, letting loose the arrow.

It pierces through his rib cage, grazing his heart. Blood seeps into his chest cavity. His eyes narrow with fury as he listens to his own heart struggle to beat.

"Playtime is over," Vladimir growls. He tosses her end over end as he leaps to his feet. He grips the arrow protruding from his chest and roars as he tears it out. The instant his gaze shifts from her she knows she won't make it in time. She barely has time to blink before the arrow slams into Nicolae's chest.

"It's me or him now, Roseline," Vladimir taunts, clutching his chest. "Your choice."

She snarls at him as she turns and leaps to Nicolae's side. Her hands feel around the wound. She breathes a sigh of relief as she realizes the arrow has missed all vital organs. "Stupid," she grunts as she turns to catch Vladimir's grin before he bolts for the exit. "He missed on purpose!"

Nicolae's groan pulls her attention back. His face pinches as he writhes on the floor. "This is going to hurt," she whispers in his ear. Without any warning, she snaps the end of the arrow and pulls the spearhead from his back.

Roseline's arm slices through the air, hurling the broken steel tipped arrow at Vladimir's back. The blood coated arrowhead burrows into Vladimir but it doesn't stop him as he dives for the tunnel. He is gone.

She should probably go after him. It would be easy to take him out now that he is injured and weary from battle, but her friends need her.

Dipping low, Roseline pulls Nicolae into her arms. She carries him to the cage and grimaces at the sight of her war-torn friends.

Fane's eyes are closed as he leans against the cool wall. Already the blood has begun to clot around the wound. Healing will be a slow and painful process, one that Roseline does not envy him. Fane's immortal blood will eventually seal over the lesion, forever hiding the evidence of his injury.

Sadie's color has returned slightly and her breathing is much less labored than before. William cuddles up to her, holding her in his arms. His face is streaked with blood; tears wash winding trails of grime from his face.

Gabriel's heart continues to beat at a snail's pace but Roseline has no idea why or even how. Each breath he takes is a miracle.

Roseline carefully settles Nicolae next to Fane, propping him up on his good side. Despite her great care not to jostle him, Nicolae still cries out in pain. "William, throw me your shirt."

Without thinking, William strips. His skin pimples against the frigid draft pouring from the open tunnel. "Hold this tightly over the wound," she commands.

Nicolae offers her a wry smile. "I didn't know you could fight like that."

She smirks. "And you never told me you were Sorin's nephew. I should have known. You're both stubborn mules!"

"Guess we both have our secrets." He winces and presses back into the wall.

"Thanks for keeping them alive," she whispers. "I owe you."

"Huh." He grins, tilting his head to the side. "I like the sound of that."

Roseline laughs as she squeezes his shoulder and hurries to Sadie's side. "Hey," she whispers as she drops next to her friend. Sadie's eyes flicker open. "How do you feel?"

"Like I've been trampled by a rabid elephant." Roseline's throat clenches. This is all her fault. If she had just kept her distance from Sadie in the beginning, none of this would have happened. "I've been thinking…" Sadie trails off, wincing as she pushed herself upright. "I'm thinking about going blonde next."

William stares at his sister in amazement. "You nearly died and all you can think about is your next hair color? Unbelievable."

Roseline smirks, shaking her head. "What's the theme this time?"

Sadie grin is a faint glimmer of her former self. "I'm thinking of going Christian."

William splutters, glancing at Roseline to see her reaction. When all he sees is a twinkle in her eyes, he reprimands Sadie. "You can't just 'go Christian.' It's a whole faith thing you know."

Sadie shrugs. "I'm thinking I might give God a try…you know, just in case," she whispers. Roseline refuses to think of what might have happened if Fane hadn't stopped her in time. Maybe Sadie is right. Getting on good terms with God is a great idea if Sadie is going to spend any more time around her.

Roseline pats her best friend's hand, grateful to feel warmth returning to her skin. "I think your mother will be proud."

Sadie grins, nodding weakly. Her smile fades as her eyes rolls toward Gabriel. "Is he dead?"

"No, not yet." Her heart shatters at the thought of losing him. "But it won't be long."

"Can you save him?" William asks. He might not have liked Gabriel much before they went on this harebrained adventure, but the guy has actually started to grow on him. If donating his blood for a transfusion can save his life, then William is all for it.

A tear slips down Roseline's cheek as she shakes her head. "He's too far gone. He shouldn't even be alive." Her voice cracks as pain ripples through her chest.

Fane slips an arm around her, pulling her close. Roseline buries her face in his chest, sobbing over the boy she should never have fallen in love with but will never be able to get over. How can she go on without him? Losing Gabriel will destroy her and Fane is the only one who truly understands that.

"Turn him," he whispers. His gaze fixes on the boy over her shoulder. It hurts far more to say the words then he could have imagined. As if he reached into his own chest and tore out his heart. This is a wound that Fane knows will never heal, but what choice does he have? He loves Roseline.

She rears back from his embrace, horrified at the thought. "I can't do that to him. I would rather die than let Gabriel suffer as we do," Roseline says.

Fane's handsome face melts into a resigned smile. "You've only suffered because you never had love."

"No," she whispers, grasping his hand. "We did have love...a long time ago."

Nodding, Fane wipes away her tears. "You know I will always love you."

He pulls Roseline into his arms and kisses her, sharing every ounce of his devotion in that one final kiss. He breaks away and lurches to his feet, unable to linger in the moment any longer. The pain is too raw. With one final glance at Roseline, Fane exits the cell and disappears into the shadows.

"He's gone," Sadie whispers. "Will he come back?"

"No," Roseline shakes her head. "Not for a very long time."

"Is it safe to leave?" William asks.

"It should be. Vladimir won't stick around now that he is injured. He needs to heal. I'd stay away from Brasov for a while though."

William shudders but nods as he wraps his arm around Sadie's back. They navigate the slippery floor, leaving Roseline behind. Neither one of them knows what decision she will make, but they know she needs to make it on her own.

Nicolae cups William's shirt to his wound as he rises. He darts one last glance back at Roseline before turning to follow behind Sadie and William. After everything he has witnesses tonight he can't decide if saving Gabriel would really be a bad thing. Surely, his uncle was wrong about some immortals. He was obviously wrong about them being vampires. Maybe they aren't all damned.

He watches as William helps Sadie to the tunnel that leads into the forest surrounding his home. He wants to follow, to be near Sadie, but there is something he has to do first.

Nicolae kneels at his uncle's side. He ignores the congealing blood and stares into the face of the man that has been the only family he's had since he lost his parents. "I will avenge your death, Uncle. I swear it."

He grasps Sorin's hand, pledging his oath. Tears fall unashamedly as he pulls his uncle's sword from his stiff hands. It is the sword that Sorin used to kill Lucien. "Vladimir is next."

Without another word, Nicolae turns his back on the gruesome scene in the dungeon. He vows this place will never be used again. As soon as the dust settles from tonight, he will blow up the entrance to the tunnel and seal Sorin into this eternal tomb. It is what he would have wanted.

Forty-Six

Warm tears stream from Roseline's bloodshot eyes. Her heart is broken and bleeding, torn in two directions. One is racing away from her, desperate to flee his self-inflicted agony after releasing her to love another. The second lies with only seconds remaining of life. She can hear the final beats of Gabriel's heart approaching.

Roseline dips low to brush her lips against his. "I'm so sorry, my love."

Epilogue

Gabriel moves through the dark, vacant of his body and yet somehow still tethered to it. If only the shadows will part so he can see. There is something he is supposed to be doing. Someone he is supposed to be looking for. Someone that needs him.

Rose.

Her name echoes through the dark, taunting him as he races ahead. His hands splay before him, desperately searching for a door that will lead him into the light. It has to be here, somewhere.

The pain from his wounds receded long ago. How long? He cannot remember. Time is meaningless here. Wherever here is.

Gabriel stops and listens. He can hear something. The sound is muffled, as if he is listening to it from under water. A girl is crying.

No. Please don't cry.

He wants to console her, to tell her that he is okay, but she can't hear him.

Rose?

Yes. It is her. He is sure of it. Even her heart wrenching sobs are delightful to his ears. He thought he would never see her again. And now he has found her—at last.

The sound changes. Something is happening. Oh, why can't he see her?

"I'm so sorry, my love."

Wait. What's wrong? There's nothing to be sorry for.

Gabriel whirls around and around, searching for her, but there is only darkness.

Rose!

His nose prickles. Something smells sweet. His mouth waters as saliva swirls in his mouth. What is that smell?

271

Gabriel feels something different. He can feel his body. Not the body that is trapped in this hell dimension. His real body. Real flesh and blood. Probably more flesh than blood now.

Something presses against his mouth. He fights to move his lips, to loosen his frozen tongue, but nothing happens. Then something wonderful drips into his mouth, oozing down the ridge of his tongue. He can hear Roseline's voice whispering an enchanting language. He feels a stirring in his soul.

The blood burns a trail down his throat, winding its fiery tendrils all the way to his belly. The warmth spreads, searing his skin as it shoots through his veins, into the recesses of his body. His toes begin to tingle. His fingers cramp, aching to move. Gabriel's mind whirls into action, frantically struggling to comprehend the changes in his body.

And then...the pain begins.

Continue the Series

Reckoning, Book II

Redemption, Book III

Evermore, Book IV

See how it all began...the Immortal Rose Prequel Trilogy

Desolate, Book I

Reckoning

Gabriel is gone.

Roseline is left with questions that refuse answers and only the memory of a man she vows to hunt and kill. But to do so, she must call a truce with her sworn enemy.

Together, Roseline and Nicolae track Fane to the underbelly of London, in search of Gabriel's kidnappers. But when Malachi—an immortal with mystifying origin—presents himself as their guide, Roseline discovers she is not the only one looking for Gabriel.

Buried within the secret chambers of the infamous Hellfire Club, Roseline discovers a grim truth: Gabriel isn't just a pawn being used by the *Arotas* prophecy, and those who seek to control its power. He is *Arotas*.

Everything Roseline has ever known about her brethren is about to change. Emotions flare, friendships sever, and the newly formed bonds between enemies are tested as she delves into realms hardly conceived. They are trapped in the midst of a battle that has been waging since the beginning of time.

The prophecy binds them all together. But will they break before the end?

Books by Amy Miles

The Rising Trilogy

Defiance Rising

Relinquish

Vengeance

The Arotas Trilogy

Reckoning

Redemption

Evermore

The Immortal Rose Trilogy

Desolate

The Withered Series

Wither

Captivate

In Your Embrace

About The Author

Author Amy Miles has always been a bit of a dreamer. Growing up as an only child, and a military brat to boot, she spent countless hours escaping into the pages of a book, only to spend the following days creating a new idea of how to twist up the story to make it unique.

Since becoming a mother, Amy has slowly nourished her love of the written word while snatching writing time in the midst of soiled diapers, tumbling over Legos and peering around mounds of laundry and dishes that never seem to go away. Once her only son started school, Amy was free to let her fingers dive into dark mythology, tales of betrayal and love, and explore human nature in its rawest form. Her love of seeing the world from a different angle bloomed.

Amy is the author of several novels, including her popular young adult immortal books, The Arotas Series, which are an Amazon and iBooks bestselling series. Unwilling to be defined by any one genre, she proceeded to flip over to a science fiction/fantasy based idea with her Rising Trilogy. She then dove into contemporary romance with her novel, Captivate and explored the depths of her own faith with In Your Embrace.

She is currently working on completing her Immortal Rose trilogy, a prequel to her Arotas novels. She has also embarked on two new journeys this year, one in the form of a co-written banshee trilogy, The Hallowed Realms, which is currently represented by GH Literary and she breached another genre with her upcoming adult horror novel, Wither.

Want to know what Amy will be working on next?

Sign up to receive Amy's Newsletter:http://bit.ly/1jkG1Hn
Join her at www.AmyMilesBooks.com
Follow on Twitter: @AmyMilesBooks
Instagram: Amy Miles Books
Facebook: www.facebook.com/AmyMiles.Author